GAMETIME

Gametime

JAMI DAVENPORT

HeartEyes
Press

To Lisa B. Kamps, good friend and fellow hockey romance author. Lisa had plans to write a book for Moo U when her life was cut short last fall by cancer. I miss you, Lisa, but I know you're in a better place and keeping those angels on their toes.

To all the children of indifferent parents: I hope you find the love and validation Paxton did in this story. Hugs to those who are struggling in these tough times. My heart goes out to you.

To my faithful readers and the new ones who found me through this book: If my stories bring you comfort and joy, I will have done my job. I love you all. You're the reason I do this.

CONTENTS

GUILTY BY ALCOHOL

Paxton

The hockey house was lit tonight. And I don't mean by lights. By drunken hockey players—myself included.

My twin brother, Patrick, had exited long ago with two hotties on his arm. We might be identical twins in appearance, but my brother always got the girls, and I got his leftovers. He was way more gregarious and outgoing. I was the quiet, serious one.

But now the party was ending. I sat down on one of the worn, beer-stained couches and tried not to think about what else it might be stained with. It'd probably be a petri dish of... Okay, I wasn't going there.

Being alone on a Saturday night after the first hockey game of the year was bad enough. I was a junior at Burlington University in Vermont, fondly known as Moo U by the locals and pretty much everyone else in the state.

Watching my brother revel in his hockey-team star status after a typically fantastic game brought out the ugly in me. I was jealous of him, and I hated being jealous of my brother. He was the best guy I knew and deserved all the good things in his life. Yet being the one always in his immense shadow proved more and more difficult. I played my supporting role as I always had, bolstering him in any way possible, sending the puck his way, and deflecting defensemen intent on mowing him down. That used to be enough, but this year was different. This was my year to break out. My year to establish myself.

Beer made me sleepy, and apparently, shots of whiskey made me grouchy.

I'd sworn things would be different this season. I'd have more fun, get more involved, shed my role as the smart, nerdy brother, while Patrick was the fun, partying brother.

Did I mention Patrick even had a cool nickname? The team called him Trick because he'd had a hat trick his freshman year, scoring three goals in one game. I, on the other hand, was merely known as Pax, short for Paxton. No good story there.

A blonde staggered by and spilled some of her beer on my jeans. I did a double take.

Oh, my God. Wait.

Naomi?

I blinked a few times, forcing my eyes to focus and focus they did.

That blonde *was* Naomi Smith, the unrequited love of my life. Naomi was petite with gray eyes that had a warmth and humor that drew me in. She'd dyed her hair blonde in the past week, rather than the caramel color I'd so loved. I wondered if the change of color had anything to do with my brother, who was currently working his way through the blondes on campus.

She wore a skintight dress showing ample cleavage. The skirt's hem teased the bottom of her rounded ass. She teetered on these really high heels. The overall look was smoking, but so not her usual style, more the style of the females my brother preferred.

"Oops, sorry," she said with words as slurred as mine were.

"That's okay." I met her gaze, and her eyes widened when she realized it was me. My heart rate sped up as a result. It was no secret that Naomi had a crush on Patrick, but he was oblivious. She and I'd been good friends since our freshman year, and I'd heard all about her pining for my twin.

She dropped down on the couch next to me, sitting way too close for comfort. "What're you doing sitting here alone?"

"Waiting for you. I've been waiting for you for a lifetime." The mass doses of alcohol I'd consumed made me bold and stupid, but I didn't have the wherewithal to shut up before I blew my cover, and I'd blown it good this time.

She laughed, and it sounded like a siren's song reeling me into my fate. I smiled back.

"Your dad's a piece of work," she noted. Not that she hadn't experienced my dad before, but he'd taken it to a whole new level tonight.

"I know."

"Don't feel bad. So is my dad. He wishes I'd been born a boy, or at least a female with skating talent. He hates that I have zero athletic ability."

We exchanged glances. We'd had this talk before, and our mutual problems with our fathers were one of the things that'd bound us together.

She snuggled close to me and leaned her head on my shoulder. While she watched the crowd buzz around us, I contemplated my next move or if there should be one. Taking a chance, I dropped my hand to her bare thigh. She sighed and snuggled closer. I slid my hand higher, and her legs parted while she made a happy little purring sound from deep in her throat.

I turned my head and Naomi lifted hers, regarding me with interest, sexual interest, and my hopes bumped up slightly. I cocked a brow at her. She put her hand over mine and guided it farther upward.

"Oh, touch me," she gasped. And then I did exactly as she suggested.

Whoa. "You're really wet." And I was really hard. Painfully so. I hoped like hell she wasn't playing me, because this was a fantasy come true.

"Do you want to fuck me?" She arched toward my waiting fingers.

I blinked several times, not sure I'd heard her correctly. Naomi wasn't known for her tact, but her proposition was still almost too good to be true. I'd waited what seemed like a lifetime to hear those words from her lush mouth.

"Well, do you?" she demanded impatiently.

"I...uh, uh... Hell yeah," I admitted, unable to keep up the charade of being good friends without any benefits. I fucking wanted those benefits. "And you?"

"I've wanted to strip you naked since I first met you."

"That's not just drunk talk?" I questioned because my insecure self required validation. I'd never picked up on her being interested in me, or I'd have gladly made the first move.

"If it is, it's drunk talk by both of us."

"We might regret this in the morning." I gave her one more chance to back out and prayed she wouldn't; all the while my fingers stroked her, causing her to groan.

"I can assure you, I won't regret a thing, other than not doing this sooner." She clumsily straddled me and rested her palms on my chest. Leaning close, she pressed those heavenly lips against mine. Any reason or sanity remaining escaped my brain faster than the team scattered whenever the police showed up to shut down one of our epic parties.

4

She grasped my shirt collar, and her mouth was hot, demanding. Two could play that game. I demanded right back. Our kiss was deep and scorching and sloppy. Just like I liked it. One of her hands slid downward past my waistband until she was squeezing the bulge in my jeans. I groaned, and I swear my eyes rolled back in my head and fireworks exploded. I slid both hands up her skirt and squeezed handfuls of her incredible bare ass.

She drove me beyond reason, and I'd have screwed her right here on this couch for the entire team to witness if one small shred of sanity hadn't invaded my horny skull.

Reluctantly, I broke off the kiss and drew back. "Not here," I rasped, breathing heavily.

She made a pouty face. "Not here?"

I briefly considered my options. Do I unzip my jeans and move aside her G-string for a quick hookup on the couch in front of everyone, or find somewhere private and make it an all-night affair?

As desperate as I was to be inside her, I opted for multiple orgasms over instant gratification.

"Let's get out of here," she said, reading my mind.

I didn't have to be propositioned a second time. I lumbered to my feet and grabbed her hand. "Where to?"

"You live with your twin, and I have a private dorm room."

"Your place then."

We half ran, half staggered the several blocks from the hockey house to the dorm, laughing all the way there and stopping on occasion for brief make-out sessions. Once we stepped inside the dorm room, I kicked the door shut and locked it. We didn't bother turning on the lights. Sex by touch worked for me. Any sex with Naomi worked for me.

Naomi grabbed the collar of my button-down and ripped the buttons off—and I do mean ripped. Seconds later, my jeans were pooled at my ankles. This girl didn't waste any time. I shrugged out of what was left of my favorite shirt, kicked off my shoes, and stepped out of my jeans.

Naomi was still wearing all her clothes. Time to rectify that. I reached for her, barely able to make out her sexy silhouette. Her mouth was hot on mine as she clawed at my bare chest.

"You're still dressed," I panted.

"Let me fix that." She kicked off her shoes, and the dress and G-string followed, then we fell onto the bed together. I'd have liked her to leave those shoes on, but now wasn't the time to get hung up on details. She pushed me onto the bed and was on top of me in no time, rubbing her delectable body across mine and grinding into my painfully hard cock.

I needed her and now, but I wouldn't be that guy who didn't give as much pleasure as he got. Besides, Naomi was special. I'd dreamed of this moment for two years. Another few minutes wouldn't kill me. I had to make this last for her. Naomi had other ideas.

She ran her hand up and down my dick. "You're so big. I knew you'd be big." She fisted it and pumped her hand up and down. As much as I loved her hand job, I was going to blow all over if she didn't stop.

"Naomi, I—"

"I get it." She once again read my mind. "I want you inside me. We can take it slow the next time."

There was going to be a next time? My heart sang with joy.

She leaned across me and opened the small drawer on the nightstand, pulling out a handful of condoms. I banished doubts from my mind that I was just another one of her conquests. And Naomi had a lot of those, if the rumors were true. She was as big of a heartbreaker as my brother. *Enjoy the moment*, I told myself. *Don't overthink this.*

Straddling my thighs, she rolled the condom onto my cock

with expert efficiency. Unable to be an observer a second longer, I flipped her onto her back. She parted her legs and arched her hips toward mine, begging me to take her. I didn't have the willpower to resist the invitation; taking it slow would have to happen later.

"Bury that big cock deep inside me," she begged.

I gladly obliged.

As soon as the tip entered that wet, inviting entrance, she dug her fingernails into my back, wrapped those beautiful legs around my tortured body, and met me halfway.

I was in fucking heaven. Being inside her felt better than any fantasy or wet dream I'd ever had and far surpassed any woman I'd ever been with, and I'd had my fair share.

She pressed against me, moaning and thrashing her head on the pillow. What a beautiful sight she was all hot and sweaty and primed for me and me alone.

I began to move inside her, attempting to take it slow, but Naomi would have none of that. She made it clear this was raunchy, down-and-dirty sex, and I was on board every stroke of the way. She met my desperate thrusts with thrusts of her own as we banged each other into oblivion and beyond.

My cock twitched and my impending orgasm pulsed through me. I gritted my teeth to hold myself together a little longer. I wasn't coming without her. Reaching between us, I found that little nub and worked her into a bigger frenzy than we were already in. Her body told me it was time, and I exploded at the same time she did.

We clung to each other as wave after wave of pleasure rolled over us, each one more powerful than the one before it, until I was certain I'd die of a pleasure overdose. Surely, a mere mortal wouldn't survive such emotional extremes. Yet somehow, I managed, which had to be the eighth wonder of the world.

As we came down off the greatest natural high known to man and woman, I hugged her close. She nuzzled my shoulder and planted lazy kisses on my collarbone.

I'd never experienced such perfect bliss, such contentment, such a feeling of being right where I needed to be. This was everything. She was my everything. My heart sang with joy, and I reveled in the moment. I'd never known sheer perfection until now. Naomi was perfect for me, as I'd always suspected she'd be.

"I love you. I've always loved you. You are my one and only." I blurted out the truth I'd been holding in since I'd first met her in Psych 101.

"I love you, too." Naomi murmured her agreement before she faded off to sleep.

I was giddy from our mutual declaration of love for each other. We were finally on the same page with an entire future in front of us, and I couldn't wait to read the rest of the book.

BLAME

Naomi

I woke up feeling like my life was finally on track.

The guy I'd been lusting after the past two years was finally in my bed, and we'd had sheet-scorching sex all night long. We were explosive and insatiable together and hadn't fallen into a deep sleep until three or four a.m. But who checked the time when you were experiencing something timeless? We'd dozed here and there.

Through the slowly lifting fog of drunkenness and fading haze of lust, I attempted to reconstruct what we'd done and said last night.

I'd had sex before. Actually, a lot of it, but this was different. This experience was almost Zen-like. Like two halves coming together to make a whole. Like finding your soul mate. Like my wildest fantasies come true. If that wasn't Zen, I don't know what was.

And I wasn't a Zen-like person.

I was a numbers person. I loved my stats and my details.

Numbers didn't work in this situation because numbers didn't feel, and I was definitely feeling.

Patrick, or *Trick* as some of his teammates called him, opened one eye and then the other. He smiled at me as brightly as the sun streaming in the window of my dorm room. Since the sky had been cloudy for a week, and I was feeling my inner Zen, the rays of light warming my naked body were a good sign.

I stretched in the bed like a lioness who'd had a good hunt the night before. Patrick propped his head on an elbow. His hot gaze seared a path across my naked body. I wasn't modest, and I enjoyed knowing he liked what he saw, because I sure AF loved what I saw.

"Good morning," he whispered in a raspy voice full of sleep, sex, and contentment. His smoldering blue eyes contradicted the lazy way one of his hands kneaded the flesh on my waist.

"That was epic." My smugly satisfied smile backed up my words.

"Yeah, it was." He sounded in awe, almost as if he hadn't expected this, which was weird because I'd been pursuing him for two years.

"You have some incredible stamina."

"So do you," he said with a chuckle.

Sometime in the early-morning hours, he'd told me he loved me, and I'd said it back. I wasn't going to hold him to that particular declaration just yet. I'd give him time for things to sink in. After all, people were often their most honest when they were drunk. Now that he was sober again, he'd back off, but I'd wait for him to come to terms with his feelings, once he'd let them be known.

Patrick rolled onto his back and put his hands behind his head, still watching me closely. I gave him one of my best sultry smiles, pretty sure we'd be going at it again this morning. I ran my hand down his rib cage to where the sheet rested against his hip. Licking my lips, I rose up, ready to go down on him, as I edged the sheet lower and lower to reveal a cock once again hard, ready, able, and willing. I traced the tat that rode low on his flat stomach between his hip bone and his dick. I'd wondered last night if he'd had any tats. I'd figured a guy like him had to have tats.

Leaning in, I licked his tattoo with my tongue. His tat was simple. Crossed hockey sticks with his jersey number in the center in Moo U green and white.

I blinked a few times, certain I was dyslexic. I stared harder.

Fifteen?

One five?

Patrick's jersey number was fifty-one. I knew his number better than I knew my own cell phone number.

I had to be reading it wrong. That brain fog thing from drinking and fucking.

I squinted at the number as I absently traced it over and over again.

Patrick held still, not even breathing.

Fifteen.

Fifteen.

Fifteen.

Why would Patrick have his twin brother's number on his—?

His identical twin brother.

Identical.

I gaped at the tattoo in horror.

The reality of the situation slammed into me harder than a rabid defenseman slamming me against the boards.

Oh. My. God.

What have I done?

I was going to be sick, throw up, or die of embarrassment. I'd slept with the wrong twin. I'd slept with my friend. My very good friend. My confidant. The guy who was always there for me.

And he'd told me he loved me. I'd said those three words back thinking he was someone else. I'd had sex over and over believing he was someone else. I'd been shameless in my lust for him—no, not him, someone else.

For two years, Paxton had listened sympathetically as I crushed on Patrick, and he'd never once let on that he had a thing for me until last night.

I was mortified, but not for myself, for him.

If—correction, when—he realized my mistake, he'd be humiliated beyond belief. Our friendship might not survive this. Damage control must happen immediately. The truth would deal his pride a mortal blow, but he had to know the truth. To continue with this charade would only make things worse.

But how to do to it? How to let him down carefully with his dignity intact but tattered?

"Naomi, what's wrong?" Patrick, no, Paxton asked. Concern weighted his tone. My reaction aroused his suspicions. He wasn't stupid. In fact, he was pretty damn smart.

"I...I..." My brain churned through possible solutions to handle this mess in the kindest way possible. I averted my eyes, certain he'd read the truth there before I had a chance to decide on a course of action.

"Naomi?" His voice shook, taking on a more frantic tone. He knew something had gone wrong, horribly wrong.

Finally, I raised my head to meet his gaze.

And the excruciating truth of what I'd done was mirrored in his horrified blue eyes.

He realized I'd thought he was Patrick.

I'd banged the wrong twin and loved every moment of it, while giving him the courage to pour out his heart. I'd bludgeoned his pride and irreparably harmed one of the nicest guys I'd ever known. Shame crashed over me, mortification for what I'd done to him.

I'd been in hot messes before but nothing that'd so humiliated someone I deeply cared about.

And I had no one to blame but my drunken self.

3

DAMAGE CONTROL

Paxton

Adequate words didn't exist that did justice to my soul-deep humiliation. My pride had been laid to waste by a nuclear explosion of massive proportions, and my ego had been slammed against the boards with a hit so monumental it should've been shown repeatedly on all the sucker-in-love highlight clips. If only the earth would open up and swallow me, never to be heard from again.

I had to come up with a plan to save face by wiping the pity and absolute mortification off Naomi's face. That'd happen later. Right now, I was too raw to devise a plan beyond being buried alive, which really wasn't a viable option.

After wandering aimlessly, I sought refuge on the ice that afternoon. Skating had been my personal therapy whenever life was more than I could handle, such as when my dad was being a bigger asshole than usual. The night my mother died in a car accident, I'd gone to the rink and skated until I almost passed out from exhaustion. Being on the ice was healing, and I desperately needed to heal my fractured heart right now.

Only this time, my dad hadn't crushed the joy out of me, Naomi had.

I took to the ice, glad that no one else was around. Even though Sundays were our days off, sometimes guys showed up to skate. Not today. Most likely too many hangovers after the victory party last night.

I tortured myself by running back through the events of the prior night. I'd played a mediocre game. Patrick had been the star. My dad had been present for the first game of the season, and he'd barely acknowledged my presence while raining criticism down on Patrick. I don't know which was worse—neglect or verbal abuse. All par for the course.

After the game, when he wasn't tearing Patrick's performance apart, he'd disgusted us both with his bootlicking of Naomi's dad, Gene Smith. Mr. Smith was an NHL legend and Moo U grad, and my dad craved his attention like a small child craved the last cookie in the cookie jar.

His cruel indifference had driven me to get wasted drunk that night. I wasn't thinking clearly. I only knew I needed someone to show I mattered. Naomi had, or I thought she had.

The most epic sex I'd ever experienced was followed by the single most demeaning experience of my life. Naomi had tried to cover it up, but one look at her, and I knew. I'd laughed it off, claimed it was all drunken nonsense and didn't mean anything. Then I'd gotten my ass out of there.

I'd avoided going home to the apartment I shared with my twin. Patrick would see the devastation in my eyes, and I couldn't tell him the truth, even though we told each other everything.

Well, not everything. Patrick didn't know how much I hated being in his shadow or how much I hated being the forgotten, insignificant brother. He also didn't know there were times I was insanely jealous of him. If I had anything to say about it, he'd never know. Patrick was one of the good guys, and he'd be ruined if he knew some of the shit rolling around in my head regarding him.

I skated around that rink like a demon with his ass on fire. I skated until my lungs burned and my legs threatened to give out. I skated until I didn't have any gas left in my tank.

I coasted to the boards and leaned over, hands above my knees, gasping for breath.

Only then did I get the feeling I wasn't alone.

Shit.

Someone had witnessed my crazy-assed insanity, which would be all anyone who was watching would be able to call it.

I closed my eyes for a moment and willed my brain to remain calm. Slowly, I straightened and met the gaze of assistant coach Magnus Garfunkle. He was an odd duck, and though his methods were effective, they were a little too new agey for me. I was more of a see-it-to-believe-it guy.

I'd pretty much flown under his radar last year, his first season with the team, but by the intense look on his face, my obscurity had ended. He'd given a few of the guys crystals and rocks and talked to them about auras and chis. I'd been hoping to escape that particular insanity.

"Paxton, that was quite an impressive display out there. I knew you were a powerful, fast skater, but I had no idea how fast. I've seen flashes of brilliance, but nothing like you demonstrated just now." If only he knew what had driven me. He wouldn't be so impressed.

I shrugged, embarrassed by his words. Essentially, I was being called out for not giving 150 percent, whether Coach Garfunkle meant his words that way or not.

"Skating helps me work through problems." Skating had always been my solace from a father who considered me expendable, the bone-deep ache of losing my mother at ten years old, and being smothered in the shadow of my uber-talented twin.

"Did you?"

I frowned. "Did I what?"

"Did you work through them?"

"I don't know."

He laughed. He was an intense guy with moments of joy. Coach lived by his instincts and emotions, and he loved his hockey. He'd played college hockey but didn't have what it took to go to the next level. Now he poured his heart and soul into teaching. I suspected he'd be our next head coach after Keller retired.

If he ever retired.

Our head coach was an institution. He'd been here forever, and he was a star maker. Patrick and I wouldn't have gone to school anywhere else. Moo U was the college hockey mecca and our ticket to a career in professional hockey.

"Got time to talk?" Coach Garfunkle's smile was contagious, and I found myself smiling back, lifting a bit of the weight off my shoulders.

"Yeah, sure." I didn't know why the sudden interest in me, but in my current state of mind, I assumed he wanted to discuss my brother. That was usually the only reason my dad or coaching staff singled me out. Okay, probably not true but I didn't want anything raining on my pity party.

"Get changed and meet me in my office in ten."

I nodded and headed for the locker room, took a quick shower, and dressed. In nine minutes, I was in his office.

He gestured for me to sit on the couch stacked with mounds of magazines and papers. I moved some aside to sit, while he rolled his desk chair to a spot in front of me.

"Coffee?"

"I'd love some. Black, please." The coffee would give me something to do with my hands rather than fidgeting. I'd never been comfortable being the center of attention. Patrick did those honors.

Garfunkle sat back, studying me as if he was stripping away all my protection and saw deep into my soul. He steepled his fingers on his chin. "I watched you all last year, waited for you to mature and come into your own, but you never quite met my expectations. The ability is there, but you're not consistent," he began.

I squirmed, uneasy with the direction this conversation was taking. He was focusing on me, not on what I could do to make Patrick be a better player, and I was caught a little off guard.

I sipped the hot, nasty brew. Coach didn't have good taste in coffee, but it was better than nothing. I stayed silent, uncertain how to respond and figuring zipping my mouth was my best shot.

"Last night's game wasn't an improvement over last year."

Oh, shit, was I being kicked off the team? Or even worse, moved off the first line? Patrick and I had played on the same line together since we were toddlers. We were in each other's heads. We knew each other out there on the ice.

He met my gaze, as if waiting for a response, so I gave him one. "I wasn't feeling it last night. I was off," I offered lamely with a shrug.

"I see great innate talent in you, and it's squandered. You have a confidence problem. Not only do I want to fix you, I want you to become the best player on the team."

I started to laugh, but he was dead serious. "My brother is the best player on this team. In fact, he's one of the best college players in the country right now."

"And you're his identical twin. The talent is there. The

confidence is not. Your brother plays hockey balls to the wall. He's aggressive, constantly on the attack. He's easy to coach because we just let him play his game. He's used to being the go-to guy when a score is needed, and he expects to be. What do you expect, Paxton?"

"I, uh, I do my best to be a team player." By the look on his face, he didn't appreciate my answer.

"And how do you do that?"

I felt like I was being grilled for a final exam and didn't know the subject of the test. "I watch for the best scoring opportunities for my teammates. If they have a better shot, I pass the puck."

He nodded as if he'd expected my answer. "And you often pass that puck to your brother."

"He's our top scorer."

Garfunkle nodded sagely and leaned back in his chair, propping his feet on an end table and crossing his arms over his broad chest. I was six foot three of solid muscle, but he was stouter and shorter.

"What do you want out of hockey, Paxton? Do you want to make a career out of it?"

"Yeah, I want to give it shot."

"You want to give it a shot?" His brows crept upward.

"I…uh…I, yeah," I finished lamely. "I want to contribute."

"You'll have to up your game now to make it in the pros. You aren't there yet, and you're going to be older than a lot of those hungry rookies. How hungry are you, Paxton? How badly do you want it?"

"I love hockey."

"The Sockeyes will expect you to be ready to play, not have to go back down to a minor league for a few more years. College is your minor league preparation."

I nodded. I knew all this.

"Did I ever mention that I know the Sockeye head coach? We're good friends."

"You do?" I hadn't heard this before.

"I do. We played some hockey together and kept in touch over the years. Were you surprised when the Sockeyes took you in the first round? It wasn't expected."

"Yeah, really surprised. So was my family."

Garfunkle rubbed the goatee on his chin and nodded like a sage Buddha. "I've had a few conversations with Coach Gorst since they drafted you. Gorst is an out-of-the-box thinker. He took a chance drafting you as high as he did, considering your stats. He sees in you what I see. I won't lie to you. They wanted your brother and didn't get him. They picked you because Gorst and I both think the only thing holding you back is your own perception of your abilities and perhaps others' perpetuating that belief."

He spoke the truth. I swallowed hard and wished the knot in my stomach would lessen. I had no idea Garfunkle had been speaking with Coach Gorst. In hockey a lot of guys were drafted at eighteen like Patrick and I were. Then they played in the minors or went to college. Being drafted wasn't a guarantee you'd make it to the NHL. In fact, I'd guess most guys didn't. Yet the Sockeyes might have a slot for me if the timing worked out. No hockey player in their right mind turned down an opportunity like that.

When I didn't offer any excuses or explanations why I wasn't living up to my potential, he continued. "The Sockeyes want you at the end of this season. They predict they'll have a few offensive holes to fill next season, and Gorst thinks you'd be a good fit with their current roster."

"Next season?" I'd been toying with going pro at the end of this year. I had enough credits to graduate early.

"Yes, next season. Do you see a problem with that?"

"No, Coach Garfunkle."

"Call me Coach G or Coach Garf. Garfunkle is a mouthful."

I nodded, surprised the team hadn't awarded him with a nickname previously. I guess we were still trying to figure him out. "Okay, Coach Garf." Coach G seemed more impersonal, and Garf fit him.

"Now that we've settled that, are you willing to go for what you want? Make some uncomfortable changes?"

"I'm not a slacker. No one works as hard as me on the team. I—"

"This isn't about working hard or playing harder, this is about taking risks during the game because you believe in yourself and your abilities. This is about confidence, not talent. The raw talent is there."

"Okay," I said. This was too much to absorb at once and went against everything I'd been programmed to believe about myself over the years by my family, coaching staff, and friends. Fuck, even unintentionally by my brother.

"Your brother won't be around to lean on when you go pro, which might be the best thing that ever happens to you."

"You think so?" To me, it was the worst thing to be without him skating by my side.

He nodded, and his eyes were full of intense determination. "You'll be contending with a bunch of other rookies for a few spots on a team, and no one holds back, no one lets another teammate have all the glory at their own expense."

"But I'm a team player," I insisted.

"Plenty of time for that once you have a spot on the team."

"Okay, sure, but I have a spot on this team."

Garf sighed as if I was too dense to understand, and so far, I was.

"Do you want to be the best player you can be or to merely be a good player?"

"The best I can be." That was a no-brainer.

"Is that what you really want?" He was pushing me out of my comfort zone, and we both knew it.

"I work my ass off for hockey. I love hockey. Hockey's my life, even if I don't express my enthusiasm as clearly as some of my teammates do."

"Good. We're going to make you the best you can be, and if my instincts are correct, you're going to be the premier player on this team."

I opened my mouth to argue, then shut it.

"You have to really want this, Paxton. You have to get beyond your doubts and believe in yourself and your ability. When you see that shot, you have to take it. I never thought I'd ask a player to be selfish, but when it comes to you, you need to be a little more selfish. Don't always pass to your teammates. Trust your instincts; if you have the shot, take it. Your shooting percentage is quite good, you just don't shoot enough."

"I'll try."

"No, you *will*. I believe in you, Paxton. Has anyone ever believed in you before?"

Our eyes met, and he saw the tragic truth written there.

He clapped me on the shoulder. "I believe in you. We need you to step up if we're going to win it all this year. Don't let me down."

"I won't, Coach. I promise."

"One more thing, your grades look pretty good. Do you spend a lot of time studying?"

"I do my reading, go to class, and take good notes. I'm lucky in that I remember stuff really well, so I have to do minimal studying compared to a lot of people."

"Good. You and I will be working on some confidence-building exercises every day after practice starting in a week.

In the meantime, I have homework for you." He riffled through one of the piles and pulled out a dog-eared book titled *How Bad Do You Want It?* "I want you to read, take notes, and we'll discuss and implement what you've read at our first session in a week."

I blinked a few times, trying to process everything. I stared down at the book.

"I appreciate your help. Thank you."

He laughed. "Don't thank me. I'm doing this for the team. If you become the player I know you can be, you'll bring the team up with you and challenge others to reach deep within and find that extra something they didn't know they had. Even your brother." He dug in his desk drawer and pulled out something. "Here, this will help."

"What is that?" I stared at the rock necklace he'd placed in my hand.

"It's a moonstone."

"Okay." I'd heard about Coach Garf's fondness for rocks, but I'd avoided any such gifts from him until now.

"The moonstone is a crystal that increases clarity regarding your self-worth. Wear it always for renewed vitality and to energize your confidence."

"Uh, thanks, Coach."

He must've read skepticism because he explained further. "Crystals aren't magic, but they do positively interact with your body's chakra, or energy field. They're just another tool in your tool kit."

"Okay."

He stared at me until I realized he wanted me to put it on. I did so, and he grinned.

"Thank you." I nodded, we shook hands, and I walked out of the building clutching the book and feeling a hell of a lot better than I had going in.

THE CHALLENGE

Paxton

I glanced at my phone for the first time in a long while, having avoided the thing since I'd left Naomi's dorm room early this morning. There were several text messages from various friends but multiple ones from Patrick and Naomi. I sighed and fought off the guilt that I was being disloyal to my brother by vowing to up my game.

As far as Naomi went, the humiliation was still too fresh to deal with her. I'd been dealt a severe blow, but despite my dented and crumpled ego, I didn't want to lose her as a friend. I wouldn't be able to bear the complete absence of her in my life, even if being around her tortured me with memories of our night together.

Instead of responding to her, I read Patrick's last message:

Where the fuck are you? A bunch of us are at the Biscuit.

I wanted to ask if Naomi was there. Part of me hoped she

was, while another part hoped she wasn't. I considered crawling off to my apartment and licking my wounds, but I'd been licking them all day. Time to stand up and take my blows like a man.

On my way, I tapped quickly and hurried down the sidewalk toward the Biscuit in the Basket several blocks away. The Biscuit was a fave hockey team hangout, known for their cold beer and awesome chicken wings. My mouth watered and my stomach rumbled, reminding me how long it'd been since I'd eaten anything substantial. The soggy convenience-store English muffin I'd wolfed down this morning had long ago worn off.

I pushed open the door. The place wasn't all that busy on a Sunday afternoon, but my teammates were sitting at our usual table and already consuming beer. A few empty pitchers littered the large table.

The chair between Patrick and Tate was open so I took it. Everyone always left room for me to sit next to Patrick. Today that rubbed me the wrong way. I hated being treated like an extension of Patrick rather than my own person. Shit like this was a good example of all the little things that happened throughout my day reminding me most people considered me one half of a whole, instead of my own whole.

Barely acknowledging my presence, Patrick chatted up the waitress, Carly, pouring on the charm. He'd been hustling her all semester with zero luck. Tate and Michael debated hockey trivia, as usual. Jonah and our goalie, Josh, had their eyes glued to the football game on one of the big-screen TVs around the room.

Carly took my wings order and hustled off, and Patrick turned his attention to me.

"Where've you been?" His tone was slightly accusatory

and somewhat hurt. "You didn't come home last night and weren't answering texts this morning."

While it wasn't unusual for us to spend the night elsewhere without notice, we always checked in the next morning, as part of our unspoken twin code. I hadn't done that.

"I was home briefly. You were passed out," I lied.

"I didn't hear you come in. Yeah, wild night last night. Last I saw, you weren't feeling any pain."

I nodded. No sense denying what everyone at this table had seen. Patrick's gaze softened with understanding, and the last thing I wanted right now was anyone's sympathy.

"I get it. That wasn't one of your most stellar performances last night."

Not on the ice it wasn't, but the sex had been epic right up until she'd seen the number fifteen tattoo on my hip. *Shit.* I shuddered at how far this charade might've gone if she hadn't seen it.

I banished those mortifying thoughts from my head. Tonight, in the privacy of my own bed, I'd go over the past twenty-four-plus hours again and examine everything in minute detail. Right now, I had other worries. Such as whether or not to tell Patrick about my deal with Coach Garf.

Even as I debated, I realized with a bit of a shock that I wasn't going to tell him. We never kept secrets from each other. He even knew about my crush on Naomi, but I don't think he realized how bad I had it and probably thought it was old news. He'd left her off his conquest list because of it.

This thing with Coach was personal, and I didn't know if he'd take it well or read something different into my desire to up my game. I'd always had his back on the ice, and this possible change in our status might be perceived as a threat. Even worse, he might laugh it off and deflate my severely deflated ego all the more.

My brother wasn't cruel. He was a great guy, but sometimes his confidence in his abilities caused him to unintentionally say something hurtful. Like the time he was telling a scout how he was the better, more-talented player of the two of us. He didn't mean to rip out my heart with his words, but he did. In fact, both he and our dad told me not to expect to be drafted in the first couple rounds. Yet I had been, I reminded myself.

"Hey, Omi," Tate shouted from down the table and interrupted my musing. I stiffened. The entire team knew Naomi because of her father, an alumnus of the Bulls and a huge contributor to the hockey program. We were all in awe of him. Sometimes he'd show up at practice and give us pointers and took a special interest in Patrick. Naomi was also a staple at hockey games, which she often attended with her dad.

I didn't have to turn around to know she was walking toward us. I felt her presence as she closed the distance between our table and the door.

"Hi," she said cheerfully, and the guys all responded with waves or greetings. I, however, did not until I caught the puzzled sideways glance from my brother. He was already suspicious.

I turned in my chair and offered her a blazing smile. "Oh, hi, Omi. Didn't see you there," I gushed, overdoing it and drawing more attention from Patrick.

She ignored everyone else at the table with a laser focus on me. I squirmed a little, wishing she'd quit staring at me like that. We'd seen each other naked, and I struggled to return to the friend zone when I wanted so much more. When you'd tasted paradise, how did you go back to mac and cheese? I fingered the crystal under my T-shirt in a last-ditch attempt to bolster my chakra or energy or whatever.

"Pax, could we talk for a moment? I need some help with a small problem I have."

"Uh, sure." I stood, grabbed my beer for a little liquid courage, and followed her to a remote table as my brother's gaze bored into my back.

REGRETS

Naomi

On Sunday evening, I found Paxton at the Biscuit in the Basket. He sat with a few teammates at the large table in the middle of the room.

He'd ignored my multiple text messages all day long. I'd been left with no choice but to hunt him down. I'd checked the Biscuit multiple times during the day and finally hit pay dirt late afternoon.

We had to talk. I had to make sure things were okay between us. Paxton was one of my dearest friends, and we had to get through this mess with our friendship intact. I was my father's daughter in that I tended to push things in the direction I wanted them to go, while Paxton was more deliberate and thoughtful when it came to his actions. I'd given him all day to think; now it was my turn.

He avoided my gaze as he pushed back his chair, grabbing his beer. "Be right back, guys."

Most of his teammates barely noticed, with their attention focused on a hockey game on one of the overhead flat-screens, except Patrick. I saw the wheels spinning in his head. He knew something was up. Maybe Pax had told him about my epic blunder. God, I hoped not.

Paxton followed me to a table away from prying eyes and sat across from me. He focused his attention on his beer glass as if he'd never seen one before. I clasped my hands under the table, wishing I had a beer, but the thought made my stomach rebel after all I'd consumed last night.

"Did you tell Patrick?" I asked.

His head shot up, and he met my gaze with surprise. "Fuck no."

"Then why is he staring at us like that?"

Paxton glanced over his shoulder. Patrick rubbed his chin and studied us, trying to figure shit out.

"Because he senses a disturbance in the twin connection."

I laughed, but it was a hollow, empty laugh.

"Naomi, your secret is safe with me. We were drunk. We said shit— Okay, I said shit I didn't mean. We had sex. That's it. Nothing else. I know how you feel about my brother, and I would never do anything to damage your chances with him."

"Okay, good, I mean…" I trailed off. What did I mean? I hadn't intended this conversation to revolve around Patrick. I wanted to talk about us, what last night did to us. Paxton was my best guy friend, and I hoped I hadn't irreparably fucked that up. I'd come on to him, made him an offer no guy would refuse, and then made it clear I'd mistaken him for Patrick. How did friends get beyond such a thing?

I didn't know, but I had to try.

"I didn't come here to talk about Patrick. I came because I don't want what happened to ruin our friendship. You're too important to me."

Why hadn't I ever noticed what a strong chin he had? Patrick had this little cleft in his chin, but Paxton's chin was slightly different, squarer maybe. His eyes didn't have the twinkling mischief of his brother's but were deeply serious. Yet he had a playful side. I'd seen it last night. He was so panty-dropping handsome, with straightforward goodness and a quiet strength. I was getting hot just thinking about him minus his clothes.

I shook my head to clear it. I was lusting over Paxton. *My friend.*

Paxton nudged my foot to get my attention. "Don't worry. We're good. Lots of friends hook up. Doesn't mean anything. Don't give it another thought." He winked and gave me a cocky smile. If I hadn't known him as well as I did, I'd have believed him. He wasn't fooling me. Lots of friends did hook up, but they usually knew exactly who they were hooking up with. I had not known.

"Are you sure? We're good?" I studied him intently, drawn to those deep blue eyes with the laugh lines in the corners. Patrick's lines were more pronounced than Paxton's. I'd never noticed that before. Now that we'd been as intimate as two people could get, I saw things I hadn't seen. Perhaps I'd been guilty of viewing Paxton as an extension of his twin rather than as his own person.

I glanced toward Patrick. He regarded us quizzically from across the room, and my heart didn't do that pitter-pat, pound-pound thing it always did when our eyes met. I turned back and met Paxton's gaze, and my heart pitter-patted and pound-pounded.

What the fuck?

My brain was confused because I'd slept with the wrong twin. That had to be it.

Right?

"Naomi?" Paxton's dark brows knit together as he watched me. He ran his hands through his wavy dark hair, which he'd let grow longer than usual. In fact, so had Patrick.

"Uh, yeah, uh, I just want to make sure everything is good between us."

"We're good," Paxton insisted with forced lightness. He signaled to Carly, who was walking by. "I'd like to buy Naomi a drink."

Carly smiled at me. "What'll you have?"

"I'll just have whatever light beer you have on tap."

"You got it." Carly hustled off.

"You won't tell Patrick what happened, will you?" I didn't want Patrick to know about Pax and me, but not necessarily for the obvious reasons. Things had gotten way more complicated than simply not wanting the guy I'd been lusting over to find out I'd slept with his brother. Correct that—we hadn't slept. We'd had sex so epic I feared sex with Patrick or anyone else would be a letdown.

"Not on your life. If I did, then he'd know how you felt about him, and I'd be betraying your confidence."

I was relieved, but I wasn't sure I cared if Patrick knew I'd been crushing on him for two years. More importantly, I wanted—needed—to protect Paxton's pride.

"Then we're good?"

He rolled his eyes and smiled. "Yeah, I said we're good. It's not a big deal, Naomi. Let it go." He sounded annoyed. I guess I was driving the point home a little too strongly.

"How're your classes this semester?" I asked, changing the subject.

"I'm carrying a full load and then some. I might graduate early and go pro."

"Really?"

"Yeah, but don't mention this to anyone. I haven't even told Patrick."

Since he was revealing something Patrick didn't know, we were back on solid footing, or so I hoped.

We talked about classes and hockey and issues with our dads for a few minutes. Shortly after my beer arrived, Patrick ambled over to join us. With an assessing gaze, he looked from his twin to me and back to Paxton. I suspected he'd been having a serious case of FOMO.

"Can anyone get in on this secret?" he asked and verified my suspicions.

I licked my lips and guiltily glanced at Pax. "Uh, no secrets."

"Right." Patrick studied us as if he were calculating his chance at a clear shot at the net. Only he had more time to dissect our behavior than he ever would his scoring chances.

Speaking of scoring chances, we were in luck because a couple senior girls flopped down next to him, claiming his attention. He flipped on the charm and flirted outrageously, forgetting his twin and me.

Paxton shrugged apologetically. "What can I say? My bro's a ho."

I laughed. Watching Patrick in action didn't hurt me nearly as much as it would've even a few days ago. In fact, I wasn't certain it bothered me at all.

WTF was going on here?

One of the girls turned her attention to Paxton, and he fell into an easy conversation with her. She scooted close to him, placed a possessive hand on his muscular thigh, and snaked an arm around the back of his neck. He smiled at her, but his expression was mildly disinterested and didn't sizzle with the heat he'd shown last night. Or was I imagining he had a special smile just for me?

Patrick would go home with one of these women, and Paxton might also. My stomach twisted at the image of Pax having sex with someone else less than twenty-four hours from our night together. Thoughts of them together smothered me, and I gasped for breath. I had to get out of here.

Abruptly I stood and grabbed my purse. All four pairs of eyes looked up at me. "I have to go study. See you guys later."

I didn't wait for Paxton's reaction, but I got the hell out of there.

Paxton might be the good twin to a point, but he wasn't an angel. He got his share of action if campus rumors were to be believed, and this particular senior appeared to be one of his hookups hoping for a repeat performance.

Seeing her cuddle up to him upset me, and I didn't know how to deal with this bit of information. I was suffering from twin confusion and had to get my head on straight. I didn't like things out of order or not following my plan. Patrick was my crush, not his brother. Patrick was the guy destined to be a superstar and the guy my dad thought I should date so he could relive his glory days through him. Patrick was the guy I'd lusted for since my freshman year.

Paxton was a friend with one-time benefits. *That's all.* Patrick was the one. My attraction to Paxton was temporary confusion due to scorching-hot sex. Nothing more. Nothing less.

But what if I was wrong? What if there was more?

HIRED

Naomi

By the end of the week, Paxton and I settled into a weird new normal. Nothing was the same, even though we both pretended it was. Even weirder, after two-plus years of ignoring me, Patrick suddenly woke up and noticed me. It must be the blonde hair.

Instead of being thrilled, I was torn. I'd entered the twilight zone for sure.

I couldn't for the life of me stop thinking about Pax. I made excuses all week to be where he was, eating in the dining hall at the same time, being outside the rink when he finished practice, or walking by his apartment about the time he left for class. At first, I'd denied these things were anything but coincidences, but I knew in my heart they were not. Then I tried to convince myself I was actually stalking Patrick. I wasn't.

I was stalking Paxton. Even at the height of my crush on Patrick, I hadn't stalked him like this. I'd like to think I was a concerned friend making sure we were okay. But I feared there was more to it than that.

On Thursday, I got home from classes in the early afternoon to multiple calls and texts from my father. Nothing unusual there, but the urgency in those messages alarmed me. Immediately, my mind raced to all kinds of conclusions. A person tended to do that when they lost their mother at a young age, just one more thing I had in common with both twins.

We understood each other's pain with controlling, critical fathers and no mom to balance things out. We knew what it felt like to get a knock on the door late at night and have our lives be forever changed after that. Paxton and Patrick's mom was hit head-on by a drunk driver, and my mom's SUV was T-boned by someone running a red light in a stolen car. I suspected the driver was also drunk, but he ran from the scene, and they never found him. My dad had been on a road trip. I'd been alone with the nanny. Part of me blamed him for not being there for me, as unfair as my blame might be.

Shaking my head to clear those disturbing thoughts, I called my dad's cell. I'd worked myself into a frenzy by the time he answered on the sixth ring.

"Dad, is everything okay?" I blurted out. Desperation shook my voice.

He chuckled at my tone. "Yeah, calm down, honey. Everything is good."

I expelled all the oxygen I'd held in my lungs and collapsed in the only chair in the room. "What's going on then?"

"Good news. I pulled some strings and got you an internship with the team."

"What?" I stared at the phone as if it were the enemy. My dad interfered in my life on a regular basis, but he'd never gone this far. He'd been pushing Patrick and me together since the end of last season, and his efforts were embarrassing, especially considering Patrick resisted them and pretended to be oblivious to my dad's machinations. I knew what Dad was doing even if he didn't acknowledge it. My father missed playing the game, the glory, the cheers, the adulation. Originally, I'd been thrilled at his attempts because I'd gotten my Patrick time. This year, I wasn't so sure how I felt.

"I know you don't need the money. I give you plenty, but a job with a stellar college team will be good for your resume."

"I know, but I'd have preferred to get that job on my own merits. If I'd known they had an opening for an intern, I might've applied." This job had been created by the athletic department to appease the great Gene Smith; I'd bet my best pair of shoes on it. The Moo U athletic director was so far up Dad's butt he never saw the light of day.

"The least you could do is thank me. Why are you so ungrateful, Naomi? I bust my ass to make your life comfortable, and all you can do is complain?"

Here he went with the guilt trips. While I was somewhat immune to them, this time he got under my skin.

"I didn't ask for your interference in my life. I appreciate your efforts and know you're coming from the right place, but, Dad, I need to stand on my own two feet and make my own decisions."

"Considering I pay for everything, that ship has sailed, and now you're balking at an opportunity to make some of your own money?"

"Dad, I—"

"It's settled. You'll meet with the coach today after practice. You'll be on the bus tomorrow for the away games. I'll be attending, and we can talk then." Dad bulldozed right over me, just like he always did. No wonder I'd rebelled so completely in my teens. He'd barely noticed, though, having been wrapped up in dealing with the end of his career and a brief sojourn into sportscasting.

"But—"

"You'll love this job. It's right up your alley. Numbers, stats, analyzing…"

That did sound like something I'd love to do.

"I'll see you tomorrow night. Let Patrick know I'll take you both to dinner after the game."

"What about Paxton?"

"Paxton?" He sounded confused, as if he'd forgotten Patrick had a twin. "Uh, yeah, sure, he can go," he added magnanimously, as if he were giving Paxton a great gift. I wasn't sure Pax would see it that way. My dad surrounded himself with people who adored and worshipped him. Paxton did not. Patrick, on the other hand, gobbled any tidbit of hockey knowledge Dad chose to bestow upon him.

There were other alums from Moo U who were outstanding hockey players. My dad had one of the longest careers and probably won the stats game, but he'd been lost ever since he retired a few years ago. I almost felt sorry for him. He didn't have a life after hockey, so now he was trying to live vicariously through the young guys. I think he spent a lot of time watching his old pro team practice, too.

"Naomi, did you hear me? You need to talk with the coach today to make sure you understand your duties."

"I will. I promise."

"Good." He hung up without even an *I love you* or *goodbye.* That was my dad. I knew he loved me, but he had a hard time showing it.

A week ago, I'd have been thrilled at the opportunity to spend more time in Patrick's presence. Now, my befuddled brain bounced between the two twins. I had to get a handle on myself.

I checked my makeup, grabbed a jacket, and headed for the coach's office, bolstered by the possibility of running into Pax, uh, Patrick. Much to my dismay, I didn't run into him. He wasn't in the dining hall either. I headed for the library to do some much needed studying.

The basement of the library was usually deserted, and I wasn't in the mood for company, so I went downstairs and cracked the books. Instead of studying the business principles of sports management, I recalled the heat in Paxton's eyes when he'd entered me for the first time. The pure heaven of it all.

"Hey, Naomi."

I jerked my head up and stared straight into the bright brown eyes of a guy I knew from some of the frat parties. We'd dated a few times my sophomore year, but he'd been a self-absorbed jerk. I'd dumped him pretty quickly. That didn't stop him from trying on occasion to hook up again.

"Hey, Bart." I turned away and stared at my book, hoping he'd get the hint and leave me alone. He didn't. He sat down next to me and scooted his chair closer. I moved away from him until my chair was wedged between his chair and the wall.

"I'm bored. Why don't we find some other source of entertainment?"

A girl couldn't be subtle with a guy like Bart. You had to clobber him over the head to get through to him. With his looks and money, I was sure he'd rarely heard the word no.

"Thanks but no thanks."

"Ah, come on." He wrapped a lock of my hair around his index finger and leaned in close. I smelled beer and the overpowering scent of his cologne.

"I'm waiting for someone," I lied.

By his knowing smirk, he didn't believe me. "Ditch him. I'm way more fun."

"Actually, you're not." I spoke from experience. Bart was too selfish to care about anyone but himself.

He scowled at me. "I don't like to be disrespected." His syrupy-sweet tone turned menacing. I glanced around, but the basement appeared empty.

"I don't like to be harassed." I lifted my chin defiantly and stared him straight in the eyes.

He leaned in closer. Both hands held my arms in a vise-like grip. My heart pounded in my chest, and I fought down the panic rising inside me. I was all alone down here without a chance anyone would hear me. It was well known by the students this area of the basement had no security cameras since there was nothing of real value stored down here.

"Naomi?"

I was never happier to hear Paxton's voice.

IN THE BOOK STACKS

Paxton

I was a glutton for punishment. Naomi kept popping up where I was, and I didn't mind one damn bit. If her frequent appearances weren't a coincidence, they most likely had more to do with my brother than me, but tell that to my lovesick heart.

By Thursday, I'd had too many cold showers and late-night fantasies. Thoughts of Naomi were making me crazy to the point I was irritated with myself and itching for a fight. I'd been an ass at hockey practice that afternoon and relished slamming my brother up against the boards. Patrick was furious at me, and I didn't blame him. It was a cheap hit. Coach Keller made me stay after practice and do skating drills for twenty minutes. Then Coach Garf, disturbed by my aura, insisted we work on sports psychology stuff for another half hour.

By the time I showered and dressed, my teammates had deserted me, most heading for the Biscuit. I'd neglected my studies all week and wasn't in the mood to hang out with my boisterous buddies. My mood was darker than that. Besides, Patrick needed time to cool off, and so did I.

I grabbed a bite at the union building and trudged over to the library, where I'd hunker down and attempt to study, even though my concentration level had been shot to hell since last Saturday night.

I slipped downstairs to the basement, not wanting to be recognized or, even worse, mistaken for Patrick. No one liked studying in the basement. The place was poorly lit, a little spooky, and smelled funny, like it leaked or something. And if I was being honest with myself, which I wasn't, Naomi was known to study down here. In fact, she'd showed me this location our freshman year.

I paused, listening.

I heard voices, one very familiar. In fact, so familiar that voice lived in my dreams, day and night. Only this time, it wasn't husky with lust or sleepy from a great orgasm. Instead, that voice of an angel sounded frightened.

I rounded the corner of the book stacks to the space where several tables were and took in the situation.

"Naomi?" I said, assessing the situation. Naomi was wedged between the wall and some guy who had his hands on her and not in a good way. I was going to put my hands on him and show him just how tough hockey players were.

The asshole loosened his grip on her when he heard my voice. Naomi looked up, spotted me, and met my gaze. Relief filled those beautiful eyes of hers. Before I had a chance to react, she leapt to her feet and ran to me, throwing her arms around me.

"You're late, honey," she chastised.

Confused, I slid my gaze to him and back to her. Her expression implored me to go along with her.

"Sorry, got held up at practice." I said the word *practice* extra loud because hockey players were gods on this campus, and I wasn't beyond throwing my weight around when necessary. Who I was dawned on the guy. Whether he thought I was Patrick or me was a moot point.

The guy stood, all bravado gone, his hands shaking. "I–I was just leaving."

I held Naomi to me and glared over her head at the frat boy. I'd seen him around and had a vague idea who he was. I racked my brain for his name. He needed to know I knew his name. Then it came to me.

"Bart," I called after him before he'd managed to escape from sight. He paused and turned around.

"Yeah?" Because of the distance between us, he'd bolstered the courage to smirk at me.

"You touch her again, and you're in deep shit. You'll find out just how jealous of a boyfriend I am."

The bravado drained from him. "I won't. I promise. Nothing was going on. We're just old friends." Before I had a chance to respond, he scampered away and disappeared between the book stacks. I waited until I heard his feet pounding on the metal stairs.

"Are you okay?" My arms went around her, and she hugged me tight, burying her head in my chest. Her shoulders shook, and I thought she was crying until she lifted her head. She was laughing her ass off.

"The look on his face… I bet he peed his pants."

I chuckled, distracted by how good she felt in my arms. "I'm glad I showed up."

"I am, too." She leaned into me and sighed a contented sigh.

"You do know I'm Paxton?" I joked, though I was half-serious.

"Of course I know. I can tell you two apart, especially when I'm sober."

"Good to know."

She looped her arms around my neck. "Thank you. Really. I dated that guy briefly, and he occasionally wants a repeat."

"He's a jerk. I've heard about him."

"He is a jerk. But being a nice guy wasn't a qualification for a date my first couple years here."

"And now?" I couldn't help but ask.

"Now it is."

Our gazes locked, and everything I'd done and sworn to do in the last few days flew out the window, totally forgotten. Naomi was my heart and soul, and I didn't know how to get beyond her.

She stood on tiptoes to reward me with a thank-you kiss, but I had other ideas. All reason escaped me as I buried my fingers in her hair and deepened the kiss. Naomi pressed her sweet body harder against mine, and we did the tongue tango. I'd never made out in a library before, but there was a first for everything.

Never breaking the kiss, I backed her up until she was pinned between me and shelves full of books. After four days of not touching, our hunger for each other swept through us, overwhelming any resistance we might've managed to muster. Instead, we abandoned all pretense of being just friends and let our bodies take control.

She cast a spell on me as she had Saturday night, and I had no chance of resisting, not that I wanted to. She felt so good, so right, so mine. Despite her diminutive size, our bodies fit together as if we were made for each other by a higher power.

We were insatiable, controlled only by our fever for each other. Nothing mattered but this woman, and I didn't care about consequences. I had to have her.

Had. To. Have. Her.

"It's been too fucking long," I panted against her cheek.

"Way too fucking long." She slid her hand down my chest and cupped my balls, squeezing gently. My pelvis jerked in response. I shut my eyes and moaned. She broke off the kiss despite my protests.

Grabbing a handful of my T-shirt, she pulled me along the stacks to the darkest, most private corner of the basement behind an oddly angled bookshelf, almost as if it were placed there for this very reason.

She pushed me against the cold concrete wall, but I didn't notice or care. My eyes widened as she sank to her knees.

"*Oh, please, yes. Oh, fuck,*" I pleaded, having absolutely no shame. I wanted those luscious lips and talented mouth on my dick.

She tore at my jeans, yanking down the zipper, opening the fly, and scratching my skin in her desperation to slide them down my legs. My hard cock sprang free, and she purred. I grasped the shelves on either side of me and held on as Naomi lowered her mouth and licked the pre-cum off my dick.

I was a mouthful, but she handled me well. Really well. I arched my back, angling my hips and pushing myself deeper. Naomi took more and more in her mouth until my entire length was inside her hot sweetness. I pumped several times, lost in my private nirvana, and forever craving what she did to my body, my mind, and my soul.

I came in a heated rush, and she took it, licking me clean afterward. I leaned against the bookshelf, panting, trying to gain my bearings, attempting to hold on to the last vestiges of a glorious orgasm as long as possible. But all good things must end, and so did this one. As I floated back to sanity, I gazed down at her, still kneeling, still holding my dick. She smirked with satisfaction, knowing she'd given me the blow job of my life in the Moo U library.

She slid up my body until she was standing.

"Naomi, I—"

Naomi shook her beautiful head and placed a finger across my lips. "No words of regret, Pax. We both knew what we were doing and what we wanted."

"I'm glad you knew it was me this time." The words slipped out with a trace of bitterness before I had the where-withal to stop them, effectively pouring cold water on the moment.

"I had a fifty-fifty chance of guessing correctly," she said, infusing some humor into a tense moment.

I barked out a laugh. "Well, I'm glad you guessed right."

Her smile was secretive, as if she knew something I didn't know. She stood on tiptoes, kissed me on the mouth, and turned.

"See you tomorrow." I gawked at her as she gathered up her things into her backpack and sashayed past me. She started up the stairs and turned. "And Pax?"

"Yeah," I said huskily.

"You might want to zip your jeans before anyone sees you trolling the book stacks." On that note, she clambered up the stairs, her soft laughter like the sweetest bird's song drifting down the stairwell.

CONFESSIONS

Paxton

I bounded up the stairs to the team bus late Friday morning. We'd play a game that evening in Connecticut and then travel to New York for a Saturday night game.

After my last class, I'd hung out near Naomi's dorm, hoping to see her before leaving on the road trip. We hadn't spoken since last night, and things were so unsettled between us. I didn't know if the blow job was another won't-happen-again moment or if I should read more into it.

I'd been tempted to text her, but this subject required personal contact. If I had my way, a lot of personal contact. I waited around as long as possible and had to hustle to get to the bus on time. I was five minutes late instead of my usual half hour early.

Coach Keller gave me *that look* and made a show of checking his watch. I glanced around for an empty seat. Patrick sat in the back of the bus, playing cards with a few of the seniors. I started toward the back. Lex waved to me from the middle of the bus and pointed to the empty seat next to him. Upperclassmen usually had their own seats, but I didn't mind sharing. I welcomed a conversation with someone who didn't share my DNA.

"You sure you don't want to save this for Kaitlyn?" I asked him.

"No, Keller hates it when we sit together. You know how he is." At the mention of his girlfriend, he smiled the same goofy smile he'd had on his face since he'd fallen for Kaitlyn last year. She was abrasive and rude at the best of times, but the girl did know her hockey, and she was one hell of an equipment manager. Like Naomi, her dad was also hockey royalty. Moo U had quite a few alums who'd gone on to be hotshot pro players. Our program was one of the best in the nation for turning out professional-caliber athletes, and I hoped to be one day added to the list.

I checked my phone for the hundredth time, hoping for a message from Naomi.

Nothing.

Lex nudged me with an elbow. I glanced up and did a double take. A petite, curvy female with a face so delicate it should be carved of porcelain followed Kaitlyn toward the bus. My eyes widened, unable to believe what I saw.

Naomi?

I still had a hard time with Naomi as a blonde. I loved her caramel-colored hair. But the blonde about to board the bus was definitely her.

"What's she doing here?" I wondered out loud.

"You didn't hear?"

"Uh, no," I said with my eyes glued to Naomi's beautiful face.

"Her dad got her an internship with the team. She'll be traveling with us, helping with stats."

"This could get complicated." I was overjoyed and

concerned at the same time, not knowing what was going on with us.

Lex frowned at me, puzzled. "Complicated? Does this have to do with you two making out on the couch last week?"

I snapped my head toward him. "You saw that?"

"Oh, fuck, are you dense? Everyone saw that. Except your brother and a few others who were already too wasted to notice or indisposed."

Of course we'd been seen. I'd be stupid to think otherwise. Oddly, no one had given me shit or brought it up until just now. My gaze slid to the bus door as Naomi climbed the steps and stopped at the top. She surveyed the bus, looking for a seat. Our eyes met, and her smile was slow and inviting. I welcomed the sight of her, and I grinned back. She glanced away as if not wanting to call attention to us, but she was too late. Lex noticed. I could tell.

She took a seat next to Kaitlyn near the front.

"You and Naomi?" Lex's eyes were wide with curiosity. "I thought that was just a drunken make-out session that didn't go anywhere."

I forced my hungry gaze from Naomi to Lex, and he must've noticed my misery.

"That bad?"

"Worse."

"You can tell me. I'm one of your biggest fans, and I'd never betray a confidence."

I took a moment to check for possible eavesdroppers. Hockey players could be the biggest gossips. The bus buzzed with separate conversations and debates as the team embarked in its first road trip, and no one paid attention to us.

"This is beyond humiliating."

"Go ahead. We've all had our share."

"Nothing like this."

Lex cocked his head. I'd aroused his interest, and there'd be no backing out now.

"She came on to me. We were both pretty drunk, and I wasn't thinking clearly. You know I've carried a torch for her for a while."

Lex nodded. He did know. I'd confided to him on occasion.

"We were making out, and she suggested we go to her dorm room. I won't give you the details, but the next morning, I noticed her staring at my number fifteen tattoo. From the stunned look on her face, I knew the mortifying truth."

"Truth? What truth?" Lex scratched his head and squinted at me.

"All night long she thought she was with Patrick."

"Fuuuucckkkk. Oh, man, that's brutal. Beyond brutal." Lex let out a long, low whistle. His expression was one of sympathetic horror.

"Tell me about it." I sank down in my seat so I was no longer able to see the top of her head.

Lex's eyes filled with sympathy. "I'm sorry, man, but she's stupid if she's disappointed you weren't your brother. If I was so inclined, I'd do you in a heartbeat."

I laughed, grateful for Lex's humor. "Thanks for the vote of confidence."

"You get my vote any day of the week."

I'd spent a lot of time helping Lex out last year, and the guys joked we had a bromance going. I was glad they didn't hear his latest vow of loyalty.

"Being mistaken for my brother is normal, but being mistaken to the point the girl didn't know who she was fucking has never happened to me before. It's pretty demoralizing."

"If she still wants Patrick after that, she doesn't deserve you."

"Thanks. We talked and agreed to be just friends, then last night, I ran into her at the library, and we were more than friends." I didn't give him the details. He knew enough to understand my dilemma.

"Did she know which twin you were?" When he saw my grimace, he said, "Sorry, I had to ask."

"Yeah, she knew. I was late getting on the bus because I was hoping to catch her after class. I don't know what's going on with us, if anything."

"Well, sounds like something is. If she's confused, it's not right for her to lead you on."

"I don't know that she's purposely doing that." I appreciated his support even if I didn't agree with him. Everything with Naomi was too raw, too up in the air. Talking about her might give me a little relief, but this conversation also made my stomach clench in frustration.

"Can you keep another secret?" I asked in an attempt to change to a safer topic.

"Buddy, I am your secret keeper."

I told him about my deal with Coach Garfunkle and his quest to make me the best player on the team.

"I've been telling you that you sell yourself short. He sees what I see."

I shrugged, suddenly embarrassed. "I don't know. We start on Sunday afternoon. I have no idea what to expect."

"I've got your back. If you need an extra stick, I'm there."

"I appreciate that. The last person I'd ask is my brother, and I don't want the other guys to know I'm getting special attention. I feel weird about it."

"Why is Patrick the last person you'd ask?"

"I don't know how he'd take it. We're tight, but we're also uber-competitive."

"Sibling rivalry?"

"Yeah, twin rivalry. That's even worse."

"I can only imagine."

"Hey, Pax, get your ass back here! We need another player for poker," Patrick shouted from the back of the bus. I looked at Lex, reluctant to desert him when he'd been so good to me.

"Go ahead. I hate poker. I'll stay here and lust after Kaitlyn."

I laughed, feeling better now that I'd gotten a load off by telling him my two secrets.

I got to my feet to make my way to the back of the bus, not able to resist one more glance in Naomi's direction. She was half-turned in her seat and our eyes met briefly. I swallowed hard and looked away.

Cal, Tate, Jonah, and Josh hunkered over a deck of cards sitting on a suitcase. I joined them, keeping my back to Naomi so I wouldn't obsessively stare at her, but I wasn't as successful at keeping my mind off her.

CHOICES

Naomi

I stared at Paxton's fine ass as he walked down the aisle to the back of the bus. I knew what that ass looked like naked with all those tight muscles and—

OMG, last night. I still didn't know what to do about that. We shouldn't have, or I shouldn't have done that. But the look of ecstasy on his face when I made him come had made my misgivings worth it. Still, what was I doing? Did I see Paxton as a surrogate for Patrick, or were my feelings more complicated than that?

"Oh, my God, it *is* true," Kaitlyn declared. Startled, I jerked my attention away from Pax's ass. Heat rose up my collar to my neck and cheeks, causing Kaitlyn to snort with amusement.

"What's true?" I adopted my best innocent tone, but I'd already blown my cover, what little cover there was.

"You have the hots for Pax, don't you? And here I thought you wanted Patrick all this time. I was so wrong."

"Shhh," I whispered, glancing around to make sure no one heard her.

Kaitlyn snickered, totally entertained by my discomfort.

"I don't know why you say that." I made a feeble attempt at denial. Guilt was written all over my face, and Kaitlyn was a smart cookie.

"I saw you two playing tonsil hockey on the couch of the hockey house a week ago. I can't believe you were sitting on that couch. Do you know what kind of biological material is on that ratty old thing?"

"I was drunk, and I don't want to think about that couch."

"That makes two of us. I've spent a few drunken nights on it myself. Soooo, do we have a twin love triangle going on here?" She waggled her eyebrows and drew a scowl from me, which delighted her all the more.

"No, we do not. Paxton and I are friends. We were just drunk, that's all." I hadn't been drunk last night, but I squashed that thought.

"Really? So you're still wanting to get into Patrick's pants?"

Did everyone on campus but Patrick know about my long-time crush on him?

"I don't know. A girl can't graduate from Moo U and not have a piece of that, can she?" I made fun of my entire sticky situation and hoped she'd drop the subject.

Kaitlyn lowered her voice. "I haven't."

"You haven't?"

"Nah. And then Lex came along, and nobody measures up to him, but if I were forced to choose between the twins, I'd choose Patrick for a one-nighter and Paxton for an every-nighter."

"Really?" Now she had me intrigued.

"Really." She winked at me conspiratorially but didn't elaborate.

54

"My dad's pushing me to date Patrick, like Patrick doesn't have a say in it. He's already got me married with kids while he sits in the stands and tells everyone Patrick is his son-in-law."

Kaitlyn was taking a drink of water and almost spit it out. She swiped her face and gaped at me. "You're kidding? And I thought my dad was bad."

"Mine got me this job."

"They're so much alike."

"Tell me about it." Most people didn't like Kaitlyn, but we'd bonded last spring over our mutual experiences having fathers who were hockey legends. I wished my dad had a business like Kaitlyn's dad, though, because lately he'd spent too much time focusing on me and my personal business.

"What is your job exactly?"

"I'm interning with the statistician. I'll be doing some advanced stats and stuff like that."

Kaitlyn screwed up her face. "Sounds interesting." Sarcasm dripped from her voice.

"It actually does to me. That's my area of interest. There are so many stats that aren't tracked by most teams and tell a more complete story about a player."

She waved me off with a hand. "Now you sound like my dad."

"Sorry. Not sorry."

I liked it better when my own dad was neglecting me and letting a series of girlfriends and nannies take care of me. Not that I didn't have a good time, especially with some of his twentysomething girlfriends. One of them had taken me to get breast implants at seventeen. He still didn't know about that.

Speaking of breasts, Paxton had loved my tits. He'd been completely mesmerized by them and had worshipped them with his clever mouth and sensuous tongue.

Oh, God, I was getting wet thinking about sex with Paxton while surrounded by a team of hockey players, coaches, staff, and Kaitlyn.

She raised a perfectly sculpted brow. "I know what you're thinking."

She couldn't possibly know, but my face flamed from embarrassment.

"It's okay, I think about it all the time. Frankly, there've been a few times when I've made myself feel better late at night when the bus is heading home, and it's dark inside."

"You didn't?"

Her smile was sly and wicked. "Maybe, maybe not."

I wouldn't put it past her, nor would I put it past her to go into the bathroom and have a quickie with Lex. None of my business, and I banished those thoughts from my head. I had enough sexy thoughts of my own without allowing others to enter into the weird-enough metrics flying around in my jumbled brain.

"Back to your twin dilemma," she said.

"I don't have a twin dilemma."

"Bullshit. You have a big twin dilemma. So, how was he? Paxton's the quiet type, and I've found more often than not they're the best lovers. In fact, hotter than fuck in most cases. All that quiet intensity focused on you and you alone."

"That about sums it up," I admitted, dropping all pretense of how much we had or hadn't done.

"I knew it."

"Then you understand my dilemma."

She nodded with a superior smirk. "Pax is a great guy. He's done so much for Lex's confidence and his game. He should do as much for his own game."

"You think?" I knew hockey, but Kaitlyn *really* knew hockey. She'd actually played some hockey, while I had an ice-skating phobia. And I do mean full-blown, panic-attack-gener-ating phobia from a childhood trauma on the ice.

I'd long thought that Paxton had the stuff to be an even more exceptional player than he was. He was a hard, powerful skater, but he needed to show the same aggression when it came to taking more chances at the net.

"Don't get me wrong. Patrick is going to take the NHL by storm, but Paxton might do the same thing only in a quieter, less flashy manner."

"I hope so," I whispered, because I cared about Paxton, and I wanted the best for him.

"The best thing that could ever happen for Pax's career is to get out from under his brother's shadow."

"Really? But they're so close." I didn't disagree with her necessarily. I'd thought so myself a time or two, but I wanted to hear her reasoning.

"They lean on each other, and taking away that crutch will make them better players."

I nodded. I'd watched them play for two years, and I knew exactly what she was saying.

"So when are you guys hooking up again?"

"We aren't. It was just a drunk fuck."

"Maybe it didn't mean anything to you, but I'm positive it does to Paxton."

"Why would you say that?"

"Because he's had a crush on you for a long time, and you've been oblivious."

"You noticed that?" I felt like an idiot for being in the dark about Pax for so long. How had I not seen it until last week-end? Maybe I hadn't wanted to see it?

"I notice everything when it comes to this team."

"I didn't realize he was"—I paused to find the right words that wouldn't reveal Pax's drunken declarations of love

—"uh…interested, until we slept together. I guess there were signs, but I didn't want to see them. I've always been more attracted to Patrick."

"Really? Why?" Kaitlyn cocked her head and regarded me as if I were a foreign species she wanted to study.

"I guess because everyone thinks he's the better player, and I'd score more points with my dad."

"That's as good a reason as any."

I narrowed my gaze and studied her, trying to discern if she was being sarcastic or not. She was unreadable at times, and this was one of those times. She merely smirked at me.

"If I were you, I'd be taking Pax up on what he has to offer. At least you'll know he won't be sharing that same offer with half the female student body, because he's a one-woman man. At least when he's dating someone."

"He doesn't really date much." I craned my neck to look to the back of the bus. Paxton was staring at me, and our eyes met. He ducked his head and concentrated on the cards in his hand, refusing to look my way again.

I was so confused.

GOOD GAME

Paxton

I played a good game Friday night, inspired by Coach Garf's faith in me and Naomi's presence. Her presence inspired me, and that blow job last night didn't hurt. I skated that much harder to impress her, wanting her to see I was every bit as good as Patrick in more ways than one.

I even slanted a few looks her way and did catch her staring at one point, giving me an even bigger boost. We hadn't had a chance to talk about what was going on between us, and part of me avoided that conversation. Sometimes ignorance was bliss.

A few minutes into the third period, Patrick and I took to the bench after our shift.

He slanted me an odd look. "You're playing differently."

I shrugged.

"I mean what's up?" He wasn't altogether comfortable with my increased aggressiveness. I'd taken a few shots I'd have normally passed to him. I got that. My play messed with our twin mojo, and we weren't reading each other like we normally did.

"Just trying to help us win." I turned away from him to shout encouragement to Lex, who streaked down the ice after he'd stolen the puck.

Lex scored. The bench rose as one, pounding our sticks on the boards. The score was tied. Except for a few perplexed glances, Patrick didn't say anything else about how I was playing.

With a few minutes left, I was on the ice with my line, and we desperately wanted to put this game away. Patrick had the puck and passed to me. It was one of those plays we'd done a thousand times. He'd pass to me. I'd give the impression I was going to shoot, then flip it right back to him, and he'd shoot. Only this time, I didn't pass to him. I saw an opening in the goalie's stance, and I lasered one toward the net. The puck hit the top of his pads and bounced in for a score.

A minute later, the final buzzer sounded, and we won. My teammates flooded the ice with backslaps and shouts of victory. I clambered over the boards to celebrate.

Patrick grabbed my arm and spun me around. At first his expression was almost angry, then he grinned.

"Great shot, bro."

"Thanks," I shouted over the din.

We headed for the locker room, but not before I caught Naomi's smiling face near the entrance to the tunnel.

"Good game," she said and winked.

I winked back, hope filling me with joy. I had a shot at Naomi, and that felt better than scoring the winning goal.

We were staying in the hotel tonight and would make the three-hour drive tomorrow morning to our next game. I was always starved after a game and looked forward to the huge food buffet the hotel set up for the team after our away games.

I showered and dressed, feeling cocky, as if I had the world at my fingertips. I walked out into the hallway to wait for the bus with the rest of the team, scanning the crowd for Naomi.

Her dad, Gene Smith, held court several feet away, surrounded by many of our players, including my brother. In fact, Patrick stood next to Smith as if he were the heir apparent to the throne. Judging by the attention Mr. Smith was showering on him, he probably was.

Coach Garf and Coach Keller were the last to arrive as we milled around.

"Guys!" Keller clapped his hands together to get our attention. "Mr. Smith has generously offered to buy everyone dinner tonight. We'll be walking down the block to Milano's Pizza, where we'll have the run of the entire restaurant."

The crowd cheered, and I went along, even though I'd prefer the buffet with more choices.

"That means no beer," Tate said in my ear.

"Yeah," I said, distracted by my brother and Naomi. They were deep in conversation, and he was making her laugh. The hopefulness drained out of me. Tate's eyes flicked to them and back to me.

"Your brother is making a move on her."

"He makes a move on anyone who's female and still breathing." My words came out with more bitterness than I'd intended.

Tate's brow shot upward. "Did I hit a sore spot?"

"No, not at all." I snuck another glance in Naomi's direction. She leaned into my brother and gazed up at him with those big gray eyes. Jealousy wrapped itself around my heart and squeezed hard.

"You're wearing your emotions on your face. You might want to tone it down if you don't want the entire team to know your secret."

I snapped my head back to Tate. "It's that obvious?"

"Only if you're looking. The good thing is I'm the only one who was."

"I'm so fucked," I muttered.

"Ask her out before your brother does."

"She doesn't want to date me. She wants Patrick. Look at her." Misery washed over me. After last night, I'd thought we had a chance, but now... She'd been toying with me until she got what she really wanted.

"What I see is someone who's playing the game for her dad's benefit, but she keeps stealing glances in your direction."

"She does?" I forced my gaze to stay on Tate. I wouldn't be caught ogling her again. Horror of all horrors to have my brother catch me. Hope soared inside me, and I tamped it down with a fresh dose of skepticism.

Tate didn't answer. Instead, he stared at a spot below my chin.

"Is something wrong?" I wondered if I had food on my shirt or something.

"Garfunkle got to you, didn't he?"

"Huh?" The shift in conversation caught me off guard. I had no idea what he was talking about.

Tate pointed at the crystal hanging around my neck and then pointed to one of his own.

"Oh, that. Yeah, he did."

Tate chuckled.

Our group shifted and moved as one toward the double doors leading out of the arena. I hung back. Lex fell into step beside me.

"Great shot at the end of the game. I've always admired your slapshot."

"Thanks," I said. Most of my good feelings about the game

had faded after watching Patrick hustle Naomi. I hung back, reluctant to subject myself to more torture.

My phone rang. It was Dad. Normally, I ignored his calls, but tonight I embraced any excuse to prolong the agony of watching Naomi and Patrick flirt with each other. I wanted to hear Dad's praise so badly I answered.

"I have to get this. I'll meet you at the pizza place."

"Sounds good. I'll save you a seat."

I waited until Lex was out of earshot and pressed the answer button. "Hi, Dad."

"Paxton, what the fuck was that play at the end of the game?"

Huh?

I blinked a few times and squinted at my phone.

"I scored the winning goal." I was confused, thinking he'd missed the end of the game.

"Your brother had a clear shot. Why the fuck didn't you pass to him?"

His words wouldn't have hurt more if he'd physically slapped me.

Patrick. It was always about Patrick. To hell with me.

I was speechless. He'd always treated me as an afterthought, but he'd never stooped this low. I guess because I'd never stolen the limelight from Patrick.

I took a deep breath, attempting to control my anger after years of neglect and verbal abuse at the hands of this man. I failed.

"Fuck you, Dad," I said and ended the call.

11

COLD SHOULDER

Naomi

Paxton and I barely saw each other all day. Something had to be said about last night, but I was still figuring out what that something was.

After Coach announced my dad was buying pizza for the team, ravenous hockey players eagerly headed for the door. I noticed Kaitlyn hanging back.

"Aren't you going?"

"No, I'll meet up with Lex later. All this shit reminds me too much of my father. This isn't about the team, it's about them craving the limelight."

"Isn't that the truth."

"Enjoy your dinner. I'm outta here." Kaitlyn ducked out the side door. I wished I could join her. I glanced around for Paxton. He stood off to one corner with his back to me. I walked toward him but stopped when I heard his words. Something was very wrong. He was defending his play to someone, but he'd played fantastic. Why would he have to defend that unless he was talking to his asshole of a father?

I didn't want to be caught eavesdropping and backed away, just as my dad took my arm, not noticing my distress. He steered me toward the sidewalk with Patrick flanking him on his other side. I glanced over my shoulder, but Paxton was gone.

He'd played one of his better games tonight, and I was proud of him. I wanted to tell him and talk about last night, but reluctantly I went with my father.

We walked the short block to the restaurant. I allowed myself to be ushered to a table with my dad and Patrick. The remaining chairs were taken up by a few of the senior players.

I tried not to roll my eyes as Dad gave his opinion on each player's game, and they hung on every word. It was disgusting how everyone groveled to him, even Patrick. No wonder Kaitlyn had ducked out on this. She hated it when her dad did this shit, too.

Patrick scooted his chair closer to mine. In the not-so-distant past, I'd have been flattered he was flirting with me, but I was too worried about Paxton.

I dissected Patrick's behavior with a more cynical eye. There were only a few women in the room, so really no competition, and he'd been paying more attention to me since I'd slept with his brother. While I didn't think he knew what had happened, something had changed enough in his eyes to spark a little sibling rivalry. The twins were competitive, and Patrick was used to getting what he wanted. Not that Pax was a complete pushover. I'd seen him stand his ground more than once, but he was more selective regarding his hills to die for, while Patrick picked every hill and wanted to win every battle and every competition—and he usually did.

My gaze slid to the door for the hundredth time, and this time my diligence was rewarded. Pax walked in looking like a dog beaten by its master. Only a few minutes ago, he'd been flying high after that game-winning score.

He paused in the doorway and swept his gaze around the room. Our eyes met briefly before he tightened his jaw and looked away. My heart sank as fast as a stone thrown in a stream. There weren't any seats left at my dad's table, or I'd wave him over. He skirted past me and joined Lex and Jonah across the room.

My sneaking suspicion regarding who'd been on that phone call earlier had to be correct. There was one person who beat Paxton down faster than anyone—his father.

He needed a friend, and I wanted to be there for him. Plotting my escape, I slid from my chair. Patrick had forgotten all about me and was basking in the praise my dad heaped on him. Meanwhile, my dad was in full hockey advice mode and didn't even know I existed.

I walked to the soft drink station closest to Paxton. Doing a short detour, I snagged a nearby chair, sliding it between Lex and Paxton. Lex scooted over to make room.

"You can only listen to that bullshit for so long," I said to no one in particular.

Paxton, deep in conversation with Jonah and Lex, nodded in acknowledgement. I waited for a lull in the conversation, which happened when a harried waitress dropped another pizza in the middle of their table. The guys grabbed for pieces like a pack of dogs. I sat back, afraid I'd lose a hand or fingers if I tried to snag one for myself.

Paxton took a bite and chewed. His gaze swung around to me.

"Great game tonight. That goal at the end of the game was wicked." I flashed my most brilliant smile.

"Thanks." He turned his head and regarded me with a hurt expression.

What had I done?

"Is everything okay?"

He frowned, picked up a napkin, and shredded it. I surely hoped he didn't imagine me being that napkin. "Yeah, sure. Why?" His indifferent tone chilled me.

"I saw you on a phone call earlier. You seemed upset."

"It's nothing. Just the usual parental BS."

"We need to talk."

Paxton sighed as if he'd been expecting and dreading this. "Fine." He pushed back his chair, not waiting for me. I hurried to catch up with him as he stepped outside.

"What's wrong with you?" I hissed, pretty upset with his attitude.

"With me? What about you? After last night, I—" He stopped and clenched his jaw. I waited for him to finish his sentence, but he didn't.

"What? You what?"

"Nothing. It doesn't fucking matter."

"It does matter. Last night was—" I searched my brain for an answer, because I didn't know what it was. I'd been struggling with what I'd done ever since it'd happened.

"A mistake. One more mistake." He was in a mood, and I wasn't going to get anywhere with him.

"Yeah, it was a mistake," I shot back. I leaned into him to punctuate my point and jabbed at his chest with my finger. Our eyes met, and before I knew what was happening, we were in each other's arms and kissing as if the end of the world would happen any second. I didn't know who made the first move or if we both did, not that it mattered.

There was nothing tender about our kisses. They were deep and rough with raw emotions as our frustrations bubbled to the surface and manifested themselves in a hot make-out session. His big hands grabbed handfuls of my ass, and I slid mine up his shirt, digging my nails into his back. We were hungry for each other like two feral creatures with raging hormones and uncontrollable needs.

"Oh, my fucking God. Can't you two find somewhere else to do that?" I heard the words, but it was several seconds before they sank in, and I realized someone was talking to us. Paxton released my ass, and I staggered back a few steps. Blinking to get my bearings, I turned to see Kaitlyn standing on the sidewalk, hands on hips, with disgust lining her beautiful face. Before either of us had a chance to respond, Kaitlyn pushed past us and through the door. The mood was broken.

"Shouldn't you get back to your dad and Patrick?" Paxton jerked his chin toward their table. Then, dismissing me, he followed Kaitlyn into the building.

I'd been given my walking papers.

He'd never treated me so callously before. Never. I felt used. I wasn't going to let him get away with it, but now wasn't the time to confront him regarding his behavior. I wasn't sure what last night had been or what had just happened or if this attraction between us led anywhere. I did know one thing, though. He was one of my best friends, and we needed to figure our shit out.

He'd just had a big argument with his asshole father, and maybe he was butt-hurt over Patrick flirting with me. Whatever. We'd be having words. Soon.

I stalked inside, unable to resist a glance at Paxton. He didn't look my way. Sighing, I went to my table.

And began to plot my next move.

SIZED UP

Paxton

Okay, I was an asshole, and I'd taken my misery out on Naomi.

I owed her an apology. She'd made herself scarce the rest of the weekend, and I couldn't blame her to a point. I'd been a grouchy jerk and deserved her cold shoulder. On the other hand, she sent mixed messages, leaving me confused as hell. But, damn, that blow job and the sex from the week before haunted me and gave me no peace.

By Wednesday evening, I still hadn't seen her. I wasn't sure who was avoiding whom. Maybe it was both of us. I'd done a lot of thinking and come to a few conclusions about my life.

I carried my heaping tray of food to a table and sat down next to Patrick and a few other teammates, along with the gaggle of females currently in Patrick's fan club.

I bit into my hamburger and chewed. The food in the dining hall was actually good, and the choices were endless. Pretty much something for everyone. And all a guy could eat.

Considering the energy hockey players expended, the endless supply of food was a definite plus.

I ignored the girls sizing me up, knowing I was their second choice if they couldn't snag my brother. I must've put out not-interested vibes, because they soon dismissed me and went back to drooling over Patrick.

I'd had a few workouts with Coach Garf, if you could call them that. The guy was decidedly weird. We did very little hockey and a lot of visualization and positive thinking exercises, along with reviewing a few chapters in the book, which I actually did read, even highlighted some paragraphs. The book had been a welcome distraction from my Naomi problems.

Coach insisted once the mental aspect of my game improved, the physical would fall in line. I was all-in, especially after being snubbed by Gene Smith and tortured watching Naomi with my brother. The negative talk in my head had to go, and I was making an effort to ban it and replace my thoughts with more positive affirmations. Coach did some of this work with the entire team, but he was drilling down with me, getting deeper into my psyche. The emotional intrusion bordered on uncomfortable at times, but mostly I kept an open mind and gave it all I had.

I knew I was screwed up. You couldn't have a dad like I did and not be. Patrick and I'd turned out pretty well considering, thanks to those first ten years with a loving mother.

"Hey, are you in la-la land or what?" Patrick snapped his fingers in front of my face. I fucking hated it when he did that and snarled at him, drawing a hearty laugh from the asshole.

"What?" I said, shoving his arm away from my face.

"What's with you? You've been weird lately." Patrick lowered his voice so his admirers wouldn't hear. He probably could've shouted as they were too busy giggling and chattering.

I shrugged and took another bite of the burger.

Patrick narrowed his eyes and studied me. "What've you been doing after practice every day? You haven't joined us at the Biscuit."

"I have stuff to do. I'm not your shadow, you know. I have my own stuff going on." My words were harsher than I meant, and Patrick reared back as if I'd slapped him.

"Shit," he said, shaking his head. "What's stuck up your ass, bro?"

"Sorry," I mumbled. "I'm just…going through some things."

His eyes clouded over briefly. "I'm here, you know. I'm always here."

"I know." *Way to make me feel like shit, bro.* I'd shut him out, and he knew it.

"Okay, well— Hey, there's Naomi." Patrick waved at her as she stepped into line at a serving station. She smiled and waved back. I looked away, irritated at him and irritated at myself for being irritated. How's that for skewed logic?

I felt Patrick's gaze on me. "I wonder why I never noticed her before. She's hot."

"You were too busy working your way through all the blondes on campus." I hunkered down over my fries and stuffed several in my mouth so I wouldn't say something stupid I wouldn't be able to take back.

"Variety is the spice of life, and now she's blonde." Patrick angled his head toward mine. "You don't have a problem with me asking her out, do you? I know you've had a thing for her over the past couple years, but you've never asked her out."

"No problem. Go for it."

"You sure?" Patrick narrowed his gaze, and I looked down,

afraid the miserable truth would be reflected in my eyes. I was crazier about her than I'd ever been, but I didn't like being jacked around, either, by a woman who couldn't figure out which guy she wanted.

"Positive."

"Hey, Naomi, have a seat." Patrick was all smiles as Naomi sat down across from us, which drew jealous stares from the gaggle.

"Hi, Patrick. Hi, Pax."

I mumbled a hello and didn't look up. If she and my brother were undressing each other with their eyes, I didn't want to witness it.

I bolted my food down and stood abruptly. "I've got a study group I'm late for. Catch you guys later."

Before either of them responded, I was out of there. I chanced a look over my shoulder as I dropped off my tray. Naomi stared thoughtfully at me while Patrick stared at her. He was moving in, and she'd finally get the guy she really wanted. And that guy wasn't me. She wouldn't need a surrogate anymore. She'd have the real thing.

Think positive, I warned myself.

Naomi and I'd had our fun. No blame on either side. I had to concentrate on other priorities in my life, such as graduating college and going pro or not. Of all the things holding me back, leaving Patrick behind was one of them. And perhaps leaving Naomi behind was another, even if I chose not to admit the truth.

I didn't have a study group, so I wandered to the hockey house. The guys were watching a game, which happened to be Seattle versus Vegas. My team versus my brother's team. Someday we might be on that ice playing against each other instead of with each other. The sheer weight of that thought caused my shoulders to droop even lower.

"Hey, Pax, have a seat," Lex called to me. I dropped down onto the couch and propped my feet onto the scarred coffee table currently littered with textbooks, popcorn, and empty beer bottles.

"Where's Kaitlyn?"

"Girls' night out."

I wondered why Naomi wasn't with her but didn't ask. None of my business.

I nodded to Jonah and Tate, lounging in the two beat-up recliners.

"Beer?" Josh asked as he stood in front of the refrigerator.

"Yeah." A beer flew toward me, and I managed to snag it before it crashed against the opposite wall. I twisted off the top and took a swig.

The door opened ten minutes later, and Patrick and Naomi entered. I'd half expected them to go back to our apartment and have loud, obnoxious sex the rest of the night. My mood lightened considerably seeing them here instead.

"Can you two scoot over?" Naomi pointed to the space between Lex and me. Lex moved over, and Naomi squeezed between us. I shifted my ass to make more room, but even so, her thighs pressed against mine, reminding me of our night together. Then again, anything reminded me of our night together.

"Patrick, get me a beer," she ordered. Much to my surprise, Patrick obeyed. This was getting weirder.

My brother came back with three beers and sat in the chair across from us. He kept two for himself and gave her one, then turned his attention to the game on TV. "Hey, that's our two teams, bro," he said, stating the obvious.

"Duh." I rolled my eyes, and he threw a fistful of popcorn at me. Normally, a move like that would start a food fight, but I wasn't in the mood. I brushed the kernels off my shirt.

"You missed one." Naomi leaned over so close to me the intoxicating scent of her filled my nostrils. She plucked a kernel from its resting place at the collar of my shirt. Her fingers brushed my neck, and I breathed in sharply. She leaned back and smiled—a smile full of false innocence. I knew what lay beyond that smile. The girl was anything but innocent. She was wicked in the best possible way, and she'd been my drug.

No more. Armed with some of Coach's techniques, I wasn't falling for it. I deserved better than my brother's leftovers. When the time came, that special person would find her way to me. If I believed it, my subconscious would do its damnedest to make my beliefs come true. Coach Garf and his book said so.

I looked at my phone, pretending to see something what wasn't there. "Oh, crap. I have a project meeting tonight. Totally spaced it." I stood quickly, nodded to my teammates and Naomi, and was gone before they had time to react. I'd performed my second disappearing act of the night.

I glanced over my shoulder before exiting the house. Naomi threw back her head and laughed at something Patrick said, and he gave her one of his *you're the next notch on my bedpost* grins as he drove the final nail in my Naomi coffin.

For the next several months, hockey would be my end-all, be-all. Sports were a lot easier to figure out than the rest of my life. But all that being said, Naomi was still a friend, and I'd treated her like crap last weekend.

I had to settle up with her.

13

NOT SO EASY

Naomi

Be careful what you wish for.

I'd never understood that particular saying until now.

For whatever reason, Patrick was definitely interested. Almost overnight, I'd moved to the top of his ask-out short list. After Paxton left the hockey house, I didn't want to stay either, despite Patrick's heavy flirting. I left, claiming I had to meet a friend at the library.

The next day after practice, Patrick offered to buy me a drink at the Biscuit. While such an invitation wouldn't be considered a date in most cases, with Patrick it was. Three weeks ago, I'd have died for the chance, but I asked for a rain check, and I really wasn't sure why. Patrick seemed surprised but took my answer graciously and without any personal offense. I did appreciate his ability to let most things roll off his back and enjoy life. I wished I was more like that.

While I had a mind for numbers, my personal life wasn't nearly as ordered. I often wondered if my love of numbers and stats came from the chaos in the rest of my life.

Currently, things were more tumultuous than usual because of my conflicting emotions when it came to those gorgeous twins.

As I was heading back to the dorm, I got a text message. My heart rate spiked when I saw Paxton's name on the screen.

Paxton: Can we meet?
Me: Sure, where? The library basement?

What made me type that and send it? And what if he accepted the invitation? Instead, crickets.

Me: Just kidding.
Paxton: How about the coffee shop in the union building?
Me: Just passing there now.
Paxton: See you in a few.

I got there first, ordered a decaf, and sat down in a seat next to the window where I'd be able to spot him. About five minutes later, he came in the door carrying a shopping bag.

He smiled when he saw me and sat down. "Hey."

"Hey." I grinned at him, genuinely glad to see him. "You got your hair cut." It had been somewhat unruly and longer than usual.

"Yeah, it was bugging me." He ran his hand through his now short-cropped hair as if checking the length. Pax had never been much for his appearance. He didn't need to be; he was gorgeous without putting any effort into it. I felt this insane urge to slide my fingers along his scalp and check things out for myself. I liked the longer hair on him, but this look was good, too.

We grew silent, neither knowing what to say to the other. Paxton looked down, fidgeting with his phone, oddly nervous.

I waited him out. He'd called this meeting, and I'd let him say what he'd come to say.

Pax looked up and met my gaze. "I'm sorry. About a lot of things. I was an ass to you last Friday night, and I owe you an apology. I sorta lost it."

"Apology accepted." I reached across the table and grabbed one of his hands. He wrapped his fingers around my hand. He stared into my eyes, and that one look sucked my breath away. So much was reflected in his eyes, longing, regret, uncertainty. I felt the same way.

"I miss you," he said in earnest.

"I miss you, too."

"I have something for you." He held the bag out to me.

I took it and peeked inside, but the item was wrapped in tissue. I pulled it out and unwrapped it, holding it up. The green and white Moo U jersey was emblazoned with number fifteen. I didn't know what to make of it. Fridays were jersey days, and most of campus wore the jersey of their favorite player. I'd always been jealous of the girlfriends who wore their guys' jerseys. Was Pax trying to tell me something? I glanced up questioningly at him.

"It's to help you remember which twin is which." He laughed, and I realized with relief and a tiny bit of disappointment, this jersey didn't mean anything more than a peace offering in the way of our private joke.

"I'll wear it proudly," I declared, and I meant it.

He beamed at me. "So, we're good?"

"We're good. We've always been good. Pax, you are very important to me, no matter what happens. Don't forget that."

He squeezed my hand and ducked his head. I wondered if he was getting as choked up as I was. He meant so much more to me than I was able to articulate. In fact, maybe more than I understood myself.

"This physical thing between us is really fucking up our friendship," he said, not meeting my gaze.

"I don't want to hurt you, but I'm so confused right now. I don't know what's what."

Disappointment flickered across his handsome face. I hadn't given him the answer he was hoping for. He forced a smile. "I'm okay if you want to date Patrick. I may not like it, but I'm okay with it."

"I don't know what I want, and that's not fair to you."

"Then let's stay friends."

"If we can." I laughed, and he joined in.

"It'll be hard."

"I know, but you need to concentrate on hockey, and I need get my head on straight."

"Friends?" His blue eyes sparkled as he held my hand to his lips.

"Friends. Always."

He kissed my knuckles and released my hand. "I have to get going. See ya."

"See you." I watched him leave, as confused as ever. I needed honest advice from someone who wouldn't sugarcoat their answers and would give it to me straight.

I knew just the person.

I found Kaitlyn in the laundry/equipment room off the locker room, cleaning another endless round of hockey jerseys. This place was the epitome of organization, everything perfectly aligned, folded, and arranged, almost frightening in its tidiness, at least to someone who was inherently messy.

A pile of towels sat on the opposite counter. Kaitlyn efficiently and uniformly folded each one and placed it in a neat stack. She glanced up when I walked in. Typical of her, she didn't greet me with a smile but something more akin to a scowl. I'd come to know her well enough not to be put off by her unwelcoming demeanor.

"Hey, could I help you?" I offered, not sure how else to start this conversation.

"I've seen your room. Can you fold like this?" She pointed at her precise stack of towels.

"Uh, no, I can't."

"Then you can't help me, but you didn't come here for that, did you?" She got right to the point, no polite small talk for her.

I shook my head and slumped into a plastic chair. Kaitlyn regarded me with a smirk, which was oddly sympathetic. "Guy problems?"

"Yeah, how did you know?"

"I recognize that look. I've seen it in the mirror a time or two." She continued to fold in a fascinatingly efficient manner as she talked.

"Pax and I settled our differences."

"You looked like you'd settled them last Friday night."

"I mean we talked it out and agreed to stay friends."

"Why? When there seems to be so much more?"

"I don't know. I'm torn," I admitted.

"You're torn?"

"Uh, yeah. Patrick asked me out. I've waited so long for this moment, and now I don't know. I asked for a rain check."

For someone who came across as selfish and mean, Kaitlyn was very perceptive. People didn't give her enough credit. Probably because she had one hell of a resting bitch face. She wasn't nearly as harsh as she portrayed. Usually, people like her were deeply insecure. I doubted she was an exception. The intimidating wall she put up kept people from getting too close.

But enough psychoanalyzing her. I'd come here for no-nonsense advice.

"I can't stop thinking about Paxton. It's insane. What if I'm using him as a surrogate for Patrick, because Patrick is such a player, and Paxton is the safe option?"

"That would be a bitchy thing to do." Kaitlyn raised one perfectly sculpted brow and regarded me pointedly. "If you don't know what you want, spare the boy. Keep it as friends. He needs to play the best hockey of his life this year. Don't mess with his head. He doesn't need that."

"I know." We'd had countless discussions about how badly he wanted a career in hockey.

"Then he'll need to show he's close to ready, especially if he's going pro after this year."

"Do you know something more?" Kaitlyn had connections via her father.

She smirked and shrugged, not willing to divulge any further information. "Back to your twin problem. Seems simple to me. You've decided to limit myself to being friends with Pax. That's settled. See where it goes with his brother or don't. It's your choice."

Leave it to Kaitlyn to break things down into their most basic components.

I wasn't convinced it'd be so easy.

14

PUSHING THROUGH

Paxton

I ached for Naomi.

Ached to the point my joints hurt. Ached inside. Ached in my soul.

I freaking loved her, and nothing she said or did seemed to dissuade my smitten heart.

I'd even taken to writing poetry in class when I was bored. Now that's desperate.

Friends, just friends.

This friend crap was killing me, but I had to respect her wishes. Deep down, some part of me knew it was for the best. She didn't feel like I did. Maybe physically but not emotionally.

I wouldn't be good enough once again, especially not in love.

For the next week, I consumed my thoughts with hockey as best I could, even though thoughts of a naked Naomi snuck in when I was least expecting them. I strove to compartmentalize my two obsessions and reduce Naomi thoughts to bedtime or during an incredibly boring lecture in my calculus class. Sometimes I succeeded; other times I failed.

Last weekend had been one of ups and downs. My usually consistent play had been very inconsistent. I'd had a good game Friday night and a mediocre one on Saturday. More often than not, I slipped back into old habits and struggled with new ones. Coach Garf told me not to fret about it, just keep pushing through.

Hanging out at the hockey house Saturday night had been torturous with Naomi there. She'd started popping up wherever I was. It was weird. She must've been trying to make my brother jealous or something. Or I was reading more into it, which was more likely.

Now we were in Michigan for back-to-back games. Of course, Dad would make the nine-hour drive, and I dreaded his attendance. I hadn't seen or spoken to the man since he'd reamed my ass for scoring rather than giving Patrick the opportunity.

He'd go postal on me, and I readied myself. I'd changed the rules without his permission. Eclipsing Patrick's stardom was not an option. My job was to feed the puck to Patrick. That was how he saw it.

Not anymore, according to Coach and the Sockeyes. I fought to realize the potential they'd seen when they'd drafted me. I wouldn't let them down, even if those closest to me were uncomfortable or angry or both.

We were in first place in the league going into this weekend, and Coach Garf insisted I take more shots rather than passing the puck. Not that he wanted me to hog the puck but to take the good shots when I saw them and trust my instincts.

Regardless, I was torn about my new role on the team and wished I was able to discuss my concerns with Patrick, but I held back for fear he wouldn't understand, or worse, would unintentionally destroy the fragile confidence I'd struggled to build.

Change wasn't easy. Change was difficult and painful.

I absently rubbed my fingers over the moonstone tucked under my jersey, but I didn't feel any magical improvement in my self-confidence. Maybe crystals didn't work like that. Maybe their effect was more subtle.

Michigan played a very physical game Friday night, and we lost in a hard-fought battle. I played like shit, and everyone avoided me afterward, as if some of my bad juju would rub off on them.

I pulled off my jersey and found Patrick studying me quizzically, his hair wet from showering and a towel slung over his shoulders.

"What's going on with you?" he asked, scratching his bearded chin.

"Nothing. Why?"

He narrowed his gaze and looked at me hard. I ignored him and toweled off. Because of that twin connection thing, he'd see my inner struggle even if he didn't understand its source. He didn't push the issue, much to my surprise.

With a shake of his head, Patrick wandered off to give some advice to a couple freshmen who'd cracked under the pressures of an intense game.

I put my head in my hands and closed my eyes for a moment.

"Pax."

I lifted my head. Coach Garf sat on the bench next to me and lowered his voice. "You're working on a new style of play. You're going to get worse before you get better."

"The whole team is mad at me for not passing the puck to Patrick."

"Just stick with the program. I'll worry about the team."

"Maybe I should've passed to Patrick more."

"You did fine. Just what I've been expecting. We win as a team, and we lose as a team. Everyone bears the weight of this loss." He stood and patted me on the shoulder pads. "Believe in yourself as much as I do."

"I'm trying."

"No, you will do this."

"I *will* do this." I chuckled, unable to help myself.

"Good boy." He grinned and sauntered off to give a few words of encouragement to our goalie, who'd had a far worse night than the rookies or I had.

I sat up straighter, stripped off my clothes, and took a long, hot shower, after which I dressed and boarded the bus for our hotel. I sat by myself on the bus. Even Tate and Lex left me alone, which I appreciated.

Within five minutes, the bus pulled up to the hotel, and we unloaded. As usual, my gaze sought Naomi, but she'd disappeared. We had an hour before curfew, and several guys headed for the Chinese place across the street. I started to follow and froze.

"Oh, fuck," I muttered under my breath as I saw my dad in the lobby. I half expected Naomi's father to be with him, but he was nowhere to be found. Glancing left and right, I plotted an escape, but I was too slow.

"Paxton," my father ordered in that tone I rarely defied. Better to take my verbal licks without complaint and get it over with. Sensing Dad was preoccupied with me, Patrick attempted to skirt past us, but Dad grabbed him by the arm and pulled him into our happy little family group.

I met Patrick's gaze and sighed. He gave me that *we're screwed* look back. We were both in for a butt chewing.

"What the fuck was that performance tonight?" Dad perched his hands on his hips. His angry gaze slid from me to

Patrick and back. Obvs, we were both the focus of his ire this time around.

I shrugged, knowing there was no good answer, and silence was probably best.

"Don't get smart with me, young man." He shook his finger in front of my face. I held my ground and didn't flinch.

Patrick, who had less patience for our dad's bullshit, stepped forward. "He didn't say a fucking word. How is that getting smart with you?"

"And you? You shot like shit. You wouldn't be able to score a goal tonight if the goalie had left the net wide open. Your shooting was way off."

"We can't all be perfect like you," I muttered and deflected his anger back on me. Patrick and I often ping-ponged our responses to make it harder for him to focus on one of us. We liked to think of it as a survival technique.

"I don't know what the fuck is up with you lately, but your job is to handle the puck and pass to your brother unless you have a sure shot."

"A sure shot? What's that? Do you mean if the goalie passes out or takes a coffee break, I can shoot?" I ignored my brother's shocked expression. I wasn't usually the defiant one. I left defiance to Patrick and usually suffered in silence. I preferred flying under the radar with Dad, which I'd accomplished because Patrick was the chosen child, and I was merely an afterthought.

"Look, you insubordinate little bastard." He moved closer to me, his posture threatening. I held my ground. I was bigger and fitter than him. "Don't you fucking ever speak to me the way you did last time."

"I'll speak to you in a manner you deserve."

Patrick's eyes grew big, and he regarded me with a new respect.

"Ah, Mr. Graham, I've been looking for you." Coach Garf appeared alongside us with a huge smile on his face. Dad's expression switched from angry to pleasant like he'd flipped a switch. Patrick rolled his eyes and prepared to bolt. I'd be right on his heels. Coach had run interference for us.

"Hello, Coach," Dad said in his smarmy suck-up voice. Patrick made a gagging sound, and I had to clap a hand over my mouth to stop my snickering.

"I'd like to spend some time with you, pick your brain. I know you played in the NHL and might have some insight into coaching strategies."

Dad puffed up like a peacock in a parade.

"Dad, looks like you're busy. We'll see you in the morning." Patrick grabbed my arm and turned.

"Yeah, certainly, boys, I'll text you. We'll meet up for breakfast." Our father was all smiles and niceties now. His behavior was disgusting, and I owed a debt of gratitude to coach. Maybe he'd attempt some of his psychological tricks on our Dad, but I wished him luck with that. The man wouldn't be a willing participant.

We bolted for the elevator.

"Damn, we need to buy Coach a drink," Patrick said. "What'd you say to Dad that has his boxers in a wad?"

"Last time he called me, I ended the call with *Fuck you* and hung up on him."

Patrick grinned at me and slapped my back. "Pax, you are my hero. I'm sure he deserved it."

"You know he did."

Patrick caught the eye of a few thirtysomething businesswomen standing off to one side of the lobby. Their faces lit up when they saw us. My brother winked at them, and they took that as an invitation.

"Later," I said, not interested tonight in hooking up with

anyone—except Naomi, and I didn't need to be reminded we were staying in that damn friend zone.

I walked toward the pub, the only place open in the hotel to get a bite to eat. Not only was I irritated by my crappy play, but my brother was flirting with these women when he could have Naomi. I shook my head and slid into a booth in the nearly deserted seating area.

Slumping in the booth, I wallowed in my foul mood until a shadow crossed over the table.

I looked up to find my own personal angel smiling down at me, and my crappy mood wasn't so crappy anymore.

15

KINDNESS LECTURE

Naomi

I slipped out from behind a large potted plant and checked to make sure no one had caught me eavesdropping on Mr. Graham and his sons. I was furious at the depth of cruelty and selfishness in that man. Pax needed me, and I was determined to find him.

I startled a hotel worker who was dusting the nearby coffee table. She jumped backward, clutching her duster to her chest.

"I'm sorry." My face flamed red, and I hurried past her. Near the main doors, Patrick flirted with several women. I barely gave them a second glance.

I stopped in front of the hotel pub and peeked inside. Paxton was slumped in a booth, nursing a glass of water and hunkered down over a menu. His shoulders were slumped and his body language signaled defeat like a blinking neon light.

I hesitated, not sure being alone with him was a good idea. But he needed me, and he was one of my besties. I slunk across the room, keeping my eyes on him, still reluctant to approach him. My feet had no such problem and carried me right to his booth.

"You look like you could use a friend?" I said.

His head shot up, and he regarded me warily. "I guess I could."

I sat down across from him. "I was nearby when your dad accosted you and Patrick."

"How much did you hear?" He frowned and rubbed his eyes wearily. Heaving a sigh, he met my gaze. I wanted to wipe the devastation off his face, make all his troubles go away, and give him something good to think about. My thoughts had started down that more-than-friends path once again. I jerked myself back from the brink of propositioning him.

"Enough," I said.

"So you heard my dad?"

"Yes, pretty much everyone did."

He sighed and slammed back his water, signaling for another. I ordered one, too. I hated for a man to drink water alone.

"He's a little harsh," I offered sympathetically, tempering my words. Frankly, I wanted to slap the man for how he treated his boys. Coach Garf had way more patience than I did when dealing with obnoxious parents. Maybe my patience had been worn thin by my own dealings with an overbearing parent. Regardless, I knew my dad loved me in his own way. I wasn't sure I'd say the same for the twins' father. He seemed more interested in what they might be able to do for him.

"That's one way of putting it." Paxton took a huge gulp of his newly delivered water glass.

"You might slow down." I pointed at his new glass of water, now empty.

He snorted. "Imagine you telling me that?"

"I know. Right?" I laughed, and we grinned at each other, feeling our old mutual respect and fondness.

"Hungry?"

"You know, I am."

He ordered nachos and offered to share. I never turned down an invitation like that. We made easy small talk, teasing and joking like we once had. A weight lifted off my shoulders, and my world looked so much brighter. Pax and I were finally in sync again.

His phone buzzed, and he scowled at it.

"Your dad again?"

"Nah, Patrick telling me not to come to the room until curfew."

I nodded knowingly.

"I shouldn't have told you that."

I shrugged. Knowing his twin, my alleged crush, was hooking up with some random female didn't depress me like it once had.

"Does that bother you?"

"Not really. Patrick is Patrick. We both know that." Now if Pax had joined his brother and hooked up with one of those women... The mental picture of him screwing someone else's brains out ate at my gut, surprising me. I met his gaze. We stared into each other's eyes, not speaking but communicating with our hearts, not our heads. I dared not decipher what those two hearts were saying to each other.

Finally, I voiced what we'd both been thinking. "Pax, I really do miss you. I miss our little talks. I miss hanging with you."

"We hang out."

"Only if I initiate it, and you find any excuse to distance yourself."

"I don't want to get in the way of you and my brother." His words rang hollow and broke my heart as I'd broken his.

"Did you know Patrick asked me out?"

"I knew he was going to."

"I took a rain check. I had a test the next morning."

"I'm okay with the two of you. You know that, right? Not that I get a vote, but don't let me hold you back because of—you know—what's happened between us on occasion."

Hell yeah, did I know. It was all I thought about, especially late at night alone in my little dorm room. Thinking about him constantly was part of my own personal dilemma and confusion, since I'd been so wrapped up in pursuit of his brother for so long. Just last night, I'd dreamed that I asked him to reciprocate and go down on me. Paxton's face between my legs, giving me pleasure, while his blue eyes held mine was my newest naughty fantasy. At first, I'd convinced myself I was really lusting after Patrick, but once Paxton cut his hair and Patrick's was still long, I knew the truth. The image haunting me was Paxton with his now-short hair and number fifteen tattooed below his hip bone.

"You should go out with him. You've wanted to for a long time," Paxton pushed.

"I might." I was telling the truth. The one way to get one of them out of my system was to date the other one and see how they compared. But the idea of sleeping with Patrick after that epic night I'd spent with Paxton didn't appeal to me as it once had. And seemed like such a betrayal of Pax. I was such a fucking mess.

"I want to make sure we're okay, because from where I'm sitting, we're not," I forged ahead.

"We're fine." He smiled at me. While his smile was filled with sadness, there was also sincerity. I hated to see him sad, knowing I'd played a part in his struggles of late. Instead of harping on whether we were really fine or not, I decided to test his claims by talking with him as a friend.

"You're wearing the jersey," he noted with a grin. I looked down. I'd forgotten that, on a whim, I'd put it on before the game.

"I am. I like it."

"Good." He smirked as if at some secret joke.

"What's going on with you? You've altered the way you play. Any reason why?"

"Are you going to criticize me, too?"

"No, not at all. I think it's about time."

"You do?"

I nodded.

Paxton glanced around, as if not wanting to be heard, and lowered his voice. "Coach Garf is working with me. He has contacts with the Sockeyes, and they'd like to see me step up my game, realize my full potential, that kind of thing. They'll have a few spots on the roster next fall due to retirements, and they think I might work out well in one of them." As he talked, he rubbed something under his shirt, but I couldn't tell what it was.

"So that explains it."

"Garf thinks I've lived in my brother's shadow long enough."

"And what do you think?"

"I think I'm on the verge of not having that shadow around, and I'll be forced to handle life and hockey without Patrick. He's been my crutch for too long."

"I think Garf is a smart man, and you're not so dumb yourself."

Paxton laughed, and I loved hearing his laugh. I hadn't heard it nearly enough lately.

"It's causing stress with my brother and, to a lesser extent, the team."

"And your dad?"

"My dad never approves of anything I do."

"Patrick's having a hard time dealing with you not playing a supporting role?"

"I guess he's confused and irritated. He has his own future to consider."

"So do you."

"I know." His blue eyes met mine, and my heart did a little dance all around my rib cage. We stared at each other for a good long while until Kaitlyn and Lex showed up.

"Hey, sit over there so I can sit by my girl," Lex insisted.

Paxton didn't argue but got up to move to the booth seat next to me. I scooted over to make room for his big body. A body I was hyperaware of. A body I craved. A body I saw naked every time I looked at him.

Paxton rested his elbows on the table, and my gaze was drawn to his muscular arms, easily discernable through the sweater he wore. That man would make the worst Christmas sweater look like a million bucks.

I licked my lips and grimaced at Kaitlyn's knowing smirk. She'd caught me looking, and I was guilty as charged. The guys didn't notice. They were busy talking about the game, while Kaitlyn and I sipped our water. Coach Keller would frown on any of us drinking alcohol while on the road.

"Your dad is brutal, Pax," Kaitlyn noted during a lull in the conversation.

"Yeah, he's a little intense."

"That wasn't the word I'd use for it. Maybe more like asshole." Kaitlyn's blunt honesty didn't bother Paxton. In fact, he wasn't put off by her assessment of his dad. He probably agreed with her.

"You can't pick your relatives," was his only comment.

"Tell me about it." Kaitlyn's smile was kind and sympathetic. She had her own daddy problems.

We made small talk for a while longer before Paxton excused himself to get some sleep and Lex followed. Kaitlyn stayed with me.

"He's still stuck on you."

"You think?"

"I do, but he's gun-shy."

"I really burned him. I don't blame him for not wanting to go there again. Paxton is in a bad place right now. Coach Garf is pushing him out of his comfort zone and forcing him to take more risks. As a result, his play is going downhill."

"Needs to get worse before it gets better," Kaitlyn said confidently.

"That's what Coach told him."

Kaitlyn grinned. "I am my father's daughter."

"Yes, you are."

"Let him settle in. See where things go with the two of them."

"Dad's pushing me toward Patrick. He's got it all figured out. Patrick will be the heir apparent to his hockey throne since he doesn't have any sons, and I'm scared to put on a pair of skates, let alone get on the ice with them."

"You're afraid to skate?"

"I tried to learn to skate, but I fell down more than I skated. I had a particularly bad fall in which I broke my leg, and the bone actually pierced my skin. There was blood everywhere. I tried a few times after that to skate but had such extreme panic attacks, my dad quit asking. I was afraid to skate, and such fear galled him. He found me lacking in courage and athletic ability."

"Wow, that's brutal. I don't know if I'd skate after that either."

"Well, Dad doesn't feel that way."

"Your dad's like mine. They're tough men who see skating ability as a measure of worth."

"But you skate?" It was a question, somewhat.

Kaitlyn only shrugged. "Something I've noticed about you. You're a pleaser. You become the person you believe others want you to be. Why don't you please yourself for once? Be who you want to be?"

"I am."

"You are? You altered your appearance to be more like the type that Patrick goes for culminating in the blonde hair and skanky clothes."

I sat up straight as if she'd slapped me. "I did not."

"What's your natural hair color?"

"Light brown."

"Why don't you embrace you, instead of copying the women you see hanging all over him?"

I didn't have an answer to that.

"Figure out what you want. Until then, steer clear of Paxton. That would be the kind thing to do."

Imagine a lecture from Kaitlyn on kindness? Wonders never ceased.

Her words rang true when it came to Paxton.

I had to make some decisions, and not just about which twin I preferred.

I had to decide who I was.

Myself or someone else entirely.

GOODNESS

Paxton

Naomi and I had reached a comfortable place. We weren't as close as we once had been, but we were getting along, and she was always ready with an encouraging word when it came to my game, or lack of. The chemistry didn't go away, but I was dealing with it as best I could.

I continued to struggle, pissing off my brother on more than one occasion. I might be getting discouraged, but I wasn't a quitter. Coach Garf believed in me, and I wouldn't let him down regardless of the consequences.

Today after practice, Patrick and I had a heated exchange of words in the locker room with the entire team as our witnesses. We'd never done that before. When he attacked, I unleashed my frustration on him and fought back. Usually, I walked away from our arguments. Not this time. Tate, Jonah, and Lex had to get between us.

After nearly coming to blows with my twin, my first inclination was to crawl off and lick my wounds. *Not this time. Damn it.* I joined the guys at the Biscuit for drinks. I'd prefer hiding out in the library, but that wasn't me. Patrick's presence wouldn't prevent me from doing the things I wanted to do.

Lex and Kaitlyn saved me a seat and waved me over when I walked in. The team went out of their way to pretend nothing had happened this afternoon, but we all knew differently. Patrick's and my differences were beginning to affect the team.

My brother sauntered in a few minutes later, looking as if he owned the place, which he somewhat did. We locked eyes, and he narrowed his gaze. Giving me the cold shoulder, he breezed past and commandeered a seat at the other end of the table from one of the freshmen.

I blew out a long breath of relief. We needed space from each other. It was hard enough living in the same apartment. I hated this wall between us, but I was at a loss when it came to fixing it. I tried to put myself in his shoes. He'd always been the star of any team we'd been on, the coaches' favorite, and the go-to guy for the puck. He was struggling with the changes I'd made to my play, not just because they were affecting his game but because Patrick had been perfectly happy with the way things were. He would see no reason to change.

I, on the other hand, wanted to get out of this box I'd been locked into for all these years. I needed to do so if my pro career was going anywhere.

I considered explaining what was going on, but a gut feeling he'd balk or worse held me back. I wished he'd see what had been going on all these years and understand what being in a support role had done to me.

And I was missing Naomi horribly. I wanted things I couldn't have with her, or so it appeared, though I'd seen no sign of her dating my brother. Given our current situation, surely he'd have rubbed that in my face.

I glanced at my phone to see if I had any text messages from her. Nothing. I hadn't texted her either since yesterday, even though it was killing me not to do so. Appearing desperate and needy was not a good look.

"Hey, miss me?"

My head shot up at the sound of the voice from my dreams. I couldn't stop the huge smile spreading across my face. She'd answered my prayers like an angel from above.

Naomi settled into the empty chair next to me, rather than moving to the end of the table where my bro was.

I did a double take. She'd changed her look. She wasn't a blonde anymore, and her makeup was more understated. In fact, she looked like the girl I'd first met our freshman year. I liked this version of her a whole lot better, though any version of Naomi was hot AF. This woman was the most gorgeous thing I'd ever seen with her casual Moo U hockey T-shirt and jeans. Her caramel hair cascaded down her back in waves of pure silk and beckoned to me to bury my hands in all that sensual luxury, tilt her head back, and kiss the hell out of her.

"Pax," she nudged in that breathless voice which reminded me of our night together.

"Hi," I said. "You look great. I like the change."

"I'm going back to my natural color, and I'm leaving it wavy instead of straight."

"I like it. A lot."

She ducked her head almost as if embarrassed by my comments. When she lifted her gaze and met mine, she smiled shyly. "Thanks."

"You're welcome."

Patrick's loud laughter reached us, and we both glanced at him. When she turned back to me, I didn't see the longing in her eyes I used to see when Patrick was in the room.

"You seem down," she said, reading me like a book in that way she always had.

"A little," I admitted. The reason I was down had more to do with her than anything, though my crappy relationship with my twin was second in line.

"What's up?" She snagged one of the wings the waitress had just delivered to our table. Holding my breath, I watched as she nibbled the meat off the bones and sucked on her messy fingers. OMG. I was dying inside. Flashes of how well she sucked a certain part of my anatomy dominated my thoughts.

"Are you okay?" Her concern was palpable, and I rushed to make excuses.

"Patrick and I had an ugly scene at practice today. The entire team saw it."

"I'm sorry." She meant those words. She hated seeing Patrick and me at each other's throats. So did I. I also hated not seeing more of her, especially in less clothes.

I nodded and took a long pull on my beer. "If all this shit keeps up much longer, I'm going to be an alcoholic. I seem to be drinking to dull the pain."

Naomi's smile was kind and caring, giving me false hope I couldn't afford to feel. Did I dare believe she was looking at me the way she used to look at Patrick?

"Pax, hang in there. Don't go back to old habits." She patted my arm. "You've got this. I watch. I see. Your timing is off by a fraction. Once you take care of that fraction, no one will be able to tell you from Patrick. Hell, I think you might be a better player."

I choked on my beer with it almost coming out my nose. She was making shit up to help me feel better, and it was working. My head hurt as I struggled to come to terms with who I was on and off the ice. Breaking out of your carefully constructed belief system sucked and was way harder work than I'd ever anticipated. The physical work I dealt with just fine. It was the mental aspect that threw me more often than not.

"Dad always says it's ninety percent mental when you get to the professional level," Naomi added.

"So does Coach."

"Does that apply to you and your skating?"

"I don't have the physical ability and never will. My balance sucks." She shot back almost defensively making me sorry I'd asked the question.

"I didn't mean to hit a nerve."

"Thanks, I know you mean well, but I'll pass. I suck at skating. I'm my dad's biggest failure."

"Now who needs an attitude adjustment?"

"I won't deny that. I'm a realist. My dad wanted a boy, and he got a clumsy, uncoordinated girl."

"He should be proud of you. You're smart and bright and beautiful."

She blushed and squeezed my hand. "Thank you."

"You're very welcome."

We were quiet for a long moment as we were both lost in thought. Naomi spoke first.

"Do you miss her?"

I blinked, confused. "Miss who?"

"Your mom."

Just this one mention of my mom caused a vise to close over my heart and my throat to close up. I nodded, not trusting myself to speak just yet. Naomi waited patiently for me to gather my wits about me. "She was always there for Patrick and me, always positive and encouraging. She was loyal to a fault. She put up with our dad and all his issues, always painting a cheerful face on everything. Dad hated that I was closer to her than to him."

"I can understand why you would be. He'd be hard to be close to."

"Do you know what he said to me after she died?"

"What?"

I swallowed hard and cleared my throat. I'd never mentioned this to anyone but Patrick. "He said maybe now I wouldn't be such a mama's boy."

Naomi's mouth dropped open. "What an insensitive thing to say to a little boy who's grieving." She grabbed my hand and held it tightly.

"I thought for the longest time her death was somehow my fault because I'd displeased my dad, and as a result, I lost her forever."

Her gray eyes met mine, but I didn't see pity there. I saw understanding and sympathy. I gripped her hand, gaining a measure of comfort from the closeness.

"What about you? Do you miss your mom?" It was a stupid question, but I wanted to remove the focus from me. I also wanted to hear from her. I didn't let go of her hand, and she didn't pull away.

"Horribly. You'd think all these years later, it'd get better, but there are times it hurts as much as the night it happened. I'll never forget our nanny opening the door to the policeman. Dad was playing somewhere. I heard the words he uttered as he told her about the accident."

"I get it. Worst night ever." I did get it. We'd both lost our moms under similar circumstances.

"Every time there's a knock at the door after eleven at night, I get sick inside."

"Me, too, and I miss the sound of her voice and her laughter."

"We have to embrace the good memories, Pax, because that's all we have."

I shook my head and smiled. "No, it's not all we have. We're both a piece of our mothers. They live inside us. We have to remember that. I like to think that she's watching over me like a guardian angel."

"I'd like to think that, too."

We smiled at each other, and I didn't feel so alone anymore. "I'm lucky to have a friend like you."

"So am I. I'm glad we found our way back to each other."

"I missed our talks." She leaned into me and gave me a hug. I hugged her back, and over her shoulder, I caught Patrick watching me with a frown on his face.

To hell with him. He didn't have a claim when it came to Naomi. She'd been my friend first, and she'd be my friend afterward, if there was an afterward. He burned through Moo U co-eds faster than a wind-fueled fire burned through a forest.

I'd done my share of burning, too, but this year I'd lost interest in casual hookups, especially since Naomi showed me how good it could be, and my greedy heart and soul wanted more of her brand of goodness.

LOST ITS LUSTER

Naomi

Saturday night the guys won at home after a bye Friday night. Patrick had been stellar, scoring two goals, and Paxton continued to struggle. I tried to find Pax afterward to bolster his ego but didn't have any luck. He wasn't at the hockey house or the Biscuit.

Sunday night the hockey house was having an epic Halloween party, which I wouldn't miss for the world. I loved dressing up for Halloween. My dad had taken the liberty to send Halloween costumes to both Patrick and me.

I arrived at the twins' apartment a little after six p.m. on Halloween at Patrick's request. He was going as Captain Jack Sparrow and asked me to do his makeup. I was going as a serving wench. The costumes were incredible and also a thinly veiled attempt to force us together. My dad wasn't all that subtle, even if he thought he was. Despite my irritation at his manipulations, I grudgingly appreciated the gesture.

My dress was cut so low the girls threatened to escape if I bent over. I was pretty sure Dad's latest girlfriend picked this one out. He wouldn't have bought anything like this. He'd rather see me wrapped in duct tape. I didn't usually balk at showing skin, but this time I was more reluctant than usual.

Patrick met me at the door, dressed in his swashbuckling outfit complete with a long-haired wig. "Good, you're here." He pulled me into their messy apartment. Neither guy was big on house cleaning. Someday I'd come over and give the place a good once-over, not that I was tidy either, but this was even too much for me.

"Let's get moving. You're late." Patrick glanced at his watch and scowled.

"Only by a few minutes. What're you in such a hurry for?"

"I don't want to miss the festivities. Since it's a school night, it's starting early and ending early."

I seriously doubted that. The hockey house's legendary parties never ended early unless someone called the cops, and Patrick was often one of the last to leave.

I steered him to a battered barstool at the counter, and he compliantly sat down. Opening the makeup case I'd brought, I went to work. Unfortunately, or fortunately depending on how you looked at it, my boobs were at eye level to Patrick's face from his perch on the stool. His hot gaze seared my bare skin. Instead of being aroused, I grew increasingly uncomfortable.

I glanced around for Paxton but didn't see him. Either he wasn't here or he was sequestered in his room. I'd hoped he'd be a superhero in tights that showed off his muscular body and big— I squelched that line of thinking. Lusting over Pax right now would only get me in trouble, but what fun trouble that'd be.

I grasped Patrick's chin and yanked his head upward to better work on his eye makeup and force his gaze upward.

"Ow. That hurt," he groused, and I laughed.

"Wuss. Now don't move or you'll be wearing eyeliner on your cheeks."

He groaned but complied to my orders. After all, I was doing him a favor.

"Where's Pax?" I asked conversationally in the same tone I'd use when discussing the weather. Inside, I wasn't nearly as indifferent. I kept glancing toward the hallway for any sign of him.

"Who knows?" Patrick dismissed the subject with a wave of his hand. "That dress is hot on you." He grinned at me and his voice was laced with promise.

"Thank you, dear sir." I forgot about my low-cut peasant blouse and bowed low. Patrick's guttural growl told me all I needed to know without looking down. I whipped around, giving him my back, and tucked the girls back where they belonged.

"I'll show you how dear I am, wench." He attempted a pretty lame imitation of a pirate accent. I'd watched Patrick's moves for over two years, and now he was making them on me. His blatant interest should be a dream come true. *Should* being the operative word. Eventually, I'd have a personal day of reckoning regarding what was going on in my head and my heart. For now, I had a job to do.

"Maybe we should forget the party and have our own party here," Patrick hinted not so subtly with a wink-wink. I rolled my eyes.

"Ah, Captain, but your crew is expecting us. Duty calls."

"Fuck duty," he said. He was serious, but so was I. We were not staying here and doing the nasty under the same roof as Paxton. I had my scruples, and I wouldn't hurt Pax like that. I'd done enough damage to his ego. Not to mention, the possibility of getting naked with Patrick didn't hold the thrill it once had.

Someone cleared their throat behind me. I turned to find Paxton a few feet away. His expression was completely unreadable. Judging by his clenched jaw, he wasn't happy.

"Hi, Pax." I grinned at him, and his returned smile was more of a grimace.

"Nice makeup job," he muttered as he crossed to the kitchen and grabbed a beer from the fridge. "On both of you."

I'd applied my own makeup thicker than normal. "Thank you," I said in a voice that quivered a bit. Pax had that effect on me, and I was tired of fighting what was becoming more and more obvious every day. Every day I searched for a glimpse of Pax as I walked across campus or went to the library and the Biscuit to find him or appeared in the dining hall about the time he usually did. Denial was getting harder and harder.

"Where's your costume?" I looked him up and down. In my opinion, he looked way hotter wearing his Bulls sweatshirt and faded jeans than Patrick did in his swashbuckling outfit.

"I'm not going in costume." He set his jaw stubbornly, as both Patrick and I regarded him.

"But you have to," I said. "We'll come up with something. I'll help."

"Leave him alone. He can do what he wants even if it's being a poor sport," Patrick hissed.

"I heard that," Paxton grumbled as he grabbed a bite to eat from the kitchen.

His twin opened his mouth for a retort but shut it at the chastising glare I sent him.

"What do you think?" I said, distracting Patrick as I held up a mirror for him to view my handiwork. I'd done an awesome job, too.

"Damn. That's me?" He grinned into the mirror and tried a

few pirate glares, drawing a laugh from me and a snort from Paxton.

"I think you're a better Jack Sparrow than Johnny Depp." I bent down to fix his eyeliner, which I'd laid on thick. It'd run slightly. "Don't touch your face or sweat or even blink."

"How do females wear this shit all the time?"

I opened my mouth to answer when the front door to the apartment slammed. Paxton had left without saying goodbye. I met Patrick's gaze.

Patrick sighed and shrugged. "He's been distant lately. And different. Like he's pulling away."

"Maybe that's how he prepares to leave school and you."

"Maybe." Patrick's voice rang with skepticism.

"We should be going." I didn't want to be alone in the apartment with Patrick for many reasons, as stupid as it sounded. Not so long ago, I'd have made sure we never got to the party, given the opportunity. Now I wanted to escape as soon as possible.

"Are you on a schedule?" Patrick stood and walked to the mirror hanging on one wall. He adjusted his sword on his costume. And checked himself out some more. His costume was epic, and he'd be the life and focus of the party.

"No, but I promised to help Kaitlyn with her makeup. She's meeting me there."

"Kaitlyn needs help with *her* makeup?"

"Yeah, go figure."

"So, is this my rain check tonight? Are we on a date?" He prodded me for an answer. If I succumbed, I'd be nothing more than his next conquest, and this revelation no longer held the appeal it once had. Patrick was not relationship material, and what he had to offer was no longer what I was looking for.

What was I looking for? Not a quick hookup, it appeared, but something more? Hell if I knew.

"Let's not put labels on this." I refused to commit one way or another.

"I'd love to put a label on you."

"What? Like latest hookup?"

Patrick wasn't deterred or insulted. "That works for me, babe." He reached for me, and I pushed him away. He studied me quizzically but backed off.

"When you're done admiring yourself, we should go. What guy has a full-length mirror in his entryway?"

"A girl I dated for a few weeks put this up. She hated leaving the apartment without checking a mirror. It comes in handy. I have to make sure I'm looking my best for my fan base." He grinned confidently at me. Too bad there wasn't a way to share some of his cockiness with his brother.

I heaved a long-suffering sigh and shrugged into my coat. Patrick tried different angles in front of the mirror. I swatted him on the arm. "Let's go."

I didn't wait but headed down the outside stairs. A chilly wind hit me at the bottom, and I hugged myself. Patrick caught up, talking on his cell as he walked beside me.

The guy was a regular social butterfly, I thought with annoyance.

Lately, my Patrick crush had lost its luster.

My heart was trying to tell me something and I should listen.

RESCUE

Paxton

I seethed with jealousy as I walked aimlessly down the side-walk. I turned up my coat collar to ward off the bitterly cold wind. I didn't care. I kept going until I was far from my apartment and the hockey house.

Patrick and Naomi had been fucking adorable in their costumes, and seeing how cozy they were pissed me off. Envy threatened to consume me, and I fought like hell to prevent it. I loved my brother and hated this growing chasm between us but seemed powerless to stop it.

It wasn't just how he flirted with Naomi, it was hockey, too. Patrick had been the star last night, and I'd sucked. Things were way more harmonious when my brother was the star of the night, and I fed him the puck. My dad didn't rail at me in person or on the phone. Patrick didn't yell at me. My team-mates didn't give me the side-eye like they did when I kept the puck, shot, and missed the net. All in all, I felt better about myself when I was the old me.

Improvement doesn't come without risk and discomfort. The words of Coach Garf echoed in my ears.

Coach insisted everything would click eventually. Meanwhile, I wasn't convinced I was impressing anyone, especially myself.

I fully intended to go back home and wallow in my misery once I'd given Patrick and Naomi ample time to be gone. And what would that solve? How would hiding fix anything? My absence would throw up a red flag after I'd insisted I was fine with Naomi and Patrick dating. The last thing I wanted was to look like a sore loser.

Turning, I trudged several blocks back to the hockey house. The place was lit up like a Christmas tree in Times Square. Raucous music blasted from inside. As I approached, a few of the freshmen staggered up the sidewalk. They'd been partying pretty hard already, or so it appeared.

"Hey, handsome. I was afraid you wouldn't come," called a sultry voice as I stepped onto the large front porch. I glanced at the buxom brunette wearing a Wonder Woman costume. She slid up to me and pressed her spandex-clad body against my side. I didn't know her, but I was guessing my brother did. "I'm Paxton. Not Patrick."

For a split second, her face fell, then she gave me a thousand-watt smile. "One twin is as good as the other."

"Yeah, we're interchangeable."

My sarcasm flew right over her heard. She beamed even wider, leaning closer and running her long red nails down my chest. "I wouldn't mind having a go with both of you at once if you're into such a thing."

"Sorry, no thanks." I firmly set her aside and skirted past, slipping through the partially open front door. Annoyance crept through my veins at her, at my brother, at Naomi. Especially at Naomi. As unfair as my feelings might be.

Once inside, I threaded my way through the dense crowd to a table of shots and threw back a couple. Then I grabbed a beer. The alcohol warmed the pit of my stomach and gave me a nice instant buzz, taking the edge off my bad mood. I inhaled deeply, closed my eyes, and exhaled, then tried few relaxation exercises Coach had taught me along with uttering some affirmations.

I will have a good time.

I will have a good time.

I will have a good time.

I leaned against the wall and observed the crowd. Captain Jack and the wench were dancing a slow dance. Patrick's hand crept to her ass, and Naomi pulled it back to her waist. Her expression was as annoyed as mine. I perked up. Things weren't going so well for my brother. She was fending off his advances instead of welcoming them.

They stopped dancing, and Naomi stepped away from him, evading his attempt to put an arm around her. Patrick scowled, and they engaged in a brief conversation. After which, my brother shrugged and walked away. I smirked, enjoying this side show.

"Your smugness is showing," Lex said as he stopped beside me.

"You think?"

"Oh, fuck yeah. She rejected him, and you enjoyed it."

"I did. Every fucking moment," I admitted.

"Your sibling rivalry is showing."

"Yeah, it is." I stared at his costume. "What are you supposed to be?"

"Coach Keller."

"Oh, good one. You do resemble him somewhat."

Lex blew on the whistle around his neck, drawing scowls from those nearby.

Once the ringing in my ears stopped, I shook my head and laughed, more relaxed than when I'd walked in the door. Of course, seeing my brother exit the dance floor while wondering what the fuck just happened helped immensely.

"Who are you supposed to be?" Lex asked.

I thought for a moment before answering. "I'm Patrick. What do you think?"

"Funny. Really funny. You didn't wear a costume?"

"I'm not into dressing up for Halloween. Never did as a kid."

"Patrick seems to go all out."

"That's because Naomi's dad sent them those costumes. Besides, being the center of attention is Patrick's jam, not mine."

"Naomi's dad? Does he know what that costume looks like on his daughter?"

"I doubt he paid attention. Probably had his girlfriend buy them."

"Yeah, I can't see him picking out costumes and shipping them. It'd be beneath him."

"Hey, Pax." Michael, our alternate captain, squinted at me, as if trying to figure out what my costume was. I let him fret.

Jonah and Maggie joined the group, along with Kaitlyn.

"Pax, who are you dressed as, your brother?" Kaitlyn joked.

"Wow, good guess," I said.

"You should have a couple Barbie dolls stuck to your sides then." Tate snorted and fist-bumped with my teammates.

"Good idea," I said dryly, but actually, it was a good idea. Funny as hell.

Speaking of the devil.

I frowned as my brother staggered toward us. He hadn't wasted any time after being snubbed by Naomi. A woman on each arm held him up. The guys parted to make room as he pushed his way into our circle.

Patrick gestured toward me with a beer bottle. Sensing a confrontation, I stiffened. Beside me, Lex cast a quick glance between the two of us and stood up straighter, making it clear he supported me over our team captain. The other guys in the group observed us warily.

"You played like shit last night. Good thing I was on fire." My pirate brother was wasted drunk. Usually, he was a happy drunk, but he'd been doing shots. Sometimes hard liquor made him intolerable to be around. Unfortunately, he chose to focus his foul mood on me tonight.

"Fuck you." I wasn't dealing with his bullshit. I glanced around, grateful to see that only a few people outside of my group paid attention. Hopefully, they'd chalk it up to a brotherly spat and ignore us.

"Let me give you some tips, little bro, to help your game along."

"I don't need your tips." I hated it when he called me little bro, and he knew it. I was younger by five minutes. Leave it to Patrick to beat me to the birth canal.

He threw back his head and laughed. Naomi squeezed her way into the group, alarm on her face. Her alarmed gaze slid from me to Patrick and back.

My brother leaned forward, swaying to and fro. He shook his finger a few inches from my face. "Tip one—pass the fucking puck to me. Quit trying to hog the limelight, because you're failing epically."

I wanted to clock him. "Fuck you. You aren't the only guy capable of scoring a goal."

"Could've fooled me." Patrick snorted and beer actually came out his nose. He wiped his face on his sleeve.

"Hey, Trick." Tate wedged himself between Patrick and me.

"We need you in the kitchen for something." A drunk Patrick was easily distracted.

"What?" He blinked a few times as if to get his bearings.

"Come on, come with me." Tate motioned for him to follow.

Patrick half sauntered, half staggered away with the two blondes hurrying after him. He glanced over his shoulder for a parting shot. "I'm not done with you yet, bro. We have shit to discuss."

"Whatever." I turned my back on the now gathering crowd and slipped outside, needing some air and not wanting any further conversation with any of them. Lex dogged my heels, probably worried about me. Lex was a good guy, and I was grateful to have a friend like him, even if I'd rather be left alone right now.

We wandered over to a group of guys hanging out under the stars and chilled with them for over an hour. I needed to chill. My bro put me on edge. I itched to put my fist into his smug face. Over the years, we'd had our brotherly spats but always gotten over them fast. Not like what was going on now. This wall between us sucked.

Lex shot me a sideways glance. "You're way too serious for being at a party."

"Huh? Oh, sorry."

"Loosen up, Pax. Have some fun. Forget about your shit for one night."

I nodded and did some deep breathing while rubbing my crystal. "Good advice from a good friend," I admitted.

"Naomi's wandering around alone. You might want to stake a claim since she dissed your bro." Lex winked at me. "That reminds me, gotta find my girl." He wandered off to look for Kaitlyn, leaving me bored and freezing my ass off. I headed inside for a little heat and another beer and maybe another glimpse of Naomi in her peasant blouse.

I stopped to talk to Tate, Michael, and Jonah hovering over a table loaded with food. When I realized they were discussing last night's game, I dumped that convo and moved on. A couple sophomore girls eyed me, giggling as I walked by. Probably trying to decide if I was Patrick or not, I thought bitterly.

I had to get over this bullshit with my brother. Our problems were as much my fault as his. We were all we had when it came down to it, and I hated the wedge between us.

I scanned the crowd, disappointed in not seeing Naomi. For that matter, I didn't see Patrick either. My mind churned with the possibilities, making me a little crazy. She'd turned him down. She wouldn't change her mind. Right?

Hell if I knew.

I grabbed another beer, not wanting to ruin my good buzz, and ducked around the corner. I sat down on one of the couches and watched the action, attempting to amuse myself with who was hooking up with whom.

"Hey."

At the sound of that heavenly voice that lived in my dreams, my head snapped around. Naomi the serving wench, in that delectable low-cut top, smiled down at me.

"Hi," I answered with a slow smile. My gaze slipped to her cleavage, and I forced myself to look up. One glance at those breasts begging to be set free while knowing what was underneath, and I was hard as a puck.

"I've been looking for you." Naomi dropped onto the couch next to me, sitting way too close for comfort.

"I'm Paxton," I teased, even though I was half-serious.

"I know."

"Just checking."

"Don't blame you." She sounded close to sober for someone I'd seen throwing back shots earlier. "I thought you looked lonely."

"I'm not." My voice was harsh, and she flinched, making me feel like the ass I was.

"Well, I am."

"In this room crammed with people?"

"Yeah, because none of them are you." She turned to capture my gaze, and I lost myself in her beautiful eyes.

Had she really just said that?

I stiffened and looked away. I didn't want her to say shit she didn't mean, because it gave me hope, and hope would eventually break my heart. My brother was AWOL, and I was second-best. I wasn't settling for being second-best again, not even where she was concerned.

"Dance with me." Naomi grabbed fistfuls of my sweatshirt and leaned into me. My nostrils flared as I breathed in the heady scent of her. Her touch made me forget my vow not to be her second choice—almost. I mounted a resistance, as futile as it might be.

"You're drunk," I hedged.

"Tipsy."

"Aren't you here with my brother?"

"I was, but I lost him."

"On purpose?"

She shot me a secretive smile. "Maybe."

"He's probably passed out. Last I saw him, he was feeling no pain."

"He's in no shape to dance. Dance with me." She didn't wait for a response but grabbed my hand and tugged. Her stubborn expression didn't bode well for refusing. Short of making a scene, I'd have to appease her. I stood and let her drag me to the packed makeshift dance floor.

She stumbled over the feet of someone next to us, but I caught her to my chest. She gazed up at me like hapless females do in romantic movies. Not that I watched many romantic movies, but there'd been times I'd been forced to do so. Personally, I didn't see myself as much of a romantic.

Naomi draped herself over my body, and I held her as we shuffled around the dance floor. There wasn't room for much else. She felt so right in my arms, like skating off the ice after a hard-fought game to find the person who grounds you. Memories that flooded me of our night of bliss followed by extreme humiliation should have poured water on my flames but didn't. Her closeness rendered me powerless to resist.

She nuzzled my neck, sliding her lips across my skin. I turned my head to nuzzle her jaw. Purely a reaction without thought. I just did it. Didn't think. Just did. She tilted her head until our mouths were inches apart. Inches from heaven. Inches from what I'd wanted long before I'd first tasted her lips. And once I'd had that first taste, I craved more, like a junkie craved his next fix. She was my fix, and I needed her and fuck the long-term repercussions.

Our lips met. Mine were reluctant. Hers were determined. Our eyes locked, and my world turned upside down and inside out. I existed in a bubble with her and only her. Her body melded to mine, and we swayed, locked together in body, mind, and soul.

"Naomi," I whispered huskily.

"Pax," she sighed into my mouth, making me groan. I wanted her. All of her. My dick ached to be inside her. My body ached to be naked with her. I ached just to have her as mine.

"Pax, take me home with you." She kissed me again, plenty of tongue and a lot of promise.

My alcohol-laden heart soared. My convictions to make my

life about nothing but hockey flew out the window without a second thought. I deepened my kiss, pushing my thigh between her legs. She whimpered and gripped my shoulders, kissing with the same hunger I felt.

I don't know how long we made out on the dance floor. People jostled us, and my teammates teased. I ignored everyone but her. She was my everything, and I wanted to be her everything. Our mouths mated with an intensity only equaled by how our bodies craved each other.

"Naomi, oh, fuck, Naomi. I need you."

"I need you, too," she responded in that breathless voice that turned my lust up a notch.

"Pax. Pax! Sorry to interrupt."

I ignored this persistent buzz in my ear until it became too loud to ignore.

"What?" I reluctantly dragged my mouth from hers. Naomi wasn't so willing to let go, she held on to me. She tattooed my cheeks with hot kisses.

"Pax, I need help with your brother," Lex implored me. The alarm in his voice penetrated the lust-filled fog surrounding me. Even Naomi stopped and turned to look at him with concern on her face.

"What's going on?" I asked with annoyance. This better be good.

"He's wasted drunk, and he's picking fights with some frat guys. He's going to get himself in real trouble, maybe be kicked off the team. We can't control him."

"Ah, fuck." I turned apologetically to Naomi.

She smiled and nodded. "Go to your brother. He needs you."

I wouldn't be making any difficult choices tonight. Patrick needed rescuing from himself, and perhaps so did I.

THE DOUCHE

Naomi

I had a big decision to make. No more putting it off. The moment of truth had come.

The week following the Halloween party, Pax and I were back to the we're-just-friends game. He greeted me cheerfully when he ran into me on campus and was friendly and even chatty at times. But it was all superficial BS. I caught the hunger in his gaze on several occasions, and he caught me doing the same. I was growing tired of this dance we were doing. The day of reckoning was coming. We both knew it.

The team played out of town that weekend, a double-header with the same college. We won the first game. Patrick was the star, but Paxton's struggles appeared to be behind him. He played a very good game and scored one goal to his brother's two.

My dad invited Patrick to dinner after Friday's game in what was becoming a post-game ritual. Tonight, Mr. Graham would also be in attendance as he'd come to town for the games.

Paxton walked out of the locker room right behind Patrick, glanced at our little group, and looked away, but not before I caught the hurt on his face. Neither his father nor his brother had thought to invite him.

In a moment of rebellion, I tugged on Pax's coat as he walked by, making it impossible for him not to stop.

"Hey, Omi," he said with a too bright smile. His gaze slid to his dad, but Mr. Graham didn't acknowledge him.

Fine, I would.

"Great game tonight, Pax. You were on fire," I stated a little too loudly.

Pax frowned, his gaze going to his father and back. "I did okay." He shrugged, blowing off his best performance of the season so far.

"We're going to dinner. Why don't you join us?" I continued, because I really did want him there. I waited expectantly for his answer.

Before Paxton opened his mouth to respond, his father rushed forward, suddenly aware of his other son. "This is a private meeting to discuss Patrick's future. Sorry, Pax, but I'm sure you'll understand."

"Yeah, sure, I do," Paxton mumbled. He shrugged and met my gaze. I wasn't certain what I saw in his eyes at that moment. He did an admirable job of covering up his emotions, but I had no such problem. I was mad. Actually livid at his asshole father. Paxton was his son, too. I embraced my fury in preparation for the ass-chewing that man deserved. Pax touched my arm and shook his head.

"It's okay, Naomi. It'd suck joining you guys 'cause Dad get his rocks off pitting Patrick and me against each other. We're already in a bad place right now. We don't need him making it worse."

"Are you sure?"

He managed a joyless smile. "Positive. I have stuff to do anyway. See you later. And thanks for the invite." He didn't acknowledge the rest of the group but joined a few teammates waiting for him near the double exit doors. He left without looking back, his shoulders squared and his head held high.

Good for him.

I fumed as I followed our small group to the car. I didn't speak on the way to the restaurant, and no one seemed to notice or care. We sat down, and I ordered a glass of wine. Despite the daggers I sent to Mr. Graham and my own father, even Patrick, no one paid me any mind. After all, I was just a mere female, and I couldn't even skate. My skating ability, or lack of, was a major sore spot with my father. If I'd been a female hockey star or even a figure skater, he'd have been able to save face with his buddies who had sons and daughters who were born on skates and looked like it. I, on the other hand, had inherited my mother's ineptness, clumsiness, and lack of balance, compounded by my phobia.

I sipped my wine and observed. Patrick's father was making a fool of himself, and my dad was playing him like a fine fiddle.

The entire performance was disturbing and pathetic. Not just on Mr. Graham's part but my dad's too. My father needed adulation, thrived on it, and withered without it. I secretly called his first few years of retirement from hockey the dark years. He didn't know who he was without hockey. He'd tried announcing and wasn't ready to settle down to one thing. He'd dabbled in various business ventures, but none held his attention, not like hockey had. He still struggled, but he'd focused lately on his future, even if I had no idea what his plans were. He didn't share such things with his daughter.

Both men tag-teamed Patrick on going pro at the end of this school year.

"Listen to Gene, Patrick. He knows what's best for you," Mr. Graham insisted. Patrick's expression was grim. His strained relationship with his father didn't make these dinners my idea of fun.

"I appreciate your opinion, Mr. Smith," Patrick said, not wanting to insult his idol.

"I understand. You have to make your own decision, but at the same time, it must be an informed decision." My dad turned to Mr. Graham. "You know, Graham, you're one lucky man. You have two hockey-playing sons who'll be in the NHL soon. Poor Naomi, here, she can't even skate a foot without falling on her ass."

"I don't skate anymore, Dad. So it doesn't matter."

He shrugged and frowned.

"Yeah, I'm pretty lucky the boys inherited my athletic talent, especially Patrick." Mr. Graham beamed with rare pride. I caught Patrick's surprised glance. He wasn't used to hearing any kind of praise from this man.

"Paxton is good," I argued, drawing disapproving glances from both fathers. I guess I was to be seen and not heard.

"Yeah, Pax is a far better player than you give him credit for, Dad." Patrick jumped to Pax's defense, and we shared a conspiratorial wink.

"Pax isn't you." And that was all Mr. Graham had to say about his other son. The conversation turned to the current college season and who was likely to give Moo U a run for their money in the Frozen Four. Patrick and I exchanged glances of mutual suffering. This night couldn't end soon enough for me.

Finally, we were in a taxi and headed back to the hotel.

Patrick and I burst out the taxi and hurried into the hotel, grateful to be freed from parental hell.

"I could use a drink," I exclaimed.

"Me, too. Come on, I'll buy you a tall one."

I sat down in a booth, and Patrick went to the bar to get our drinks. He returned and sat across from me.

"For the record, I wasn't angling for an invitation. I—I was just expressing how relieved I was to be out of the company of those two men."

"Tell me about it. They're both overbearing, but my dad is groveling at your dad's feet. I want to gag."

"And my dad is lapping up the admiration. It's disgusting."

"They're both disgusting."

"I thought you worshipped my father?" I teased, and Patrick grinned guilelessly.

"I don't mean to sound ungrateful, your dad has done a lot for my game, and he's been really good to me, but..."

"I know, a little of him goes a long way," I finished for him, letting him off the hook.

"That's an understatement."

We laughed together. It was one of those moments when everything was right. We enjoyed each other's company, but something was missing.

I waited for that *something* to happen.

And waited.

And waited.

Nothing.

Not a damn fucking thing.

No heart pounding, no butterflies fluttering in my gut, no girlie parts responding to the pure magnetism of this man. I didn't get it. How had I fallen out of infatuation with Patrick before we'd gone on one date? He was the same guy he'd always been.

It was me.

I was different.

Sleeping with Paxton had been life-changing, and my once wandering eye and ravenous palate only wanted what Pax served.

"If our dads had their way, we'd be married off already," I noted with a wry snort.

"And I can't even get you to go on a date with me," Patrick said. He studied my face, as if I were a creature he was seeking to understand.

"I know I've been evasive."

"I thought you were into me."

"I was. I mean, I thought I was."

He frowned, as if he'd never had a woman say such a thing to him before. "And now?"

"I think I'm sitting here with the wrong twin."

His smile was slow and knowing, and he nodded. "I thought so, but Pax keeps denying you two have anything going. In fact, he's been pushing me toward you."

"Me, too."

"Something's going on with him, and he's not filling me in." I heard the hurt in Patrick's voice and my heart went out to him. I could only imagine how it felt to have someone so close to you all your life and feel him pulling away. Pax was pulling away from both of us. I wasn't sure I was going to let him.

"I'm sorry, Patrick. No hard feelings."

"Absolutely none. My brother's a great guy. Next to me, you couldn't find a better guy, even if he has been a douche lately."

"Maybe you're the douche."

"Maybe." He grinned at me, and I laughed. "If you don't mind me asking, what changed?"

I considered his question for a long moment as the answer came to me as clear as day.

"I did."

Patrick grinned and held up his glass. We clinked glasses, and he winked at me. "My brother is a lucky guy."

I laughed. "You think?"

"I know."

The weight that'd been dragging me down disappeared. I'd made my choice. Now to figure out my next move.

I BELIEVE

Paxton

After Friday's game, Naomi had invited me to join her dad, my dad, and Patrick for dinner, and my dad uninvited me, adding one more humiliating experience involving Naomi. As usual, my old man sucked the joy right out of me, and I slunk off to lick my wounds. I hated the pity in Naomi's eyes and the sympathy in my brother's.

My personal life had taken on a downward spiral, but my hockey life began to gather steam. Patrick and I didn't have long, meaningful, sometimes heated discussions late into the night like we used to or talk trash while playing video games. We were as polite AF, and I hated it. Naomi and I traveled the same polite road of denial.

My game had started to click Friday night. I'd always been hyperaware of my brother on the ice. I had a sixth sense about where he was going and what he was going to do, but what I'd felt tonight went beyond that. I saw shots more consistently, took the good ones, and passed the bad ones. I'd scored in the second on a breakaway, barreling toward the net. I lasered a shot right in the five-hole. Icing on the cake, I had two assists, both of them providing Patrick with his two goals.

In the locker room, Coach Garf had slapped me on the back and beamed like a proud father, something I'd never seen my real father do.

I'd be damned if the dinner un-invitation would ruin my night. I refused to sulk in my room and joined my teammates for pizza across from the hotel. I kicked Tate's ass at pool. Then Lex kicked my butt. And Jonah followed up by kicking his.

Sometime before eleven, I called it a night and walked across the street to the hotel. Coach had allowed us a later curfew because we didn't have to travel to the next game. I wanted to be in bed before Patrick came back from dinner. I'd pretend to be asleep so he wouldn't ask me questions or apologize for our father. Being treated like I was nobody by my own father was demeaning enough. Pity made it that much worse.

As I strode toward the bank of elevators, I heard a familiar laugh and paused. I glanced into the hotel bar.

Well, shit.

I froze and gaped at what I saw. Naomi leaned across the table, deep in a serious conversation with my brother. They were so intent on each other they wouldn't have noticed me if I'd been beating on a drum.

My stomach tied itself in knots. I'd harbored the remote hope after Halloween she might be into me more than my brother. She'd been sending out conflicting signals for a long while. Try as I might, she occupied too much space in my head. When she'd changed back to her natural hair color, I'd dared to hope she no longer carried a torch for my brother.

Seeing them all cozy dealt my heart a fatal blow. I'd been deluding myself.

My bolstered confidence eroded a little every second I watched the two of them. Jealousy curled through me like a vile blackness that gripped my heart in its hold and refused to let go.

Why the fuck did everything go my brother's way? Why not me once in a while?

I teetered on the verge of a mega pity party.

I turned away from them, unable to watch any longer.

"Hey, you took off." Lex caught up with me. His chest heaved from what had to be a sprint across the street.

"Yeah, I'm tired. Physical game and all."

Lex grinned at me, admiration in his eyes. I squirmed a bit, not comfortable being the subject of someone's hero worship no matter how minor. One more way my bro and I were different. He basked in attention, and I shrank from it.

"What's going on? You seem down." Lex craned his neck to look beyond me into the bar. "Oh. Oh, shit."

"Yeah, oh, shit."

"Maybe it's not what it seems," he offered lamely.

"I have eyes."

"That's brutal, man. I'm sorry."

"It was inevitable. She's been in love with Patrick since our freshman year, and he's finally paying attention."

"But for how long?"

"Hard to say with him, but it doesn't matter. I'm not interested in his castoffs anymore."

"Even Naomi?" Lex blinked a few times as if to clarify I was the same guy standing in front of him.

"Yeah, even Naomi. A man has to have his pride."

Lex nodded in agreement and switched to a more uplifting subject. "You're figuring it out. You played awesome tonight."

I'd felt good about my game tonight until my father had snubbed me and now Naomi was cozying up to my brother. The game didn't seem to matter nearly as much when I didn't have someone to share my good fortune with.

"Hey, Lex, I'm going to call it a night. I'm tired."

"Yeah, sure, me, too." Lex and I rode the elevator up to the seventh floor. He turned one way and I turned the other. I scanned the lock with my key card and heard the sound of the bolt releasing. I walked inside, yanked off my clothes, and crawled naked between the cool sheets.

I half expected to toss and turn most of the night, but the physical and emotional exertion of the game wore me down faster than I'd imagined. Soon I was sliding into a semiconscious state where my life was exactly the way I wanted it to be. Naomi was naked in my arms and nuzzling my neck. She felt so good, so warm, so soft.

So mine.

I drifted off to a night of sweet dreams and never heard my brother come in the door.

UConn was bent on revenge Saturday night. We'd soundly kicked their asses the night before, and they wanted a piece of those very asses back tonight. I was determined not to give them what they wanted, as was the rest of our team. This was our year, and no one was holding us back.

I'd slept like a baby all night long and woken up refreshed. When I finally remembered Patrick was the guy with Naomi last night, I refused to let it get to me. I'd use what happened last night to my advantage rather than let it define me. I'd show them all. Every one of them. My dad, who thought I was unworthy. Naomi, who preferred my brother. Mr. Smith, who barely acknowledged my existence.

I'd let my anger drive me. I'd embrace it and bend it to my will. After years of feeling inadequate and not good enough, no more. That shit stopped here. I was good enough. I was a top player and every bit as good as my brother. Time I started playing like one.

I skated onto the ice for warmups. My legs felt sure and strong. My blades dug into the ice. My heart pumped with purpose. Tonight was my night. My dad was here. Gene Smith was here. Naomi was working her statistician job. I had something to prove, and tonight felt right. The ice felt perfect. My body felt energized.

Coach Garf nodded at me. "Looking good, Pax." His smile was wide as he watched me skate around the rink with long, fluid strides.

I grinned back at him and gave him the thumbs-up, not easy to do wearing hockey gloves.

Patrick pulled beside me. I didn't slow for him. I sped up, wishing he'd go away. He didn't say anything but kept pace with me. He cast uncertain looks in my direction, as if I were a creature he'd never seen and was trying to figure out.

In a sprint, we usually tied. When I pulled away, he didn't pursue me. Even Patrick noticed something different in me, and he wasn't about to tap into that before the game. He might not know how to deal with the new Paxton, but he'd have to learn. I wasn't going back. I was going forward.

I glanced around for Naomi; I couldn't help it. She sat a few rows up from the bench. Her father was behind her. No one told Mr. Smith where he could or couldn't sit. He did as he pleased.

Lex skated past me and winked. "Hey, pro scouts are here. Word on the street is one's from the Sockeyes."

I glanced up toward the box where the scouts usually sat, not that I'd know who the Sockeyes' scout was. Shaking off a moment of anxiety, I concentrated on my warmup routine. The rest would take care of itself.

I positioned myself, feeling calm and relaxed as the first

line took the ice for the puck drop. Patrick fought for it and slapped it toward me. I spun around and raced for the net, faking out the defender blocking my way. The goalie bent down low, but my focus was laser sharp. I saw everything perfectly and time slowed down. I knew the direction the goalie was moving before he did, and I aimed a shot right through his legs. The second the puck left my stick, I raised my arms in the air to signal a goal. I was that sure.

The red light lit up. The guys on the bench pounded on the boards with their fists. My teammates surrounded me with hugs and slaps on the back. Patrick skated up to me with a grin on his face.

"Good one, Pax."

I grinned back at him. For a moment, we were best buddies again, and all the tension between us melted away. I embraced this moment of pure joy and wished I could hang on to it forever.

I was hot, and the team recognized it. Instead of feeding Patrick the puck as we so often did, I found the passes coming my way. By the end of the second, I'd scored another goal, and Patrick had scored none. In fact, my bro was having one of the worst games I'd ever seen him play.

I chanced a glance toward our father. He was red in the face and shouting. I didn't have to hear him to know he was pissed at Patrick, and there'd be hell to pay after this game. I had no delusions that he'd praise me, more likely chew my butt for taking the spotlight away from Patrick.

Striking out of frustration, my brother took a cheap shot at an opposing player and was sent to the penalty box for two minutes. Our line didn't miss a beat. We played on without him. Josh played the goalie position like he was on fire, and we fed off that. He practically stood on his head or used the Force to knock back some of the shots coming at him hard and heavy as UConn attempted to correct their three-point deficit.

With one minute left, Jonah sent the puck flying across the ice to me, and I powered ahead of the defenders. Once again, I saw my shot before I took it. The puck whizzed over the goalie's right knee pad.

I celebrated with my teammates. I'd scored a hat trick, three goals in one game. I'd scored a few before in my high school days but never in college.

I returned to the bench as the second line held the score of four to zero. I trudged wearily to the tunnel, exhausted but elated at the same time.

"Paxton!" shouted a familiar voice. I cringed inwardly, but outwardly I squared my shoulders and marched down the corridor toward the locker room. I wouldn't give my father the benefit of acknowledging him. It'd been impossible to discern whether he was angry or happy for me. I'd vote for angry because my great play made the chosen one's game even less impressive.

Okay, I was being a sore winner and gloating a little too much, but hadn't I earned it?

In the locker room, the guys surrounded and congratulated me. I basked in the glow of an incredible game.

Coach Garf stopped in front of my locker with a huge grin on his face. "I knew you had it in you."

I met his gaze, feeling an odd lump in my throat.

He'd believed in me when no one else had.

Well, except for Naomi. She'd always believed in me.

HAT TRICK

Naomi

Paxton was hot, and I was ecstatic for him.

I leapt to my feet, yelling at the top of my lungs, drawing sour looks from the home team fans around us. Paxton had stolen the puck and taken it to the net with one minute left. My dad rose to his feet and clapped. Even he was smiling.

"That's his third?" asked one of the guys down from us. "Incredible."

"Maybe the twins changed places tonight?" another asked.

"I doubt it," said another.

I ignored them, holding back on my inclination to dress them down. The game ended a minute later, and I followed my dad to the locker room area. He'd expect me to go to dinner with the group, but I wasn't going. Not tonight.

Tonight was about Paxton and me.

I had to talk to him. I'd thought this through most of the night.

In some ways, his superior play tonight made things more difficult. The last thing I wanted was for him to think I switched allegiances because he'd outplayed his brother. Truthfully, I'd probably switched allegiances long before I recognized my preference, and perhaps longer ago than that epic night I'd spent with Paxton. I burned for more of those nights.

"Paxton was on fire," I said, making conversation and boosting his street cred with my dad.

"Every player has a good night once in a while. It's maintaining that high level that separates the men from the boys."

I looked away from my dad and rolled my eyes. He was as sold on Patrick as Patrick's own dad was. Neither of them gave Paxton any credit for improving his play.

"Pax has been working hard with the new assistant coach. It shows."

My father stopped in his tracks and so did I. He turned to look at me, his brows knitted together. "Is there something you aren't telling me? Because I thought you and Patrick were a thing? He's perfect for you, and I couldn't pick a better son-in-law."

Son-in-law? Exasperated, I threw up my hands. "Dad, we're not even dating. It's a little early to marry me off. You might want to cancel the order for the wedding cake and flowers."

"But I thought you were interested in Patrick?" My dad frowned, disappointment etched on his face, and I hated that. I'd spent most of my life, with the exception of a few rebellious teenage years, trying to please him.

"It's complicated."

"Nothing complicated about it. Patrick is perfect for you, and you're perfect for him."

"How so, Dad?"

"Do I really have to explain it?"

"I think you do, because I'm not sure how you're more

certain about what I need than I am."

He heaved an exasperated sigh. "You're too close to the situation to see what I see. Besides, honey, listen to your father. I know what's best for you." His tone went from condescending to cajoling in five words or less.

"I'm not a child anymore, Dad. I do know what's good for me."

He patted me on the shoulder as if I were a wayward puppy he'd found wandering the streets. "Trust me on this one. I do know how important it is to have the right partner. You'll understand the trials Patrick faces and have the tools to deal with his absences. Your mom didn't have those tools."

I flinched at his criticism of my mother, even though I knew he was right. I recalled the constant fighting and accusations when he was home. My mom's claims he was seeing other women and his claims of her drinking too much. I'd often wondered if she'd been drinking the night she'd been hit. If she had, it'd been hushed up by the small-town police department.

"Oh, honey, I'm sorry." Dad gave me a quick hug. He wasn't great at displays of affection, but he did love me. I knew that.

"I want you to invite Paxton to join us for dinner tonight."

My father opened his mouth to protest, then seemed to think better of it. "Of course. If that's what you want."

"It is." I had the distinct impression I might be unwittingly setting a trap for Paxton, and perhaps I hadn't done him any favors by insisting he tag along. What's done was done. I'd make the best of it and attempt to run interference if necessary.

We walked a few blocks to a pizza place. Mr. Graham insisted on picking up the bill for the first time, probably because we were eating pizza, not steak. He came back with a couple pitchers of beer and four glasses. Cheap bastard.

Patrick grabbed one of the pitchers and poured himself a beer. He chugged it down and poured another. I didn't blame him. He anticipated an ass chewing by his father. Hopefully, my dad's presence tempered Mr. Graham's wrath.

I was halfway wrong. The twins' dad didn't go after Patrick. Instead, as soon as he settled in his seat, he turned the full force of his fury on Paxton.

"What the fuck were you showboating like that for tonight?" Mr. Graham barely waited until we were seated at the table before lighting into Paxton. To his credit, he didn't shy away from his dad's harsh words. He looked him straight in the eye with an unfazed expression, infuriating his dad even more.

Pax had just played the game of his career against a very good team, and his father was pissed at him for outshining his brother? What the fuck was wrong with that man?

"Showboating? The coach doesn't think I'm showboating. He was happy with my performance."

"You were showing off for the Sockeyes scout and making your brother look bad in the process."

"Was I? Did I do that to you, Patrick?"

Patrick shrugged, unwilling to participate in this conversation.

I chanced a glance at my dad. He scowled and rubbed his temples, as if the family drama gave him a headache. For once I agreed with him. Dad cleared his throat, and the entire table's attention turned to him. When my dad spoke, you listened. Mr. Graham leaned forward, expecting my father to back him up.

"The boy merely played his game. He had an exceptional night. Happens to any player at some point in time where they play beyond their abilities because the stars align or whatever. Congratulations on the hat trick, Paxton." My father thought he was helping, but he wasn't. Paxton's jaw tensed. My dad had just thrown some shade Pax's way and added to the Graham family tension.

I elbowed my dad, but he was oblivious as usual.

Patrick ignored all of us. He threw back his second beer and poured another.

"Thank you, Mr. Smith," Paxton said, not giving much away in his expression. He didn't fool me. He was damaged by his father's callous attitude.

Mr. Graham sulked and wisely kept his mouth shut. My dad filled the friction-laden silence by regaling everyone with stories about his playing days, but I wasn't sure anyone was listening. Patrick slumped down in his seat, while Paxton studied the wall.

The twins wolfed down the pizza once it was delivered and bolted for the door. I followed them. All three of us were anxious to get the fuck out of there. I deserted my dad, leaving him to deal with Mr. Graham. Dad would be able to handle him better than anyone.

Patrick split off from us and jogged across the street to where some teammates had gone.

"Go ahead and join them. I'm not great company." Paxton managed a mirthless smile.

"I'd like to buy you a drink to celebrate. You were awesome tonight."

"But wouldn't you rather be with Patrick?" He stopped on the sidewalk and faced me. I smiled up at him, but he regarded me suspiciously.

"I'm right where I want to be." Tucking my arm through his, I turned toward the hotel. I tugged on him to follow me. He hung back for a moment, then fell into step beside me.

I'd made my choice. Now to convince Paxton.

22

TAKING CHANCES

Paxton

My night so far had more ups and downs than a roller coaster, and the ride wasn't over yet. With a combination of reluctance and anticipation, I allowed Naomi to lead me into the hotel pub.

Perhaps she was merely rescuing me from another round with my dad. I'd dodged a bullet when Mr. Smith defended me, even though he backhandedly insulted me, too. I'd show them tonight wasn't a fluke. I was a damn good player, and I was only now beginning to realize my potential.

I tried not to read any more into this than two friends hanging out. While Naomi snagged a booth for us, I ordered two virgin margaritas at the bar. I didn't know if the message would be lost on her or not. We'd met at our first campus party as freshmen and gotten soused together on margaritas at a fiesta-themed frat party.

I set the drinks on the table and slid onto the seat across from her. Naomi's slow smile warmed my heart as she noted my drink of choice. Something was different about her, but I couldn't put my finger on it. Whatever I picked up on gave me hope.

"That was a good night," she said, referring to that frat party over two years ago.

"It was." I didn't say more for fear of humiliating myself further when it came to her. What I felt hadn't faded despite my efforts to squelch my emotions where she was concerned. No matter how many times she knocked me down, I kept coming back for more.

She held up her drink, and I did the same. "To many more nights like tonight."

"Hear, hear." Whether she was referring to my game performance or our being together, I hadn't a fucking clue. I wished it were both. "I just hope I can do a repeat, and it wasn't a one-off."

"That's your dad talking. Don't listen to him. He has his own selfish agenda, and what's best for his boys isn't part of it."

"It's hard after years of negative programming. I'm working on it."

"I hear you. I've had similar programming being the unwanted daughter who should've been a son and not having one ounce of athletic talent. Dad would trade me in for a different model if it were possible."

"That's not true, Omi. Your dad loves you. He might have an odd way of showing it, but I have no doubt that you're important to him."

"I know." She ducked her head as if ashamed of her lack of faith in her father.

"My dad, on the other hand, has no such predilections. He sees dollar signs and status when he looks at Patrick and, to a lesser extent, me."

She didn't deny what I said. After all, my dad was who he was, and we both knew it.

"I can handle my dad being an ass. It's Patrick's attitude I'm struggling with."

"It has to be hard for him. He's always been the center of attention and pretty secure in who he is and who you are."

"And lately I've been somebody else."

"Yes, give him time. He'll come around. He loves you."

I nodded grimly. "Let's change the subject," I said. Talking about my family depressed me, but I was about to switch to another topic just as uncomfortable. Resisting Naomi and pretending I didn't care wasn't working all that well for me, and I had to get something straight with her. I had to know. "I saw you last night in this very bar having what appeared to be an intimate convo with my brother."

Her head snapped up and her pretty mouth formed a perfect *O*. "You did?"

"Yeah, I did. Are you sure you wouldn't rather go across the street to be with him? I wouldn't hold it against you. I don't need your pity or anyone else's. I'm doing this thing on my terms no matter how much grief Dad and Patrick give me."

"I'm where I want to be." She reached across the table and grasped my hand in both of hers.

I stared at our interlinked fingers and swallowed hard. Naomi wasn't a cruel person, but she sure as fuck was torturing me right now whether she realized the effect she had on me or not. "Naomi, I—"

She held up her hand to stop me. "Hear me out first, okay?"

I nodded warily, reluctant to get hurt any more deeply than I'd already been. Here came the *we're just friends* lecture and *please don't read any more into my fondness for you.*

I braced myself, certain I was going to get my heart stomped on one more time.

"That intimate conversation you witnessed…"

"Yeah?" My voice was husky with emotion, and I cleared my throat, embarrassed I was showing too much and making myself vulnerable. Naomi squeezed my hand and smiled at me with kindness in her eyes. Other emotions shone there, too. Did I dare hope? Was it desire? Or something more lasting? Or just mere friendship my hungry mind was interpreting as something else?

"Was Patrick and me getting things straight."

"What kinds of things?" I held my breath and waited for her answer. She clenched my hand, but I didn't point out my circulation was being cut off. Instead, I hid my other hand under the table because it was shaking. My heart slammed against my ribs like a caged animal trying to break out of captivity. I'd held it under wraps for too long with the exception of one misplaced night, which forever lived in my dreams and a few partial encores.

"I've changed, too, Pax. For the longest time, I didn't know what I wanted on several fronts. I've been so confused. The majority of my life, I tried to be what everyone else wanted me to be, or what I thought they wanted. If I skated, I'd be playing women's hockey and most likely hating every minute of it. Don't get me wrong, I love watching the sport, but I'm not a competitive person and never will be."

I nodded, afraid to speak because my voice would crack.

"I crushed on Patrick because my dad wanted that for me. Really for him. After observing the girls Patrick dated, I imitated them with too-high heels, blonde hair, tight clothes. Only that's not me." She pointed to her chest. "This is me. Jeans, T-shirt, comfortable shoes, understated, no cleavage."

"I did like the cleavage," I joked to break some of the

tension. Naomi swatted my chest with her free hand. On a whim, I grabbed her hand and held it next to our other clasped hands.

"What you saw last night wasn't what it seemed."

"Then what was it?"

"I told Patrick I wasn't interested. That's the intimate conversation you witnessed. He'd asked me out several times, and I hedged, always having an excuse, until I finally came to terms with where I am right now."

"And where are you at right now?"

"A little confused, but not as much as I was."

"And what does that mean?" I was wary, and who could blame me?

"It means…" She looked at our joined hands, swallowed, and met my gaze. "It means I want to explore this thing between us."

I didn't believe what I was hearing. Even though her words weren't a declaration of love, they were the next best thing, and I'd take them. "Are you serious?"

"Yes. I haven't been able to get beyond the night we spent together. In fact, that entire night, deep down I think I knew you weren't Patrick. You two are really quite different."

"Thank you." I lifted one hand to my mouth and kissed her knuckles.

"Can we start over?"

"In what way?"

"Maybe we could date. See where things go."

"Are you asking me out?"

"Yes, I guess I am."

"Okay, sure, as long as you're buying," I quipped. A slow smile of pure joy crossed my face.

"I'd be glad to buy whatever you're selling."

Now she was talking my language. My body felt a hundred

pounds lighter, as if all the burdens of the past several years floated upward and dissolved into the atmosphere. I closed my eyes for a moment, attempting to absorb and savor every joyous emotion. When I opened them, she was still there, beaming at me with a smile brighter than a spotlight on the ice.

"I'll want a big steak."

"You got it, Pax." Steak wasn't half of what I wanted, but we'd take it one day at a time.

"Our dads won't be happy about this, and neither will Patrick. He's used to getting who and what he wants."

"They'll have to get over it. Patrick doesn't care. He never wanted me. He was doing what the dads wanted and getting one over on you, I suspect."

"Yeah, probably."

"So, we're going to give us a shot?"

"Sure." I tried to tamp down my enthusiasm. She wasn't exactly declaring her undying love or committing to anything long-term. I played it cool, too.

"Let's see where it goes."

I nodded my agreement. Both of us had baggage, and we also had parents and my brother to deal with. Despite all the obstacles, seen and unseen, my heart was singing love songs, and my body was prepping for another late-night marathon session, most likely premature.

I'd built up a measure of pride and confidence over the past few months, and I would go into this with my eyes wide open. Anything could happen, and I'd roll with the punches.

For now, I'd bask in the glow of knowing Naomi was mine even if only for a little while.

23

SENSIBLE FLATS

Naomi

That went well.

And I was walking on air in my sensible flats.

Pax and I were going on an official date. Even better, he was open to exploring this thing between us. My only regret was taking so long to make a decision, especially when my heart had made it long before my head.

After hanging out in the bar for another half hour, it was curfew. Pax walked me to the door of the hotel room I shared with Kaitlyn when we were on the road. We stood outside the door, reluctant for the night to end. Paxton's gaze was hungry and so was mine.

"I wish I could invite you in, but Kaitlyn..."

"I get it. I wish the same, but Patrick..."

We laughed together, and I briefly toyed with the idea of paying for our own room, but if Coach Keller found out, I'd be fired and Pax could be suspended.

The hallway was quiet, no one around. Pax stepped closer and put his hands on either side of my face, pinning me against the wall with his big body. My lips parted, waiting for his. He lowered his head and kissed me, brushing his lips gently across mine, then nudging my mouth open and deepening the kiss. I didn't play coy with him. We both knew what we wanted, even if we wouldn't get it tonight. I grasped the collar of his shirt and stood on tiptoes, pressing my body against his.

He groaned as I tortured him by rubbing myself against his hard length. "I fucking want you," he growled into my mouth.

"I fucking want you, too," I responded and wrapped one leg around his muscular thigh.

He cupped my breast through my blouse and squeezed, sending tendrils of desire racing through my veins. I climbed up his body, and he cupped my ass with one hand to hold me against him. I wrapped both legs around his waist, rubbing against him, wishing we didn't have a barrier of clothes between us.

"Oh, fuck, Naomi." His words were tortured and husky. I dug my fingers into his shoulders and ground my pelvis against his. I wanted him naked in the worst way.

"I want you." I nipped at his earlobe. He liked that and rubbed his rough cheek against my lips. This man was my fire, and I was his oxygen. Being with him felt so right, so perfect. I saw the truth so clearly now that I wasn't forcing myself to do what I thought I should do instead of what I wanted. And I wanted Pax. All of him. All the time. Every night. Because I was greedy like that. I'd have gladly let him do whatever he wanted to me in this hallway. I was that far gone, and I didn't care who saw us.

"Oh, for God's sake. Get a fucking room!" shrieked Kaitlyn from behind me. I hadn't heard her open the door. Other doors up and down the hallway opened and bleary-eyed players peeked out.

Okay, maybe we did care. Paxton lowered me to the floor and grinned guilelessly.

Kaitlyn, in a pair of panda bear pj's, perched her hands on her hips and glared at us from the open doorway. "You two are making enough noise to wake the dead. Either fucking get it over with or get your ass in the room." She did not like to be woken up.

"Sorry." Pax gave me one last lingering kiss and winked at both of us. "See you on the bus."

He walked down the hallway, hands in his pockets, whistling to himself and waving to his eavesdropping teammates. I longingly watched him go until Kaitlyn grabbed my arm and yanked me in the room. She launched me toward the bed as she slammed the door behind us.

"What the fuck was that all about? You and Paxton?"

"How did you know that was Paxton?" I asked, avoiding her question.

"Two things, if that'd been Patrick, he'd have been fucking you in the hallway. And I know Paxton's walk."

"Paxton has a different walk than Patrick?"

"Of course he does." Kaitlyn regarded me as if I were stupid or something. "He ambles. Patrick struts. You never noticed?"

"I'm usually too busy looking at that hockey ass to pay attention to his walk."

"Well, there's that, too." Kaitlyn laughed. She went to the small bar fridge and pulled out a half-empty bottle of wine. "Want to join me?"

"I'd love to." She filled two paper cups and handed one to me.

"Okay, spill. What's going on? I want all the deets, the dirtier the details, the better."

I told her about last night and tonight. She listened,

finished off her wine, and poured herself another glass while topping off mine.

"Are you sure this doesn't have anything to do with Paxton playing better?"

"No, not at all. I'd have made the same choice if he was still struggling."

One of Kaitlyn's perfectly sculpted brows rose high up her forehead. "Are you sure?"

"Yes, I'm sure." I narrowed my eyes in annoyance. I didn't like being questioned, especially by someone who was my friend and should have my back.

"I hope so because Pax doesn't deserve to be jacked around. He gets it enough from his family."

"I'm not jacking him around. I was honest with him. We're going to date, see where this goes, but we didn't make any promises. We don't know what the future holds for any of us. He's going pro at the end of the school year. I have another year left to finish school."

"You think you'll go your separate ways then?"

"Too early to make any long-term planning."

I wasn't able to wrap my head around anything longer than the next week or two. I wasn't known to stick with one guy for long.

But Pax was different. He was my best friend, and he was the one I burned for every night and thought of every day.

He might just be *the one.*

24

FIRST DATE

Paxton

I was amazed how quickly my life had turned around in one short weekend. I was at the top of my game, and I had Naomi. The only way life got better than this would be if Patrick and I resolved our differences.

Naomi picked me up for our date early Sunday evening in her Tesla. I'd been in her car before, but I saw things differently now. Finances weren't a problem for Naomi and most likely never had been. Yet she wasn't spoiled or entitled, quite the opposite.

Patrick and I hadn't been raised with money, and we worked all summer to pay for the extras our full-ride scholarships didn't cover during the school year. Dad, being the ass that he was, always had a hard time keeping a job, and there'd never been any extra money. Currently, he worked as a house framer, but I wasn't sure how long that'd last.

My bro and I pinched pennies to make it through every school year. I was better at budgeting than Patrick and often had to float him a loan, especially by the end of second semester.

Tonight, I went all out. I donned my best button-down shirt, one of my splurges last year, and a newer pair of jeans. The shirt was the same blue as my eyes, and Naomi had commented on how much she loved it before. I debated on wearing my one good pair of slacks, but I wasn't a guy to dress up. She'd have to take me as I was.

I swished on a small bit of Patrick's aftershave, and I was ready a half hour early. I used the time to walk a few blocks to a small gift store that sold cut flowers. I picked out a bouquet in oranges and golds, which the salesperson dubbed a fall arrangement, paid too much for it, and hurried back home.

Patrick wasn't around, for which I was grateful. In fact, I had no idea where he'd disappeared to. The days where we kept each other apprised of our location were long gone.

Naomi was fifteen minutes late, leaving me to pace and fret she might stand me up. Finally, her car pulled in the parking spot outside. I grabbed the flowers, shrugged into my coat, and took the stairs two at a time. I had the passenger door open before she had a chance to get out.

Talk about eager. LOL.

"Hi." I grinned at her, leaned over the console, and gave her what ended up being a deep kiss.

"Hi, yourself," she said when we finished, her face flushed and her voice breathless. Her gaze strayed to the flowers crushed between us.

"Oh, uh, these are for you." I held them out to her, noting a few blooms were broken or squashed.

"They're beautiful," she gushed as if I'd given her a spectacular floral arrangement instead of a bunch of wilting cut flowers. Naomi didn't seem to mind. She rewarded me with another kiss.

And another. And…we weren't leaving this parking lot if we kept this up. I reluctantly withdrew and ran a finger gently down her cheek, taking in her loveliness. Tonight she was mine. All mine.

"I guess I should've brought something to put them in," I said lamely.

"I have something." She took the lid off her water bottle, placed it in the cupholder, and squeezed the flowers inside. She beamed at me, and I grinned so widely my jaw hurt.

"Where are we going for dinner? I want that good steak."

"You'll get it. I promise."

I sat back happily and enjoyed the ride. She parked in front of a rustic restaurant called the Lumberjack. I'd heard of the place but had never been able to afford it on my college-kid finances.

"Are you sure? This place is spendy."

"Paxton Graham, are you uncomfortable with me paying the tab?"

"A little. I guess that's really backward thinking. Someday, I'll have money and—" I stopped. It was too soon to be making those kinds of plans with her, even if I'd been making them in my thoughts almost since we'd met.

"It is, but no worries, Daddy's paying for it. It's going on his card."

"That does make me feel better. When I'm playing professional hockey, money won't be a concern."

She kissed my cheek. "I don't care about money, just you, but I am starved. Let's eat."

Now she was talking. I leapt out of the car and raced to the other side to open the door for her.

"Aren't you the gentleman?"

"Sometimes, when I think of it. Just don't expect such service all the time."

"I won't." She laughed, warming me to my very soul

despite a cold wind whipping around us. We hurried into the building done in wood and natural tones, continuing the rustic theme on the outside. I liked the place. I was comfortable here, way more than I'd have been in restaurant decorated in blacks and whites with stark tables. The Lumberjack's seating consisted of solid-wood booths with high backs, giving the occupants a good amount of privacy.

I waited for Naomi to sit down and slid in next to her. We cuddled together like a couple in love. I wasn't willing to go that far yet, at least not on Naomi's part, but things were going pretty damn well between us if I did say so myself.

We ordered drinks, a shrimp appetizer, and dinner. Spending her dad's money, I asked for a huge steak, while Naomi had surf and turf. Once the garlic shrimp appetizer and margaritas were delivered to our table, we settled in. I plucked one of the plump shrimp from the plate and held it up to her mouth. She opened those luscious lips and sucked the shrimp into her mouth, chewing slowly. Once she swallowed, she licked the garlic sauce off my fingers. Watching her eat that shrimp made me hard and horny, but I had to be patient, and my patience would be rewarded later.

First, I was going to enjoy that steak.

Naomi would be dessert.

The steak was orgasmic, but Naomi was more so. I wolfed down my meal, and she wasn't far behind. The whole erotic thing with the shrimp, which we ended up feeding each other, almost sent me over the edge. I used every method of self-control in my tool kit to make it through dinner.

When the waiter asked if we wanted dessert, I blurted out, "Yeah, but not here."

He furrowed his brow in a quizzical manner, and Naomi jumped to clarify, "We'll take our bill now. Thank you."

She slanted a glance in my direction full of heat and promise, so hot I didn't know why I wasn't melting into this bench. Then the little wench did something wicked. She placed her hand on my thigh and slid it up to my crotch and rubbed my erection in a circular motion. I sucked a breath through my gritted teeth.

"I hope you replenished your condom supply," she said with a sassy grin.

"Fuck yeah." I grabbed her hand and held it away from my crotch. As much as I loved her particular brand of torture, my ability to control my lust was walking a thin line right now.

She smirked and leaned in to run her tongue up my neck. "Can't take the heat?"

"Oh, I can take it, just not here."

"I'm not wearing any underwear."

The waiter came back, all business, before I had a chance to respond. Naomi signed the tab and left a tip. I didn't wait any longer. I rose to my feet, helped her into her coat, and hustled her out of there.

"You're going to pay for that little move inside," I growled and pinned her up against her car.

"I hope so."

Our mouths mated wildly with each other amid groans and whimpers. Panting, she pulled back slightly. "I've been dreaming of this moment for too long."

"Too fucking long," I agreed. I yanked open her car door, and she got in. As soon as I climbed in on the passenger side, she was all over me again. We steamed up the windows in the car, making out like the insatiable, hormone-driven, twentysomethings we were.

Naomi, in an impressive display of limberness, climbed over the console and straddled me. "I can't wait."

"Neither can I." This was insane, but insane, daring sex with a chance of getting caught appeared to be our jam. I unbuttoned the sweet little dress to reveal her lace-clad breasts, currently heaving from sexual arousal. I hooked my thumbs under the straps and pulled until her nipples were bared. I loved her tits. They were large but not too large, just right for my big hands, and those nipples haunted my dreams. Leaning down, I sucked one heavenly tip into my mouth, then the other. She writhed against me.

Naomi's hands tore at my fly, and within seconds, my cock sprang free.

"Condom," she hissed.

I managed to fish my wallet from my back pocket after banging my elbow on the door and drawing a giggle from Naomi. She grabbed it out of my hand and unrolled the rubber over my throbbing dick.

"Fuck me now," she ordered, and that was an order I planned to obey. *Yes, ma'am. This boy aims to please.*

She lifted her hips and guided herself down onto my cock, inch by excruciating inch. She was killing me, but I let her take her time. I closed my eyes and wallowed in the sensation of my hardness entering her moist, inviting softness.

Powerful emotions rampaged through my body, telegraphing a warning I wouldn't heed. This overpowering passion wasn't just lust. We'd progressed way beyond lust into territory I'd never been in before with anyone else. We were in a zone glorious in its wonder, infinitely frightening in its power.

Naomi began to move up and down, and I threw back my head and shut my eyes, allowing my body and mind to just be one with the experience. No more analyzing, just to be.

I was where I needed to be with who I needed to be with.

I was finally whole.

And I needed that as much as I needed her.

25

SEX ON A DRYER

Naomi

Since our first official date on Sunday, Pax and I had been insatiable, horny college students. He'd spent every night in my dorm room. The bed might be small, but we weren't complaining. The size made for great cuddling. Besides, it was cold outside, and cold permeated the drafty windows.

I'd never had a relationship that sexually intense. I was in a constant state of lust, and so was Pax. We got quite good at sexting to the point I had to shut off my phone in class or embarrass myself.

That weekend the team had a home doubleheader with Boston College.

The twins' infamous chemistry was shot all to hell, but the team was still winning. Patrick and Paxton scored goals in both games. They were both playing well, just not playing well together. On more than one occasion, Coach Garf's eyebrows drew together in a perplexed expression and Coach Keller's frown deepened more than usual. Neither coach interfered with the tension between the two brothers, opting for them to work it out in their own time, and I was certain they would. After all, the team was flying high and a sure bet for the Frozen Four.

Mr. Graham didn't attend the games that weekend, nor did my father. A blessing in disguise, if you asked me. I didn't have to juggle my many conflicts in an attempt to make everyone happy.

After Saturday's game, I met Paxton outside the locker room, and we headed with the team to the Biscuit. Pax ordered his fave wings, chicken Parmesan, and I ordered Thai spiced, along with a pair of beers.

"Where's our captain?" Tate asked Paxton as he paused on his way to an empty seat.

"Don't know." Paxton shrugged and dug into one of his wings. Tate hesitated, as if debating on saying more, then continued to an empty seat at the large table.

I ran my hand down Paxton's back between his shoulder blades, and he leaned forward so I could rub his back, a post-practice/post-game ritual we'd developed in the short time we'd been a couple. No one seemed surprised to see us together, which was a relief.

Patrick strode in a few minutes later with a babe on each arm dressed exactly how I'd once dressed and balanced on ridiculously high heels. He paused when he saw us.

"Good game, tonight, bro," Paxton said. I was proud of him for making the first move and forcing Patrick to talk to him.

Patrick's eyes narrowed to accusing slits and simmering anger. "You'd be playing great if you were on a one-man team, but you're not." Without another word, Patrick navigated the tight space between tables and sat down at the end with his two picks of the night.

Paxton glared after him. "Selfish bastard," he muttered.

"It's fine if he's the one doing the scoring and holding on to the puck. It's not okay when it's anyone else."

"He likes the limelight."

"And he's always had it. Never had to share."

"Give him time. He'll figure things out," I told Pax as I continued to rub his tight, bruised muscles. Boston played a very physical game, and Paxton had been slammed against the boards multiple times. Patrick had fared far better, and I wasn't altogether convinced that he hadn't set up a few of those rough plays on purpose.

"I've been giving him time. If anything, he's getting worse."

"Maybe it's coming to a head then, and you two should bare your souls to each other."

"I don't think that's a good idea just yet." Paxton's gaze slid down to the end of the table, where Patrick had his tongue in one blonde's mouth while squeezing the ass of the other.

"Good thing you aren't going home tonight."

"I imagine he's been enjoying having the place to himself."

"Did you tell him about us?"

"Yeah, I told him at practice on Monday. Said we were dating, and I might not be around much."

"What'd he say?"

"Nothing. He said nothing."

We finished off our wings and beer, and Paxton gave me that look I'd come to cherish—the one that said, *I need you naked as soon as possible.* I was all-in.

"Let's get out of here. We have better things to do," I suggested.

"I like how you think."

"Of course you do. That's because I have a dirty mind just like you."

"The dirtier the better."

One of the blondes had her hand down Patrick's pants. Paxton made a gagging sound and grabbed my hand. We slipped out the back door so we didn't have to go past them. I didn't have my car, so we walked down the street hand in hand.

"What's the craziest place you've ever had sex?" Paxton asked me with a gleam in his eyes.

"In the living room of my dad's condo while he was sleeping in the next room with one of his friends who was twenty years older than me.

"Seriously?"

"Yeah, I wanted to be caught. I was going through a rebellious stage back then."

"How old were you?"

"I'd turned eighteen and just graduated from high school."

"Did he catch you?"

"No, but only because he was preoccupied."

"Did you see the guy again?"

"We hooked up a few more times over the summer. Always somewhere public. The possible danger of being caught was how he got it up. That or Viagra."

Paxton laughed. "And is it a turn-on for you?"

"It? Viagra?"

"No, the excitement of getting caught."

I wasn't sure where this was leading, but I had my hopes. "Oh, yeah. And you?"

"Never really tried it unless I was drunk and then I don't remember."

"You're missing out." I stepped in front of him, forcing him to stop, reached down, and cupped his balls through his jeans. I planted a trail of kisses up his neck to his ear. "Paxton, I'm not wearing underwear."

"Oh, fuck," he groaned and pressed his body against mine.

Our lips met and our kisses grew hotter by the second. Reluctantly, Paxton drew away first. "I don't think I can wait until we get to the dorm. You're making me crazy."

"Then don't wait."

The campus rocked on Saturday nights, and people brushed past us on the sidewalk. His mouth came down on mine, demanding and rough, and I gave it right back. We panted and groped at each other's clothes. This time I separated from him.

"We can't do it here in the middle of the sidewalk."

"Are you sure?" His grin was wicked.

"I'm sure."

"I have an idea," he said.

"Good."

He grabbed my hand, forcing me to hurry alongside him. We turned a corner and walked down the street where all the sororities and fraternities were located. He led me up the walkway of the loudest house on the block. Stepping over beer cans and one passed-out frat boy, we went inside.

The place was packed. The music was deafening. The beer was flowing freely. We pushed through the crowd to a back hallway. Paxton stopped and glanced around.

At the end of the hall was a laundry room.

"This should do," he said as we peeked into the dimly lit room.

"Oh, yeah." We walked farther inside a space housing cleaning supplies, a utility sink, and a commercial washer and dryer. Paxton spun around to shut the door behind us. He started to lock it. I put a restraining hand on his arm and shook my head.

"You're a very naughty girl."

"Let me show you how naughty." To prove my point, I unbuttoned a few buttons to reveal a lacy bra and cleavage.

His grin was positively feral. He put his hands on my waist and hoisted me onto the small counter next to the sink and pulled out his wallet, riffled through it. He met my gaze with a panicked expression.

"Oh, fuck, I'm out of condoms."

"I have one." I dug into my purse and opened the small packet.

"You are a woman after my own heart."

"You're a man after my horny ass."

His brows shot upward, but he didn't take my bait.

"Now come here." I beckoned him with a crook of my index finger. He stepped closer. I unzipped his fly. I tugged on his waistband and pulled his jeans and underwear down enough to free his very large, very happy to see me cock. I rolled the condom down the length of him. Leaning back, I braced my upper body with my arms.

He lifted my skirt, and his smile was positively feral when he saw I wasn't lying about no panties. I leaned back on my elbows and spread my legs wide, opening myself up for him.

"Fuck you're beautiful."

"And wet. Very, very wet."

He swallowed hard and groaned.

"Fuck me, Pax. Fuck me hard. Don't hold back."

He did as she ordered. He plunged his cock into me with one hard, powerful stroke, leaving me breathless and gasping as my body sought to quickly accommodate his size. Paxton held himself there, grinding against my crotch, while he unbuttoned my blouse and pulled my bra down, freeing my breasts. He rolled my nipples between his thumb and forefinger, exerting more and more pressure, the roughened pads of his fingers abrading my sensitive nipples. Stars exploded behind my eyes. I was coming. Just like that. I let out a yell, glad the music drowned out my enthusiastic orgasm. Paxton didn't give me any recovery time. He began to thrust to the rhythm of the bass pounding all around us. He thrust harder and harder.

Then he stopped and held himself there. I whimpered, protesting when he withdrew from me. He flipped me over as if were no heavier than a rag doll and entered me from behind. He pounded into me, holding me steady with his fingers gripping my hips.

I reached under my body and grasped my nipples, pinching them as the pain melded with the pleasure. I was coming again and so was he.

The music stopped momentarily, allowing me to hear voices not far from where we were.

"Someone's coming," I hissed, even though I was too far gone to stop now.

"That'd be me," he said, not understanding what I was saying.

He stroked harder a few more times as the footsteps got closer.

We came together in a burst of extreme pleasure.

"Fuck! Fuck! Fuck!" I screamed, not giving one shit who heard me.

"Naomi!" Paxton threw back his head and bared his teeth, like a wild beast in the final throes of passion. We ground our bodies against each other, squeezing out every last bit of passion left in us.

"Holy shit." I heard a low whistle and lifted my head to see two frat boys watching us.

BUSTED

Paxton

I wasn't aware we had an audience until I came down off my orgasmic high, and Naomi pointed over my shoulder. I glanced back to see two guys, most likely freshmen, standing in the doorway in open-mouthed awe.

"Get the fuck out of here and shut the door behind you," I growled with a menace I usually reserved for hockey games. The guys scrambled backward, tripping over each other, and pulled the door shut.

"I guess we're done here," I muttered. With great reluctance, I pulled out, tossed the condom in a nearby garbage can, and zipped up my pants. Naomi righted her skirt and buttoned her blouse, and I blocked her body with mine in case those guys returned with reinforcements. She slid off the counter, and I took her hand.

We strode past the frat boys milling around down the hallway, and I tipped an imaginary hat to them. Then we ran out the back door and down the block, laughing our asses off. I stopped on the corner, picked her up, and spun her around.

"That was epic," she chortled and planted kisses on my face.

"At least they were too mesmerized to get their cameras out."

"Too bad. I'd have loved a video of our performance to warm those cold nights when you're not in my bed."

"What cold nights?" I quipped, but the video idea was a good one.

"I'm sure there'll be some."

"Not part of my plan."

We laughed again.

"Besides, I doubt you want a video surfacing on social media for your dad to see," I noted.

"Or your coaches or the Sockeyes."

"Crap, I hadn't thought about that. Maybe we should be a little more discreet."

"Maybe." Her grimace clearly broadcast how little she thought of my suggestion.

"If you want a video, we could make our own."

"You think?"

"Yeah, just for the two of us."

"Have I ever told you how much I love the way your nasty mind thinks?"

"You have." I grinned at her and swatted her ass. "We've had enough exhibitionism for one night. Let's go to my apartment and try a new position."

"Your apartment? What about Patrick?"

"If he's there, he's preoccupied. He won't be paying attention to us."

"I guess you're right."

"Uh-huh. Plus, I can't take another night in that little dorm bed. I need to spread out some."

I did know my twin, and I was right. His bedroom door

was shut, and the noises coming from inside Patrick's bedroom indicated my love life would be the last thing on his mind.

I led Naomi to my room and picked up where we left off, minus the spectators. Sometime early morning, I fell asleep with a naked Naomi in my arms, the best way to fall asleep if you asked me.

Sun streamed in the open curtains, warming my naked body. I stretched and smiled to myself. Nothing like a long night of sex to turn a guy's bones to mush. Naomi stirred beside me. She rolled over and rested her upper body across my chest. Her tousled and half-lidded eyes were a sexy turn-on, as if I needed much encouragement. I absently rubbed one of her hip bones.

"It's quiet next door," Naomi said after a while.

"Yeah, he's probably passed out."

"Two at once could be tiring."

I chuckled then sobered quickly. "He's been drinking a lot lately. I'm worried about him."

"Patrick's always been a partier. I haven't noticed him any better or any worse than usual."

"I have."

"You would know."

"Yeah, I do."

"Someday, you need to have a talk with him."

"I will. I'm letting him adjust to our new normal first."

"You're more patient than I am. I'd confront him. He's not being fair to you."

I shrugged. "I don't think he sees it that way. I think he's more along the lines of it wasn't broke, why fix it?"

"But, Pax, it was broken for you."

I give her a kiss on her cute little nose. "He doesn't realize that because I never complained, just went along with everything." I put my arms around her, and she cuddled next to me with her head on my chest. I stroked her hair and breathed in the scent of her, some kind of heady fragrance mingled with the smell of sex. I liked it. A lot.

"I hope we never run into those frat boys on campus."

"They didn't see enough of our faces to get a good look at who we were."

"Are you sure?" she asked.

"No. I'm trying to make you feel better."

She swatted at my chest and giggled. How I loved the sound of that. We were quiet for a while, enjoying just being in the moment.

"What are your plans for next year? Have you decided?" She turned so she could see my face. Her nipples tickled my chest hairs, and my dick, not one to be left out, sprang to attention, distracting me from her question.

"Pax?" She nudged me.

"Huh? Oh. I'll have enough credits to graduate this spring. There's no reason to stick around after that and play another season. I could have a career-ending injury before I ever get to play for the Sockeyes. I don't want to take that chance. I'm playing well right now, and I need to give myself the best shot I can." I hadn't realized until I'd voiced those words that I'd made my decision, but there it was. I was headed for the pros next fall. "And you?"

"I have one more year after this."

Silence engulfed us again. Not the contented silence of before but the oppressive silence of uncertainty weighed on us. We'd finally discovered each other, and our time suddenly was too limited.

I shook off a sense of foreboding and flipped her on her

back, drawing a screech from her. Pinning her wrists over her head with one hand, I kissed her senseless, then kissed my way down her body. Releasing her hands, I parted her legs and found paradise. I worshipped this woman and every minute inch of her body, but what was between her legs had to be one of my favorite places in all the world.

I slid a finger between her moist folds and pumped, rubbing her clit with my thumb. She writhed underneath me, bucking and squirming as I added another finger, followed by my mouth. I relished the power I had over her body, the way I was able to make her come sometimes just by sucking on her nipples or talking dirty to her. Naomi was a sensuous woman, and I was the lucky beneficiary of her sensuality.

"Oh, fuck, Pax. Fuck. Fuck." Her hips arched and jerked while I worked my magic once again until she collapsed, limp and sweaty. She lay still, breathing heavily for several minutes. I stroked her bare ass, loving the silky skin sliding against my fingers.

Then she pushed herself to a sitting position, her gaze full of adoration, and I dared hope for more than that.

"My turn."

I grinned at the wicked gleam in her eye. Nothing was better than a wicked Naomi when I was the recipient of all her dirty wickedness.

She wrapped her fingers around my dick and slid her hand up and down my length. I groaned and tossed my head back and forth on the pillow as she drove me toward my erotic version of paradise. I lived and breathed this woman, day and night, and I especially loved the nights.

She straddled me in the classic sixty-nine position, giving me great views of her hot ass and wet pussy. I stroked her thighs and ran my hand up and down her ass, kissing her thighs and stroking her toward another orgasm. I took it slow, wanted us to come together this time.

She slid her hot tongue up and down my dick while squeezing my balls, and I swore the pleasure was so great I might pass out. When she took my balls in her mouth and used her tongue to caress them, I believe I blacked out for a moment or two.

Her mouth slid back on my dick now. She began to fuck me with her mouth, and I lifted my head to give her as good as she was giving me. When we were like this, touch drove my brain, and need drove my passion.

I was a mouthful, but she managed to deep throat a good portion of my dick. Hot, wet goodness surrounded me, enveloped me, ruined me for anyone else. I began to come. Instead of pulling back, she swallowed. Then with sweet care she cleaned me off with her tongue.

If I died an erotic death right here and now, and I'd die a happy man. This girl had my dick wrapped around her little finger, and I'd never be free of her spell, which was fine, in my opinion.

Lock me in chains to her bed, and I'd never ask for another thing.

THE GIFT

Naomi

After our first date over a week ago, Paxton and I had been inseparable. If he wasn't in my dorm room, I was at his apartment.

Patrick either made himself scarce or ignored us. My heart ached for the wedge driven between the twins, but my interference wouldn't be appreciated, and I did my best to stay out of their troubles.

My birthday was Thursday the week before Thanksgiving. Birthdays weren't a big deal to me, but Paxton insisted on taking me to dinner. Sensitive to his financial situation, I opted for pizza delivery and a movie at his apartment. Being with Pax was all the gift I needed.

Once the guy delivered the pizza, Pax and I settled on the couch with beers and pizza. He let me pick the movie, even though he groaned that it was a chick flick. We made out, nothing unusual for us, which led to sex. Finally, later that evening, we ventured back to the living room for cold pizza.

"I have something for you. You distracted me so much earlier I forgot to give it to you."

"Pax, I said no gifts."

He shrugged, almost embarrassed. "I know, but I had to get you something. It's your birthday."

I did love gifts. My dad had a package delivered today by the local jeweler, and I'd been ecstatic. One-carat diamond earrings. I loved them and had probably gushed a bit too much about them to Pax.

"Someday I'll be able to afford gifts like your dad can but not yet." He smiled apologetically, but I was hung up on the *someday* portion of his sentence. That someday was under a year away. Would I be in his life once the school year ended? Or would we go our separate ways and fondly remember this time we spent together?

Such thoughts depressed me, and I forced my attention to the package he placed in my lap.

"Sorry, I'm not much for wrapping." He gazed at me with such profound caring, like a guy crazy about his girlfriend. And I was his girlfriend, even if we hadn't spoken the words yet, and I was crazy about him.

"What is this?" I stared at the box in with the Dalager logo on the outside. Dalager Sports Equipment was owned by Kaitlyn's father, and they made premier hockey equipment, along with other sports. My blood ran cold. Oh, dear God, please don't let it be…

"Open it." Paxton bounced slightly on his heels, as excited as a little boy on Christmas morning.

"Is it what it says it is?" My voice was strained and sounded foreign to my ears.

"Open it," he insisted, grinning at me.

I took an excruciatingly long time pulling up the flaps on the box, removing the lid, and rummaging through the tissue.

Everything inside turned cold as I stared at the pink figure skates.

Noooo.

I fought for control. Pax didn't know about my phobia. He'd given me a thoughtful gift based on what he knew about me. I wouldn't let on how upset I was.

"Is something wrong?" His smile dropped off his face. I wasn't doing a good job of concealing my disappointment.

Preparing myself for the best acting performance of my life, I raised my head and smiled brightly at him. "They're beautiful, but why did you buy me skates?"

"I love skating, and I want to share my love with you. We can skate together once in a while. Nothing big, just have some fun on the ice."

"Don't you get enough ice time?"

"A hockey player never gets enough ice time." He grinned at me.

"What did these cost? You can't afford these." I picked up one of the skates and turned it over in my hands. I knew enough about skating and quality skates to know these cost a pretty penny. Dalager didn't make cheap equipment but they did make it to last.

Paxton screwed up his face and cocked his head at me. "Stop worrying about what I can and can't afford. It's demoralizing. I'll be fine."

"But Pax, Dalager skates are the best. And spendy. I can't accept this gift." I crossed my fingers and prayed he'd give me an out.

"Kaitlyn got me a good deal."

"Regardless, they're not cheap no matter what kind of deal."

"Let's drop the money concerns. They're yours. Do you like them? Kaitlyn helped me figure out the size."

I was going to kill Kaitlyn. She knew why I didn't skate. Why didn't she have my back and talk him out of this idea? I was an ungrateful girlfriend. The guilt of my ungratefulness smothered me, but I wasn't going to skate ever, not even for Pax. I'd secretly return them and find a way to get his money back to him. I leaned in and gave him a kiss. "They're beautiful, but I wish you wouldn't have." I made another attempt, but Pax shook his head.

"All you have to say is thank you."

"Thank you, Pax."

"I know it's almost a month away, but I want you to start thinking about something." He sat down next to me and put his arm around my shoulders, so very pleased with himself. My own smile was so fake it hurt my face.

"About what?"

"Go to the alumni skate with me the Friday after finals." The alumni skate was an annual Christmas tradition with the team. Former team members and their significant others were invited back to skate with current members and their SOs. It was actually a big deal. The rink was decorated in Christmas lights, and there was a catered buffet and a bar. I'd never gone, but I'd heard about it. A couple of the WAGs had attended and shown me pictures. They transformed the rink into a literal winter wonderland.

"I can't do it," I said regretfully. I'd love to go with Paxton, but my fear of skating overrode my desire to attend.

"I'll hold you up, and we can get some practice time in before then.

"My dad will be there with his new girlfriend. I won't humiliate myself and him like that." I attempted another tactic.

"This is really important to me."

"I'm sorry. I can't go."

"Naomi, I need you to go."

"I can't. I can't get on the ice. I'm scared. Don't you understand? I can't do it."

He frowned. His entire face fell. "I don't understand. I'll help you."

"No one can help me," I wailed and tears streamed down my face. Paxton gaped at me, not getting what the issue was.

"Naomi, this was supposed to be a happy gift, something we could do together. If you hate skating that much, I'll return them."

"It's not that I hate skating. I'm scared to death to skate. I have panic attacks whenever I step foot on the ice." I blurted out the shameful secret about my phobia, and he listened with growing horror on his face.

"I didn't know." He was stricken, and I rushed to comfort him with kisses and gentle words. "It's okay. I understand. You tried to do something special for me, for us, and I honestly wish I were stronger, but I'm not."

"I'll return these." His voice rang hollow, and I had to make this up to him.

"I'll do it for you. Kaitlyn can help me. It's the least I can do for all the trouble you went to."

I stood and grabbed his hand. "Let me show you what I'd like for my birthday."

His face lit up, and he followed me into the bedroom. The skates were soon forgotten as he wished me a happy birthday in the best way possible.

28

SURPRISE VISIT

Paxton

The skates had been a mistake, and I chastised myself for thinking I had the right to push anyone to do something they didn't like or enjoy, even if I didn't realize the depths of her phobia. Naomi didn't hold the gift against me, and next time I'd stick with jewelry. I didn't think a guy could go wrong with diamonds.

Our sex life was epic since our first date almost two weeks ago. I'd never had so much sex in my life. We alternated between nights in my apartment and her dorm room. Patrick didn't say much when we were there. More often than not, he'd leave and not return until well after we'd fallen asleep. I was a little concerned because I hadn't seen him crack a book in forever.

I adored Naomi and dared hope she felt the same way. The mixed messages disappeared, and from where I was standing, she was one-hundred-percent devoted to yours truly.

She'd taken the skates in order to return them, and we didn't bring that subject up again.

We won our away game with Northeastern Friday night. I scored twice, and Patrick didn't score at all. My brother was having a few off weeks, and I got the distinct impression he blamed me, which I resented. He didn't come out and say it, but his actions and those scathing glares he sent my way communicated his feelings quite well. Patrick was a good captain, but lately he'd been barking orders indiscriminately, causing the guys to give him the side-eye. No one said anything because we kept winning, but we weren't gelling as a team, and everyone knew it.

My father flew in for the weekend, leaving me wondering if he was maxing out a few credit cards this year in order to attend all these games. I knew he didn't have the money, but his finances were none of my concern. He didn't contribute a penny to my college education, a fact I was proud of. Naomi's father, on the other hand, wasn't present, so I wouldn't be subjected to dinner out with my family and him. Naomi and I had made plans to get a bite to eat in the hotel cafe and look for a quiet, private place to get some alone time.

The team spent the night in Boston before being bussed to UConn the next morning.

I showered and dressed quickly, anxious to see Naomi. I was putting on my shoes when Coach Garf came up to me. "Pax, you have some people here to see you."

"I do?" I racked my brain and couldn't come up with any reason I'd have visitors during an away game.

Garf's smile was secretive. "You do."

My brother stood nearby, and I caught his surprised expression. He occasionally had a visitor to the locker room, but I did not.

Garf winked at me and patted me on the arm. "Don't keep them waiting."

I rushed to my feet and grabbed my jacket, heading for the

door. I knew, whoever they were, this was big. Nervous yet hopeful, I stepped into the corridor. Unable to contain his curiosity, Patrick was on my heels.

Several of my teammates were gathered around three men nearby. I stopped dead in my tracks and gaped open-mouthed like a dumb shit.

It couldn't be.

I was seeing things.

Lex broke off from the group. "You're so fucking lucky. Can I spend an hour in your shoes just once? They came to see you. Watched the last period of the game."

"They did?"

Lex nodded. "Yeah, you lucky fucker."

"Wow, Pax, don't just stand there." Patrick gave me a gentle shove toward them.

Feeling as if I were in a dream, I stiffly walked forward. The group parted to allow me to join them.

"Paxton, so good to finally meet you." The brawny, dark-haired man held out his hand. I shook it, still tongue-tied and in awe. When I didn't speak, he continued, "I'm Cooper Black of the Seattle Sockeyes. This is Isaac 'Ice' Wolfe, and Cedric 'Smooth' Petersen."

I nodded dumbly. "I...I know who you all are." My voice cracked like a young boy approaching puberty.

"Good game tonight, kid." Smooth clapped me on the back.

"I'd have a hell of a time defending against your slapshot," Ice said.

"Thank...thank you."

"If you don't have plans, we'd like to take you to dinner. Talk to you about the team. Answer any questions you might have."

"I'm flattered. I...I'd love to."

"We're in town, played Boston last night and again tomorrow night. Thought we'd take in a college hockey game and check out our top prospect."

I was their top prospect? Holy shit. I glanced around for Naomi, wanting her to share this moment with me, but I didn't see her. Unfortunately, I did spot my father, salivating and hovering nearby. Patrick came around the corner with Naomi. I shot him a smile of gratitude. He'd gone to get her and bring her here. My bro still had my back despite this rough patch.

I stepped back to include them in the circle. "This is my girlfriend, Naomi. My twin brother, Patrick, and my dad, Donald Graham."

"Your family is welcome to join us," Coop said graciously, including Naomi in his invitation. "It's the team's treat."

"I never turn down a free meal," Dad said jokingly. Not that he was joking in the least. He was the biggest mooch I knew. I grimaced at him, but the ass beamed at me like the proud father he sure AF wasn't.

"Let's go then." Coop clapped me on the back. I grabbed Naomi's hand and winked at her. She gave my hand a squeeze. We walked to a nice restaurant specializing in steaks and seafood and were escorted to a large table near the back of the room.

Coop sat next to me with Naomi on the other side, while Smooth and Ice sat across from us, leaving Dad and Patrick on the end. Used to being the center of attention, Patrick sat in shell-shocked silence, as if he'd fallen down a rabbit hole and had no fucking clue where he'd ended up. I felt the same way myself but for different reasons. To be able to share this moment with the two most important people in my life was beyond awesome.

"My son is excited to be playing for your team next fall," my father blurted out between bites of the shrimp appetizer.

"We're looking forward to having him on the team," Coop said. "The coaches have given us glowing reports."

"Thank you. I'm humbled." I didn't need a mirror to know my face flamed beet red. Under the table, Naomi squeezed my thigh and leaned into me. I appreciated the moral support and encouragement.

"We're losing a few guys to retirement and looking forward to seeing what you bring to the table." Ice studied me with an intensity that made me squirm. He was sizing me up, and I hoped I didn't end up lacking.

"You have a wicked slapshot," Smooth said.

"Paxton has always had a great slapshot thanks to me. I was a player until an injury ended my career. He learned that slap-shot from me." Our father inserted himself into the conversation. Ice, Smooth, and Coop glanced at him, then dismissed him, as if he were insignificant. Just like I'd been dismissed so many times by that man. I mused as to whether or not they'd done any research regarding my dysfunctional relationship with my father and were making known whose side they were on. I'd done a lot of research on my future team. Ice had a more abusive childhood than I'd ever dreamed of having, culminating in his father being convicted of murdering his mother. It didn't get worse than that.

Cooper Black was my idol. I'd watched thousands of hours of his games in an attempt to absorb everything he did and how he did it. Like his nickname, Smooth made playing hockey look effortless, even though I knew the effort he expended to play at his level. And Ice, he was legendary as a defenseman. I'd love to go up against him someday. And that someday might be sooner than I'd ever imagined.

"Do you do this often?" Naomi asked. "I mean visit with prospects?"

"Sometimes. When the timing works out, which is rare. We

firmly believe in the team as family, and we want the right family members. These types of conversations give us a good feel for future teammates and how they'd fit into our current slate of players. Coach Gorst specifically requested we pay you a visit as an added incentive to encourage you to go pro next season. The window of opportunity is open but those slots fill quickly." Coop swished his whiskey around in his glass and met my gaze. I didn't look away. They were probing for weakness, and I refused to show them any.

"We won't guarantee you'll make the team next fall, but you have as good of a shot as any of our rookies. Judging by how you're playing right now, the odds are in your favor if you hold it together." Smooth was matter-of-fact, not sugarcoating my chances, while Ice sat back, arms crossed over his chest, and watched us interact. He wasn't drinking anything stronger than water, I noted.

I sipped my own beer, not wanting to appear like some drunken college boy. I chanced a glance at my brother. He observed everything with an unreadable expression on his face, but I knew him better than anyone. He was tense and upset, and probably even more upset with himself because my being in the limelight bothered him. Patrick was a great guy, an awesome brother, and I loved that guy. We were in a rough patch right now as we both struggled with change, but we'd find our way back to being best friends. I'd bet my favorite pair of skates on it.

"What can I do to prepare?" I asked.

The three men exchanged glances, secretly communicating as they once had when they played on the same line.

Ice was the current team captain, and they deferred to him. "You're young. What are you? Twenty-one?" His gaze fell on the beer I was about to lift to my lips.

I set down the beer without taking a sip. "Yes, I'm twenty-one."

Patrick leaned forward, eager to hear their words of wisdom. Even my dad shut his mouth and paid attention.

"All right then. At your age, if you want to have a successful professional career, you have to be in this one hundred and fifty percent. All hockey, all the time. Cut partying to a minimum. Cut out any drama that detracts from your game. Keep personal relationships out of your professional life. Hockey can be all-consuming, and at your age, where you are right now, it has to be. Your personal life needs to take a back seat until you've established yourself as an invaluable member of the team." He directed his gaze toward Naomi. "Sorry, but it's the truth."

"I understand. My dad is Gene Smith."

The three men studied her with new respect.

"Then you really do understand," Ice said.

Naomi nodded, almost grimly, which bothered me, but I tried to push that niggling of a bad feeling out of my head.

Ice turned his attention back to me. "Playing in the pros is the toughest thing you'll ever do, but the most rewarding. Men will be separated from the boys when they step on the ice in a pro arena. You'll need to dig deeper than you ever did in your college career. Everyone on the team is just as talented as you are. The game moves at twice the speed. It'll come down to who wants it badly enough."

Just like Coach Garf kept telling me. At the pro level, it was five percent talent and ninety-five percent mental.

Ice turned to Patrick for the first time. "I understand you were a top draft pick for the Sidewinders."

Patrick nodded nervously. My brother was rarely nervous, but Ice was intimidating no matter how you looked at it. He was the best defensemen in the league, known for his stamina, toughness, and unparalleled stick handling.

"You're good, kid. You're both good. I suspect you two have what it takes if you want it bad enough."

"I do," Patrick and I said in unison.

"My boys have never shied away from hard work, just like their old man." My father puffed up a little. Patrick rolled his eyes, and I grimaced.

Ice ignored our father but offered no further words of advice as our dinners were delivered. I dug into the best steak I'd ever had, big and juicy and cooked just right. The garlic butter on top was fucking incredible. The baked potato was loaded with sour cream and cheese, and the broccolini was fantastic. We finished the meal off with cheesecake and conversation about hockey, of course.

After dessert the Sockeyes had to get back to their hotel, and so did Naomi, Patrick, and I. Our dad disappeared into the bar, and we caught a taxi back to the hotel.

Naomi sat in the middle as a buffer between us, and I held her hand while I tried to digest everything these pros had said to me.

"Wow, they're courting you." Patrick spoke in amazement, as if he didn't quite believe it. I thought I heard a hint of envy. Imagine that. Patrick the Great envying me.

His lack of confidence in me was offensive, and I snapped at him. "You're not the only guy who has a chance at the pros."

Patrick narrowed his eyes and leveled a menacing glare at me. As his twin, that glare didn't work, but he'd had success with it in the past, just not with me.

"You're jealous," I accused him with a smirk, not able to resist rubbing in my triumph.

"Fuck you." Patrick grabbed the door handle of the taxi as

it rolled to stop and hopped out, stalking into the hotel and leaving me with the cab fare.

The bastard.

I paid the man with the last of my cash, and Naomi bailed me out on a tip.

"Don't listen to him. He's grappling with all this shit like you are, and he's lashing out. Don't take it personally."

"How the fuck else am I supposed to take it?"

"Like a brother who loves a brother who's hurting."

I pulled her into my arms and held her. "How'd you get so smart?"

"It's not smart, it's the truth."

I kissed her and let her lips wash away all my doubts.

29

THE UNDRESSING ROOM

Naomi

After dinner with the Sockeyes, Paxton and I entered the hotel and stood together in the lobby.

"So much for going to my room." Pax jerked his chin in the direction of the bank of elevators where Patrick waited.

I checked the time on my cell. "Kaitlyn warned me not to come to our room until midnight."

"I guess we could sit in the cafe." Paxton grinned knowingly but his smile didn't reach his troubled eyes. He'd been quiet and thoughtful. He had a lot to absorb, and the future of our relationship had to be part of what bothered him.

"Unless you want to find a semi-private place to make out."

"I sure as fuck do, but where would that be? We're not exactly on a college campus where anything goes."

I moved behind him and rubbed his shoulders as I considered where we could go. "You're really tight and tense. You have a lot to think about."

"Yeah, I do. Least of which is my brother."

He didn't mention us, which concerned me, but I wouldn't reveal my fears. "And your dad."

"Yeah, my dad, but that's old news. This thing with Patrick is breaking news."

"You two need to settle your differences before things blow up in your faces."

"I've been waiting for him to come to his senses and adjust to our new normal."

"Maybe you've given him enough time. He's stubborn and might need smacked up the side of the head."

"That's what I'm afraid of." Paxton shook his head. "I know my brother. He's not good with change. I think he'll get there if I'm patient with him."

I understood Pax's reluctance to confront his brother and cause more friction, but I really felt the direct approach was best. Regardless, I'd leave that decision to him. We had more immediate problems, such as where to go for some privacy.

"I have an idea," I said after consulting the directory on one wall. I led him to the elevators, and we exited on the spa floor. I used my room key to get inside the pool/spa area. The place was deserted. A sign on one wall indicated dressing rooms and showers this way.

Paxton's eyes lit up. "I know what you have in mind."

We hurried to the dressing area. "We're in luck." There were separate dressing rooms with showers, and we had the place to ourselves. We picked the closest one, and Pax locked the door behind us. We quickly stripped and left our clothes on the wooden bench.

"Do you have a condom?"

"I never go anywhere without one anymore." He fished a plastic packet out of his wallet.

I took it from him and opened the packet. Then I knelt in front of him and rolled the condom onto his hard dick. I took my time, doing a little sucking and stroking as I did my due diligence. Pax dug his fingers into my hair and groaned. I finished my job and stood before him, allowing myself the luxury of perusing his hard, muscular body. He was so magnificent. Hard in all the places I was soft.

I rose to my feet and spun around to turn on the shower, waiting for it to reach the right temp. Pax crowded behind me, his cock rubbing against my ass. He wrapped his big hands around my breasts and pulled me close to his nakedness.

I closed my eyes and leaned against him, reveling in the feel of his calloused palms on my delicate skin. The hot water was steaming up the small room, and I turned in his arms, backing into the shower and dragging him with me. He pinned me against the slick wall as water from the showerhead ran down our bodies.

"I—I need you," I gasped as he kissed the hell out of me. I kissed him right back, allowing my kisses to say things I didn't dare speak out loud for fear I'd jinx myself and him in the process. Whatever was happening to us was best not analyzed but experienced.

He knelt down, and I put one leg over his shoulder, giving him better access. I gripped his shoulders to balance myself while his tongue worked its magic on my lady parts.

"Pax, oh, Pax. Pax! Pax!" He was relentless, and I was shouting as I came.

I'd barely recovered when Paxton stood and hoisted me up his body, pressing my back against the wet tile wall. He aligned his dick and thrust into me. I wrapped my legs around his waist and my arms around his neck, marveling at the power behind his thrusts while holding me against the wall.

I rode him for all I was worth, enthusiastically pumping my hips to match his. His strokes built with my encouragement until he was pounding into me with such force my body slid several inches up the wall with each stroke.

His cock jerked inside me as he started to come, and my body responded by following him into the ultimate bliss. The pleasure was so intense I was certain I'd die, because no one would be able to survive the violent, erotic waves of ecstasy assaulting my body.

I was vaguely aware of Paxton calling my name and biting my shoulder as he buried his cock inside me one last time and held it there.

His labored breathing rasped in my ears, and our sweat mingled with the water. I don't know how Pax managed to still have the strength to hold me against that wall when I was boneless and incapable of any kind of lucid thoughts or movements.

Eventually, I slid down his body and stood on my own. He stared down at me with eyes still full of hunger.

"I can't get enough of you," he said, gulping in oxygen.

"I can't get enough of you either. You are the best I've ever had. No one has made me feel like this."

"Me neither."

"You get inside me like no one ever has."

"Literally." We both chuckled over the joke.

We clung to each other and were quiet, listening to the sounds of each other's breathing. Finally, I drew back. "We need to get back to our rooms. You have a game tomorrow night, and you'll need your sleep."

Guilt clouded his expression for a moment, reminding me of what the Sockeyes had told him. *All hockey, all the time.*

As if he was reading my mind, Paxton withdrew from me and began drying off with the towels we'd had the foresight to grab from the bin outside. He handed me one, and just like that, our magical moment was over.

Something shifted. Something so subtle I might've missed it had I not been hyperaware of a change in the atmosphere around us.

With growing unease, I dried off and dressed. We didn't say another word to each other as we walked to the elevators. Once on our floor in front of my door, Paxton gave me a deep kiss, yet I couldn't shake off the feeling he was holding something back.

"Good night, Omi."

"Good night, Pax."

I watched him walk down the long hallway to the room he shared with Patrick and wondered if we'd survive the next few months.

THE SPIRAL

Paxton

Sometimes I swore I was taking one step forward and two steps back, always waiting for the other shoe to drop. That kind of negative thinking would get me nowhere.

The Sockeyes' advice swirled around in my head, leaving me confused and conflicted.

Everything I'd ever wanted was right at my fingertips, yet I could feel it slipping away, out of reach. I wouldn't let that happen.

The next week was Thanksgiving, but we had away games on Friday and Saturday at Dartmouth. Naomi flew to Vegas on Wednesday to be with her family and would miss the weekend's games. I was at a loss without her, which was frightening in itself. She'd become a huge part of my life in a very short time, and that was a dangerous place to be, especially for someone who was on the verge of major life changes that didn't necessarily include her.

Patrick and I continued our strained relationship, neither one of us taking the initiative to finally have it out. I think deep down we both feared we were losing each other, and there was nothing we could do about it. We were mere months from going our separate ways for the first time in our lives. I was scared shitless and exhilarated at the same time. No longer would Patrick's shadow dominate my life. I'd make my own way. Yet we'd been each other's rock for so long, I didn't know how I'd find my way through a future without him playing a crucial part in it.

I got up early and worked out on Thanksgiving. Patrick stayed in bed with a redhead he'd picked up last night at the Biscuit.

I dreaded dinner with my dad. Once our mother had died, Thanksgiving with him had been an ordeal to be suffered and not a pleasant family time to be savored. Mom had been the glue who'd held us together. She'd managed Dad in a way no one else ever could, keeping him focused and positive. That'd all fallen apart once she'd died. He'd become someone else. He'd probably always been the selfish, obnoxious person he was now, but she'd hidden his true self from us.

I called Naomi as I walked home from the gym. Clouds rolled in and threatened either rain or snow. If it stayed this cold, we'd most likely get snow. I shuddered at the thought I might be snowed in tonight with Dad and Patrick. Naomi answered on the first ring.

"Hey, babe." I forced my tone to be upbeat. "Were you sitting right by the phone?"

"I was starting a text to you. I'm bored."

I laughed. The sound of her voice cheered me up. "What's going on?"

"The housekeeper is making dinner. My dad's twentysomething girlfriend is here, and she's a bitch, to be blunt. She's been picking at my hair, my wardrobe, my makeup. You name it. And Dad's backing her up, telling me I should dress like the daughter of an NHL legend even if I can't skate worth shit."

"Ouch. That's harsh."

"Yeah, is your dad there yet?"

"I don't know. I've been avoiding the apartment since this a.m. I'm heading back there now."

"I'm sorry."

"I'm sorry for you, too." I stopped in front of my apartment. "I'm here now. I should go in and face the fun. I'll call you later tonight."

"Let's video chat."

I perked up at the thought. "As in a little phone sex?"

"Oh, yeah."

I was grinning now. "Thank you for giving me something to look forward to."

"Thank you. And Pax?"

"Yeah?"

"I miss you." The longing in her voice dispelled all my anxieties of the past few days. We would make this work. We had to.

"I miss you, too."

We said our goodbyes and I ended the call. Steeling myself, I walked upstairs to our apartment and entered.

Patrick was making out with the redhead on the couch, one hand between her legs and the other on her breasts.

"Seriously? Go in your fucking room." All my good feelings dissolved with irritation, even though I had no room to talk. It wasn't like Naomi and I hadn't had our moments in public.

"Fuck you," Patrick barked back.

The redhead looked me up and down and licked her lips, making no move to button her blouse. "Twins? I've never done twins before. Are you up for a threesome?"

"No, he's not, and neither am I." Patrick glared at me as if I'd made the suggestion. "I don't do threesomes."

"You didn't object to one last week."

"I don't do threesomes with another man, especially my brother."

Insulted, she stood, straightened her clothes, and stalked out the door without even a goodbye.

"Thanks for ruining my good time."

"I wouldn't have ruined it if you'd stayed in your room. You know, Patrick, sex is so much better with someone you actually care about. You should try it sometime." I shouldn't have said it, but I did.

"You've turned into a self-righteous prick this year, and I've had enough of your bullshit."

"Really? At least you've only had to deal with my being a prick for a few months. I've had to deal with an entire lifetime."

"What's that supposed to mean?"

"You figure it out. You're not as stupid as your grades indicate."

A low blow, and I knew it, but I couldn't take the words back now that I'd released them into the wild.

"You fucking asshole. That hat trick you scored has gone to your head." Patrick closed the space between us in long, deliberate strides until we were toe-to-toe. His hands were fisted at his sides. I held my breath. In all our twenty-one years, we'd never come to serious blows. We'd had our scuffles, but mostly we'd been horsing around and one of us might get a little rough and draw blood.

"Every score you make inflates your overinflated ego. You're jealous. Of me." I angrily spit out my thoughts without meaning to. But he was jealous of me, and I never thought I'd see that day. I took no pleasure from it. Jealousy was a destructive emotion that could eat someone up from the inside out. I didn't want that for us.

"Why would I be jealous of *you*?" he shot back.

"Because for the first time in our lives, I have the things you want."

Patrick ground his jaw together, a sure sign he was about to lose his temper. Usually, he ended up in the penalty box when he did that. Only we didn't have a penalty box nor did we have referees, and I didn't know how this would end if we truly came to blows.

Our doorbell rang, and we both froze. Deciding to end this here and now, I backed away and turned to the door. I opened it and let Dad in. He looked at me, then at Patrick and frowned.

"What the fuck is going on here?"

"Nothing," we said in unison, something we used to do often but hadn't for a long while.

Dad strolled into our apartment carrying a couple bags. One contained two bottles of whiskey and the other had takeout from a nearby diner.

"Paxton, throw the food in the oven and heat it up. I need a drink." He moved to the kitchen to get a glass.

He needed a drink? I did, too. "Pour me a strong one."

Dad's brows shot up, but he didn't remark on my sudden desire for whiskey. Instead, he looked to Patrick, who nodded.

Drinking whiskey with my dad and brother was a bad idea, but I did anyway to dull the pain of my dysfunctional family. For the first hour, we talked college hockey and what teams had a chance at the championship besides our team. I started to relax, and Patrick did, too. Maybe we'd make it through this holiday unscathed.

But Dad was drinking two shots to our one and tossing them back like they were water. He wasn't a lot of fun when he was drunk, and I glanced at Patrick, who'd tensed again. He was thinking what I was thinking. This wasn't going to end well. Usually we ran interference for each other, but I wasn't sure we were on the same page anymore when it came to having each other's backs.

We ate our dinner, which consisted of overcooked turkey, soggy dressing, runny mashed potatoes, lumpy gravy, and canned green beans. I was hungry so I wolfed it down anyway. I'd never been a picky eater. Put food in front of me, and I'd devour it, not matter how bad it was. My mom used to joke that whoever married Patrick and me wouldn't have to be a good cook because we wouldn't know the difference. The pumpkin pie was good, and I had seconds.

My dad opened the second bottle of whiskey. He was drinking it on the rocks now, better than shots, I figured.

His gaze settled on me, and I held my breath. I usually flew under the radar with him, while Patrick drew his constant criticism.

"Have you given any thought to what the Sockeyes told you?"

I blinked, trying to decipher what he meant by that question. "Uh, yeah, quite a bit."

"You're playing above your abilities. It won't last, but milk it while you can. They're right. You have to focus on hockey and nothing but hockey."

"I am, Dad. I'm serious about this."

He snorted his disbelief. "Then get rid of her."

"What?"

"You're an idiot. You can't see the truth?"

"What truth?" I asked warily. Patrick watched us both and wisely kept his mouth shut.

"You always were a dreamer like your mother. Naomi is using you."

"No, she's not." Out of habit, I looked to Patrick for backup. He shrugged and didn't respond, leaving me to believe he agreed with Dad for once.

"For being so book smart, you're dumb when it comes to common sense. Let me spell it out for you. You're playing well while Patrick is having an off couple of weeks. Of course she switched to you. But, boy, you're a fool if you don't think she'll go running back to Patrick when he regains his stride and you go back to playing like normal."

I gaped at my father, deeply hurt and offended. Even worse, a tendril of doubt wrapped a painful tentacle around my heart.

"Dad, Mr. Smith offered to spend some time with me after the season working on my slapshot." Despite us being at odds, Patrick deflected Dad's attention to him. He gave me one of those *you can thank me later* looks.

Patrick's slapshot was the weakest part of his game, while it was my best. Even so, he had a good slapshot, but my brother had to be number one at everything.

Our father forgot all about me, and I was able to fade into the background while he gave Patrick his opinions on how to improve.

Thankfully, Dad got a text a few minutes later and abruptly stood.

"Sorry, boys, a lady I've been seeing here in town on occasion needs me. I need to go, but one last thing. I've been laid off, so I won't be able to attend your games until I'm back at work."

I didn't dare look at Patrick because I was pretty sure we were both inwardly cheering our father's bad news and feeling like shit for it.

He was gone before we had time to comment or say goodbye, and he took the remainder of the whiskey with him.

"I owe you one, bro." I grabbed the last of our beer from the fridge and handed one to Patrick.

"Hey, you'd have done it for me."

"I would've."

"I feel like a huge weight was taken off my shoulders when he said he wouldn't be at our games."

"Yeah, thank God." I fist-bumped with my brother, feeling closer to him than I had for a long time, despite the rock that sat in the pit of my stomach regarding their suspicions about Naomi.

We sat down on the couch and found a hockey game on TV, watching it and commenting on anything and everything, like we once had.

During intermission, Patrick turned to me. "I think Dad's right, you know. She's using you. Can't you see it?"

"She is not using me."

Patrick's pitying glance irritated the hell out of me. I was either going to thump him or I needed to get the hell out of here. I grabbed my coat.

"Where're you going?"

"To the library. Some of us study."

"Fuck you," Patrick shot back. I was being an ass, and I knew it. Patrick's sore spot was his studies, and I'd been getting in my jabs.

I hesitated in the doorway, about to apologize to him, but he turned his back on me and stomped off down the hall.

I slammed the door, getting a small measure of satisfaction from the loud noise, and trudged through the snow toward campus. I was furious with my family and missing Naomi. They were wrong about her. Damn it.

I spent the evening and next day mired in doubts and whether now was the right time to be wrapped up in a serious relationship with all the other shit in my life. Even Coach Garf's positive thinking lessons weren't overcoming the negativity and self-doubt creeping into my thoughts.

I was in no shape for two away games this weekend.

Naomi spent the weekend with her father, so I didn't have her encouraging presence to bolster my confidence. Nor did I have my brother to confide in. He'd made his position clear.

By the time I skated onto the ice for the puck drop on Friday night, I was a mess inside. No one noticed, not even Patrick, which was a testament to how far apart we'd grown in the past month or so.

As we raced up and down the rink, my feeling of destabilization intensified. The ice felt off under my blades. My uniform restricted my movements. My brain wasn't seeing the shots. I was tense and growing more desperate by the second. I forced several shots at the net and missed every one of them, drawing disapproving scowls not only from Patrick but from the other members of my line.

"I'm hot tonight. You're colder than this ice we're skating on. Be a fucking team player. Feed me the puck," Patrick hissed at me as we took the ice for the third period.

I bit back a retort. He was right. He was hot. I was a team player, damn it. I slid back into my old method of play, passing my brother the puck instead of taking a chance on my shots. Patrick was ecstatic, and I was miserable by the time the game ended, even though we won.

The next night, Coach Garf approached me during warm-ups. "Relax, kid. Don't panic. Don't fall back on old habits. You've got this. Trust yourself and your instincts."

"But the team…"

"The team is still winning. Stick with our plan."

Only I didn't. Our opponent was tied with us for first place, and they were tough as nails. The game was hard-fought and fast-paced. I was slammed up against the boards more than I had been in the previous four games.

We won, just barely thanks to my teammates stepping up, while I stepped down, considerably.

My life was spiraling out of control, and I needed to simplify things by making smart, sound decisions, rather than ones based on emotion. At the first sign of adversity, I'd abandoned my new way of playing and gone back to being Patrick's wingman.

BACKSLIDING

Naomi

I spent the long Thanksgiving weekend with my dad and his girlfriend. Dad had taken the liberty of making sure I had the weekend off from my statistician job without even asking me first. I'd have preferred going to the games, but instead we watched them on television as a *family*.

I missed Paxton immensely, but he'd been so busy all weekend we'd hardly had a chance to talk, with him being on the road and me being under my dad's thumb.

Moo U won both games that weekend. Patrick scored a hat trick during Saturday's game. Paxton didn't score either game, but he had an assist. He was slightly off. Not skating as sharply as he had been for the past month. He shot several times in the first two periods. By the end of the second period of the first game, he appeared totally demoralized and slipping back into his old role by feeding Patrick the puck. The team needed his scoring during the second game, and it wasn't there. Paxton wasn't shooting at all.

I was relieved to hear his father wasn't at the games. We'd

both speculated how long he'd be able to afford attending. According to Pax, he'd let his sons know he wouldn't be at any more games until after the new year, claiming he'd been laid off from his job.

My father had taken on a commentator position for his old team while the full-time guy was out with a medical issue. He wouldn't be interfering in my life as much either. I looked forward to being out from under his constant scrutiny.

Coach offered to keep me on as a statistician after the semester ended and my internship was done. A week ago, I'd have jumped at the chance. But something wasn't quite right between Paxton and me. He'd been different on the phone over the weekend, as if he were pulling away. Maybe we'd moved too fast, and he was getting cold feet. I didn't know. I asked Coach to give me a few weeks to decide, and he was fine with that.

I met Pax at the Biscuit on Sunday night for wings and beer. I arrived early for once and waited for him at the hockey table. I had missed him so much, and he'd consumed the majority of my thoughts for the past several days. In my pocket was a gift for him, certain to bring a smile to his face, while we had a good laugh between us.

Patrick came in the door first with a huge grin on his face like a triumphant warrior. He paused to flirt with a tableful of female fans giggling and fawning over him. Hockey players were Moo U's biggest celebrities, and a lot of the guys basked in the glow of such adulation.

Paxton entered a few minutes later. I took him in. With his dark hair he never cared much about but still looked sexy as hell whether long or short, the Moo U sweatshirt that clung to his broad shoulders, and his drool-worthy hockey ass clad in faded jeans, he was everything I would ask for and more. And he was all mine. He rocked my body and held my heart in the palm of his large, calloused hands. I was falling for him in a way both scary and unique.

He spotted me, and a grin played at the corners of his mouth.

Unable to control my enthusiasm, I lost all composure. Four days was a long time to be apart. I shrieked his name and rushed toward him. Launching myself into his arms, I clung to him like he was a life preserver from the *Titanic*. He hugged me back, holding on so tight it was almost as if he feared this hug might be our last one. Finally, we separated. He grinned down at me.

"I'm starved." He took my hand and led me away from the hockey table to a private table nearby.

"I missed you so much," I gushed, throwing my feelings out there and hoping he didn't stomp on them in return.

"I missed you, too." He looked away from me, not meeting my gaze. A red flag flew up the flagpole, and I sobered. Something *was* wrong. I hadn't imagined the subtle differences in him.

"How are you doing?" I tamped down my enthusiasm out of sheer self-preservation.

"Okay." He was anything but okay. His blue eyes were troubled, and his shoulders slumped.

"You don't seem okay." It wasn't us, it was his play over the weekend. That's all. Paxton was his own worst critic. I breathed a little easier having convinced myself his withdrawal had nothing to do with me.

"Did you watch the games?"

"Yeah, I did. You were having a tough couple nights." I grabbed his hand and squeezed it.

"I wasn't feeling it. Coach told me not to get down on myself. He says I'm bound to resort to old habits when things aren't going my way and to have faith." He looked up at me.

None of the usual sparkle was in his gaze. "What if it's not a fluke? What if my dad was right? What if I was playing above my abilities, and my improvement was only temporary?"

"Your dad told you that?" Anger at Paxton's father boiled inside me.

He nodded solemnly. "Yeah, tearing me down was part of our Thanksgiving Day dinner."

If Mr. Graham had been in front of me, I'd have thrown a pitcher of beer on his head or, even better, a plate of spaghetti. "He's wrong. You're an exceptional player. So you had a setback. So what? You can do this."

"Coach wants me to step it up and spend every spare moment I have working on the physical and mental aspects of my game. He thinks I've backed off lately, which is why I'm backsliding."

"Maybe he's right." I suppressed a twinge of guilt I might have some blame in why Pax's play had deteriorated. He'd been spending more and more time with me, compared to working on his game. I hadn't discouraged him either. I'd selfishly taken whatever time he gave me, not thinking about his future.

"You always have believed in me." His expression softened. I wanted to hold him and erase the lines of stress off his handsome face.

"I'll always be your biggest fan," I promised, maybe overdoing my enthusiasm a bit.

He looked away but not before I caught something in his eyes that looked like regret. Panic rose inside me. I'd been dreading this moment ever since he'd had that discussion with the Sockeyes. I'd been in denial regarding how he'd act on their suggestions, but now I realized how wrong I most likely was. Hockey had been Paxton's life since he'd been old enough to skate. He had to take them seriously. I admired his relentless dedication to his chosen career, and I'd never stand in the way of his success. I was hoping I wouldn't have to.

Searching for a distraction to bring the conversation back to something more positive, I pulled the small package from my pocket and handed it to him. "This is for you."

He turned the small brown paper bag over in his large hand. "What is it?"

"Look and see."

I watched as he pulled the rose-colored crystal from the sack and looked questioningly at me. I'd bought the rock partially as a joke between him and me.

"It's rose quartz. I thought you could put it on the chain with your other crystal."

"What does it represent?" He rolled the stone around in his palm, examining it.

"It's to help restore harmony in your relationships and also encourages self-worth. I thought you could use it because… you…Patrick."

He nodded slowly, took off his necklace, and added it to the chain. He pulled the chain over his head and tucked it under his sweatshirt. "Thank you."

"You're welcome." I'd left out the part about that stone representing love and healing in relationships. I wasn't sure how he'd take that right now. He met my gaze, and his smile was laced with sadness. My mouth grew dry, and my throat closed up. Something was horribly wrong.

"Let's go somewhere we can talk privately," he said, cementing my fears with his words.

"Okay." My heart pounded in my chest, and my stomach lurched. Fear about our future bombarded me with doubt. Our relationship was so new and so fragile. We hadn't had time to build a solid foundation able to weather any storm. I didn't know if such a possibility would ever be afforded to us.

I didn't feel so good and hoped my face didn't reflect my fears. Whatever Paxton said, I had to believe we'd get through this. Prematurely, I'd spent part of the weekend researching possible colleges in Seattle to finish my degree, even secretly started the transfer process to see if I'd lose any credits or not.

I'd been a fool to put this much stock into our relationship.

He put his coat on, and I followed his lead. Waving to the people at the hockey table, we walked outside into the chilly night.

"Over here," he suggested. The Biscuit had outside seating not used in the winter, but a few chairs were scattered about for smokers. Currently, no one was occupying them. I wiped one off with my sleeve and sat down. Hugging myself in a protective gesture he'd assume was because of the cold, I watched and waited for whatever came next.

Paxton pulled a chair across from me instead of next to me. Not a good sign.

"What's going on?" I asked, wanting to get this over with.

"I'm conflicted." He stared at his hands and wrung them in his lap. "I'm worried about my game, especially after this weekend. I've been giving a lot of thought to what the Sockeyes said to me."

"Wise words. You're on the cusp of your professional career."

He lifted his head, giving me a great view of blue eyes filled with conflict and indecision. "I don't know what to do. You're my rock, yet I feel torn. I don't know how much I can put into a relationship right now. Doing something halfway hasn't been my style, nor is it fair to you."

I stayed quiet, afraid I'd choke if I tried to speak. I'd never dealt with real heartbreak before other than the death of my mother, and what I was feeling now came close to that. We'd only been dating a short time, but we'd been friends for a few years. The dread ripped at my insides, and I hugged myself tighter.

I couldn't lose him right after I'd finally realized how much he mattered.

Pax was *the one*, and I think I'd always loved him, even if I hadn't admitted to it before.

Yes, I *loved* him. A moment like this should be sung from the rooftops and celebrated. Instead, fear weighed me down and settled in the pit of my stomach.

"Are you breaking up with me?" I choked on a strangled sob and dabbed at the corners of my eyes with a napkin. I would not cry. I was stronger than that.

"I don't want to, but there's so much going on, and I'm torn in different directions. I feel guilty not spending enough time with you, not studying like I should, and not concentrating all my efforts on hockey. Something has to give."

"And you think it has to be us?"

"Maybe. I don't know. I need to concentrate on school and hockey."

"Let's slow down. We don't have to spend every spare minute together. We do have finals coming up in two weeks, and so much is going on all at once." He wasn't breaking up. I breathed a huge sigh of relief, desperate to keep him in my life in some capacity.

"Yeah, I won't be able to spend much time with you."

"Let's not worry about us right now. We don't have to be joined at the hip. You take care of business. I'll be here when things have evened out. You take care of you. Don't worry about me."

Denying my problems had been my MO since my mom had died. I'd dwelled in a dream world where life was exactly what I wanted it to be. I worked hard on not overthinking things or giving concerns too much power in my life. As a result, I'd become irresponsible and wasted a lot of my high school years partying. Glossing over and burying problems was a survival mechanism that became destructive. After a few years of counseling, I'd learned to deal with pain and adversity rather than denying them. Here I was falling back into that mode. If I ignored our problems, they'd go away.

We both dropped the subject of our future for the next half hour, talking about classes, finals coming up, and Christmas break plans.

After drinking a few beers and gorging on wings, Paxton paid the bill.

"Do you want to come back to the dorm with me?" I asked hopefully.

He considered my invitation for way too long, and I rubbed my upset stomach under the table, then he nodded. "Yeah, yeah, I'd like that. It might be a while before we can get together again with everything we have going on."

We fucked that night with hungry desperation, as if somehow we knew deep down we might never be together again. A dark cloud hung over us. Paxton didn't stay the night but left by midnight, claiming again that he was tired. He'd never been tired before when it'd come to us, and I knew he wasn't now.

I wasn't able to shake the sense of this being the beginning of the end.

I hadn't known until this moment how much Paxton meant to me. How much I truly loved him. How torn apart I'd be without him. Some part of me had assumed he'd always be a part of my life, and there'd be time for us to explore a relationship. Even when I'd thought I preferred his brother, somewhere in the back of my mind, I'd felt time was on our side.

I was wrong. Time wasn't on our side, and I was running out of the most precious commodity a person had.

32

COMFORTING ARMS

Naomi

On Wednesday, my dad called. He'd be on campus briefly for an alumni hockey meeting that evening and thought we might grab dinner.

I hadn't seen Paxton since Sunday night, not even in the dining hall. We texted throughout the day, but our texts were superficial, none of the playfulness and sexy teasing I'd come to expect. I talked to him last night, and he was in a hurry to get to the rink for a late-night practice session with Coach Garf. I hoped to run into him while waiting for my dad, but so far, he hadn't surfaced.

My dad's meeting ran late, and I had a study group in a half hour. Dinner might not happen, but I didn't dare leave without at least saying hi to him. People catered to my dad, and the guilt he'd dump on me if I left before seeing him forced me to stick around.

Patrick strolled out of the weight room. He broke into a welcoming smile when he saw me.

"Hey, Omi, how's it going?"

The dam broke. I'd been holding my emotions in check since Sunday night, and they refused to be held back any longer. All my fears and frustration bubbled to the surface and overwhelmed my tenuous hold on sanity. A tear slid down my cheek, followed by another and another until the faucet was cranked wide open. A heart-wrenching sob tore itself from my chest, where it'd been lodged most of the day.

"Over here." Patrick tugged gently on my arm and guided me to a more private location off the main hallway. "Did my bastard brother do something to hurt you?"

"Not really," I blubbered.

"Then why are you crying?" He put his arms around me, and I fell into them. I needed comfort from someone who would understand, and who understood his brother more than Patrick? Sobs racked my body, rendering me incapable of coherent speech. Patrick held on to me, rubbing my back like my mother once had. Getting a handle on myself, I lifted my tear-stained face to his.

"What's going on?" he asked softly.

"It's Pax. He's drawing away. Stuff started falling apart after the Sockeyes spoke to him. It's been downhill from there. He's going to break up with me, he just hasn't done it yet."

"He's prolonging the agony?"

"You could say that."

"I'm sorry. I'm really sorry. I didn't know you guys were that serious." Guilt laced Patrick's voice, and I momentarily wondered what he had to be guilty about, but my misery overrode my curiosity. I discounted what I thought I heard from my overactive imagination.

"Shit happened so fast. I didn't even realize how deeply I was involved until things started going sideways."

Patrick patted my back and kissed my forehead. "Oh, baby, I'm so very sorry for you. Pax is going through some things right now. We all are. He's struggling and perhaps this wasn't a good time for him to start a serious relationship with anyone."

"I know. I know!" I wailed and buried my head in his chest to muffle the noise. I'd be mortified if anyone else saw us. He stroked my hair, playing the part of the big brother I'd never had.

"Naomi, you do realize how fond I am of you?"

I looked up at him, gripping fistfuls of his now tear-stained shirt and nodded. "I am of you, too."

"I hate to see either one of you get hurt, but it's probably inevitable that Pax will back off. His focus needs to be on hockey. Neither of us can afford the distractions. I understand where he's coming from. His game finally got back to normal on Saturday night."

"You like how he played Saturday night?" I bristled and pushed away from Patrick.

"Well, yeah, we were a team again, instead of him trying to be the lone ranger."

"Is that how you see it?" Anger rolled through me. Indignance replaced my sorrow as I sought to defend Pax. Patrick didn't get it.

"Yeah." Patrick regarded me warily.

"Just because he's not passing the puck so you can have all the glory rather than taking his shots when he sees them?"

"Hey, calm down. Things are rocky between us. Lots of changes coming are making us both nervous." Patrick clearly didn't want to discuss his brother's play with me or get in an argument. He patted my shoulder in a brotherly manner.

I sniffed and gazed up at him. "I'm sorry. I'm emotional right now. I shouldn't have jumped on you like that."

He shrugged and grinned at me. "It's okay. Really. What are friends for?"

I gave him another hug just as my dad showed up. His brow furrowed as he swung his gaze from me to Patrick and back. I pushed away from Patrick.

"Sorry I'm late. I have another obligation. Can you wait?" Dad said. He nodded briskly at Patrick.

"I can't, Dad." I ignored the curious stare Dad cast in our direction.

"I'm sorry. I'll catch you later, honey." After a quick hug, my dad walked away. He paused at the end of the hallway, glancing over his shoulder one final time.

"Do you think he's reading more into this than there is?" Patrick asked.

I shrugged, not wanting to deal with any additional drama. "Who knows. Right now, his suspicions are the least of my problems. I have to get to my study group. Thanks for the shoulder to cry on."

"Anytime, Omi." Patrick turned in the opposite direction toward the locker room.

I left the building and hurried to my study group, feeling a little better. Paxton and I would get through this. We had to. He needed time, that was all. He was overwhelmed right now with all the changes in his life and the pressures on him to perform.

The least I could do was take the pressure off him when it came to us.

BUSTED

Paxton

Sex with Naomi last Sunday night had been almost frantic in our desperation. We clung to each other even as our relationship slipped out of our fingers. Neither of us had a clue how to hold on to what we had.

We'd texted each other and talked last night, but I hadn't seen her since. It was already Wednesday afternoon, and I fucking missed her so much my body ached from emotional pain. A piercing headache hit me right between the eyes, and I wondered if Coach Garf had a crystal for that.

Doubts assailed me as I ran through my various conversations with Patrick, my dad, and the Sockeyes. I didn't know what to do. Without Naomi as my sounding board, I was a ship adrift at sea in a growing storm. Yet my family and future teammates insinuated Naomi was or could be part of my problem.

Was she?

Or was she my solution?

I was a hot fucking mess. This wasn't like me. I was the grounded one. The serious guy who knew what he was doing and where he was going. Or I'd thought I did. Perhaps it was all a façade, and I was as clueless as any other college student regarding my future.

I turned down the empty hallway outside the rink near the coaches' offices. I was early for my private session with Coach Garf. He wasn't in his office. I wandered down the hallway aimlessly, debating on whether or not to put on my skates and take to the ice or call it a night.

I heard muffled voices and instantly recognized both of them. Naomi and Patrick. What the fuck? My curiosity got the best of me, and I snuck closer. My headache intensified. I rubbed the crystals in a last-ditch attempt to calm myself. They didn't calm me one fucking bit.

I crept toward the side hall, my heart pounding in my chest and my body tensed.

Holding my breath, I peeked around the corner. Naomi had her back to me as she clung to my brother. Her head was tilted upward, and their mouths were too close together. Patrick was so intent on gazing into her eyes, he didn't see me. She gripped his shirt as she leaned into him, and he had his arms around her waist.

Bile rose in my throat, and I feared I might be physically sick. I backed down the hall as quiet as could be. As soon as I got to the locker room, I escaped into it. A few minutes later, I heard footsteps and an exit door open and shut.

The roaring in my ears deafened me, despite the silence in the locker room.

Naomi and my brother.

Everything she'd told me about how I was the one had been a lie. And what about Patrick? I thought his concern about my relationship with Naomi had been out of brotherly love rather than wanting her to himself. What a fucking fool I'd been.

No one would be able to fake the chemistry we had when it came to sex, but even so, our explosive love life didn't appear to be enough.

I sat down on a bench and stared at the cold concrete block walls. My mind was numb. My body was numb. Fuck, even my heart had gone numb. I might as well have been standing naked in sub-zero temperatures for an hour. Everything froze inside me.

With a great effort, I got to my feet and grabbed my skates out of my locker. After my mom had died, I'd turned to skating as my therapy. I don't know how many miles I racked up in the rink late at night, but it'd been a lot.

As my blades glided across the smooth surface, I began to unthaw. I started to feel real pain, heart-deep and gut-wrenching.

I'd fucking fallen in love with her. I'd always been crazy about her, but I'd gone far beyond that. I'd convinced myself she was my forever love or some stupid-assed romantic bull-shit like that.

All hockey, all the time. Only hockey. All I need is hockey, I chanted as I skated faster and faster around the rink. Affirmations, I had to remember affirmations, like Coach taught me. If I said it enough, my subconscious would find a way to make it come true, except when it involved other people. My subconscious couldn't make Naomi love me.

I skated harder, pushing my body beyond its limits and ignoring its protests at the abuse.

Hockey. All Hockey. Hockey is all that matters. Concentrate only on hockey.

Everyone in my life had betrayed me, but hockey was always there.

Beyond my heart straining to keep up and my lungs gasping for more oxygen, I heard something.

I wasn't alone.

Fuck.

I bent down, hands on my knees, and coasted, finally allowing my body to recover from the punishment I'd given it. The sound of skates pushing across the ice came closer. I didn't look for fear I'd see Patrick, and I didn't want to deal with him right now.

"Paxton!" The voice was familiar. I turned slightly to see Gene Smith bearing down on me. He caught me easily now that I'd stopped my frantic race around the ice.

"I'm impressed," he said as he slowed beside me. "I didn't know you were capable of skating that hard."

His words both insulted and flattered at the same time. I didn't answer him because how did a guy answer a statement like that?

Thank you for not having any faith in my abilities?

Thank you for discounting me like my father always has?

Nah, better to zip the lips than disrespect one of the greatest hockey players who ever lived even if he did disrespect me.

Mr. Smith narrowed his gaze and studied me closer. "Are you okay?"

Shit, was it that obvious?

"Fine," I lied.

"Right. Follow me. Let's have a talk." He wasn't asking, he was ordering. Skating away, he stepped off the ice and sat down in one of the seats on the glass. Reluctantly, I sat next to him. Still breathing hard and covered in sweat, I wiped my brow with my sleeve and focused on a point across the ice.

"Is this about Naomi?"

How the fuck did he guess that? I shot him a questioning look, and he nodded, knowing he'd guessed correctly.

"Paxton, you're a good kid, and I like you. I don't want to see you get hurt. Naomi is the female version of your brother. She's a heartbreaker."

I nodded, as if I didn't know.

"You have to know she's always been enamored of Patrick."

I clenched my jaw so hard I expected it to shatter under the pressure.

"You have a lot going for you. Just watching you tonight, I see what Coach Garf sees in you. I predict you'll have a long and successful career in the league."

"Thank you." I managed to choke out the words, even as my throat closed up.

"I love my daughter, but she has her faults. She doesn't know what she wants. She often changes for who she's with, trying to become what she thinks they want. I fear she used you as a surrogate for your twin. When did she start showing interest in you as more than a friend?"

I met his gaze as the realization slammed me like a fist to my gut. "When I began to play better, and Patrick struggled a little."

"I'm somewhat responsible for her behavior. I was so upset she wasn't a competitive skater or hockey player, in fact is scared to death of skating, I pushed her toward dating a hockey player who was going somewhere. It's hard to leave behind the sport you've dedicated your life to, and I'm no different. I wanted to live vicariously through a young player on the verge of an illustrious career. I wanted to witness those feelings again, even if I wasn't the one in that situation."

"You think she started showing interest because I was the star for a while and went back to my brother when he regained his star status?"

Mr. Smith—Gene—didn't answer my question directly. "You don't need to settle. You have too much going for you. Find someone who will love you for the person you are, not because they're torn between you and your brother and can't make up their mind."

"Did she say something to you? Do you know something?" Was he speculating or did he have more knowledge?

Mr. Smith smiled sympathetically and patted my arm. I hated the pity I saw in his eyes. "No, but trust me. I know."

Then I realized the truth. He was in this building tonight. "You saw them this evening, too, didn't you?"

He nodded. The sympathy in his eyes almost undid me. I wasn't imagining things. He'd drawn the same conclusions. "Naomi is confused and conflicted. Do you want to subject yourself to a back-and-forth that'll destroy your confidence and eventually ruin your career?"

"Uh, no."

"She needs several more years to mature. She's a late bloomer. Did you realize she was looking into transferring to Vegas next year?"

"She is?" That made sense on one level. Her dad lived in Vegas the majority of the time. On the other hand, she hated being under his thumb. A move to Vegas would land her right back in that situation. Which brought me to the conclusion she was following Patrick to Vegas, assuming he went pro next season.

"That's what I understand."

"Thank you, Mr. Smith, for your honestly. I do appreciate it."

"Call me Gene." He stood, squeezed my shoulder, and clomped down the hallway in his skates.

I sat in the arena for a long time, running through options in my head. As hard as I tried to find another solution, I came back to the same one every time.

NOT OKAY

Naomi

Kaitlyn might not be my most sympathetic friend, but she was the most honest.

On Thursday night, I sat in the team laundry room and spilled my woes to her. She listened without comment as she folded towels.

"Well, what do you think?" I asked when I finished my sad tale.

"I think you worry too much." She rolled her eyes and blew out an exasperated breath.

"That's not helpful."

"Fine. I'm guessing he's getting a shit-ton of advice from a shit-ton of directions. He's at a loss as to what to do, and you are being presented by some as part of his problem."

"So what should I do?"

"Stop fretting so much. Worrying only makes you crazy and doesn't solve anything. Whatever happens will happen."

"That sounds ominous."

"Look, I've seen the way he looks at you. If he wants space, give him space. He'll be back."

My phone beeped, and I looked down.

Paxton: Can we meet tonight?

"It's him. He wants to meet." I grinned at Kaitlyn, unable to contain my joy at hearing from him.

"I told you there was nothing to worry about. That boy is crazy about you." Kaitlyn smiled, as if she considered me too dense to have seen the obvious.

Me: Sure, my place or yours?
Paxton: The Biscuit would be best.

My heart nose-dived. I wasn't getting such a good feeling about this. "He wants to meet at the Biscuit?"

"The Biscuit? What the fuck? That's—" Kaitlyn stopped when she saw the stricken look on my face.

"Nowhere to make up," I finished for her. "He's breaking things off completely."

"You don't know that."

"But I do, and so do you. I can see it on your face."

"I'm sorry, Omi. I really am."

"I need to go." I sniffled and choked back a sob. I had to find a private place to break down, and this wasn't it. I hurried to the door and rushed down the hall.

"I'll be available if you need to talk. Doesn't matter how late it is," Kaitlyn called after me.

I ran all the way to the dorm, tears streaming down my face, ignoring the curious stares as I streaked by. I took the stairs rather than the elevator and didn't stop running until I was safely inside my dorm room. I threw myself down on the bed and cried until my eyes were devoid of tears and my throat was dry and scratchy.

An hour later, I showered and put on my makeup. I opted for skinny jeans and a tight blouse, which I buttoned to show a good amount of cleavage. A wicked part of me wanted to show him what he'd be missing if he ended it. Petty, but also gave me a measure of control over my fate.

I'd make this easy on him, except for the cleavage view. I'd suggest we break up before he did. If he jumped at the suggestion, I'd have my answer. If he fought for us, I'd also have my answer.

Paxton was being pulled in all directions, and I wasn't helping matters any. If you loved someone, you sacrificed for them. I'd never sacrificed for anyone before. Tonight, I'd give Pax the ultimate gift. I'd set him free and see if he wanted freedom or me.

On my way out the door, I grabbed the ice skates he'd bought me. No matter what happened, I wasn't wearing those damn things.

Paxton was sitting at a private table when I walked in. He looked up, and his gaze went right to my breasts, clearly showcased by my blouse. He swallowed and raised his eyes to my face. I glanced at the hockey table, relieved to find it empty of hockey players. The last thing I wanted was an audience witnessing whatever happened.

Determined, I strode toward him. His eyes followed me, but his expression gave nothing away except for the firm set of his jaw. I dropped into the chair across from him.

"I took the liberty of buying you a beer. I hope it's not warm. I've been here awhile." He pushed the beer across the table toward me.

"Thank you," I said primly and took a sip. I needed alcohol to get through the night. I raised my head and met his gaze with determination. He wore his game face, one of grit and conviction, but not revealing much else.

"Naomi, I—"

"Paxton, I—" We both spoke at the same time.

He chuckled nervously and gripped his beer glass. "You first."

I didn't wait for a second invitation. I'd get this over with. If things fell to pieces, I'd return to the privacy of my dorm room, wallow in my grief, and have another ugly cry.

The man was so freaking gorgeous, and I drank in his face, memorizing the curves and contours, the little laugh lines in the corners of his deep blue eyes, the furrow in his brow when he was being super-serious, that short, neatly trimmed beard, which had abraded my sensitive skin in the sexiest manner on so many occasions.

"Go ahead," he prompted.

I cleared my throat, heaved a big sigh, and barreled ahead. "Paxton, I've been doing a lot of thinking. I know you're under a lot of pressure right now, and I don't want to add to it. Maybe it's best we go our separate ways. Take care of business first. Relationships can wait."

He breathed out a sigh of relief and smiled sadly at me. "I was going to suggest the same thing."

My heart sank so low it was drowning in sorrow somewhere in the depths of my stomach. He wasn't going to fight for me—for us. If anything, he was relieved. I had my answer, and it wasn't the one I wanted, but nevertheless, at least it was an answer.

"It's for the best," I said, surprising myself at how calm and reasonable I sounded considering my inner turmoil.

"That doesn't mean that, down the road, we might not meet again."

"Of course it doesn't. In a few years, when your career is

established, and I'm—" I trailed off, not sure how to finish my statement. I didn't know where I'd be, but I was ninety-nine percent sure my location wouldn't be Seattle.

"Sure. We don't know what the future holds. I'm sorry." He took my hands in his. "These last few months with you were some of the best of my life. I'm going to miss you."

"We can still hang out. We won't be dating, but that shouldn't stop us from being friends."

"Yeah, of course we're still friends." I heard the reluctance in his voice.

"By the way, my internship ends in a few weeks. I won't be traveling with the team after break. That'll make this easier."

He nodded, still wearing his game face, not giving me a glimpse into how he was feeling or what he was thinking.

"Well, I have studying to do." I pushed back my chair and stood. Our eyes met, and for a moment, I was struck by a lightning bolt of clarity. Was I doing the wrong thing? Should I have been the one to fight for him? For us?

The moment passed quickly. I leaned down and brushed my lips briefly against his mouth. Straightening, I pointed to the ice skates. "I didn't get a chance to return these."

I grabbed my purse, spun on my heel, and ran to the door. I shoved the door open, barreling into Patrick. He reached out to steady me, but I pushed past him.

"Naomi? Are you okay?"

I kept going, grateful he didn't follow me.

I was not okay. Far from it.

35

WINNER OF THE GAME

Paxton

My heart followed Naomi out the door. Sadness weighted down my body. Grief blurred my vision. Numbness paralyzed me.

I gritted my teeth and fisted my hands when I saw her interact with my brother at the door. She was free of me, and they were free to do whatever they pleased with each other.

Please, God, don't let something happen under my nose.

I half expected Patrick to go after her. Instead, he pushed past the door and glanced around. His face reddened with anger when he spotted me.

Patrick marched in my direction like a man on a mission. I braced myself for whatever might come next. He stopped in front of me, hands on his hips and chin stuck out belligerently. I stole a glance at the hockey table, where, at some point in the past few minutes, multiple teammates and their girlfriends were now sitting. Some were watching us, like the trailers were over and the main movie had started.

"What the fuck was that all about?" Patrick hissed at me.

"Sit your ass down, Captain. We have an audience." I pointed with my chin toward the hockey table.

Patrick glanced over his shoulder and winced. He quickly slid into the chair Naomi had vacated after she'd ripped my world apart.

My twin leaned across the table, his voice low but threatening. "She's crying. What did you do to her?"

"She broke up with me, asshole. I didn't do a fucking thing." The huskiness in my voice betrayed the raw emotions too close to the surface.

He sat back as if I'd slapped him. "She dumped you?"

"Yeah, you happy now? You can't stand when I have something you don't, can you? You have to fuck it up for me because you have to be king."

"What the hell are you talking about? I had nothing to do with this. Maybe she'd had enough of your sorry ass and your pity parties. You've been moping around a lot."

"*My* pity parties?" I half rose from my chair until I caught the multiple sets of eyes intent on us. I sat back down. "You've been pouting half the season because I wasn't giving you scoring opps."

"Fuck you. I have not been. You're the moper."

"I haven't been moping. I've been thinking about my future. You should try it sometime, but maybe that's beyond what your feeble brain can handle."

"You wanna take this outside?" Patrick fisted his hands on the table. I looked down at those fists and supreme sadness washed over me. Not only had I lost Naomi, I'd also lost my brother. My two best friends in this world...

Maybe I was having a pity party.

I lifted my gaze and met Patrick's defiant glare. We stared each other down for what seemed like an eternity. Over the years, we'd gotten in a few scuffles, especially in our teenage years, but we'd never come to blows.

I looked away first, hating myself for doing it, but I did it for the team. Patrick wouldn't have backed down. It wasn't in his nature. Maybe it shouldn't be in mine either. Maybe that's the missing piece Coach was trying to instill in me—that fighting spirit that never gave up.

"Coward," Patrick whispered.

"Team player," I shot back.

"Coulda fooled me."

"What's that supposed to mean?"

Patrick sneered at me. "You figure it out." He shoved his chair back so hard it hit the person sitting behind him. "Sorry," he muttered, ignoring their scathing glare. He stomped out of the Biscuit, not even acknowledging our teammates.

I stayed where I was, not wanting to go home and not wanting to stay here.

"Paxton."

Lex studied me with his brow furrowed in concern. Not waiting for an invitation, he sat down. "You look like you could use a friend."

"Maybe." I ordered tequila on the rocks from the waitress walking past my table.

"You guys aren't fooling anyone. Every guy on the team feels the tension between you two."

I shrugged, not knowing what to say.

"Have you ever considered he might have a legit complaint?"

"What?" I gaped at Lex. He was usually on my side.

"Maybe you aren't passing the puck to Patrick when you should be. Maybe both of you share some of the responsibility in this rift between you?"

"Coach would've said something if he thought I was

hogging the puck." I defended my actions, even as doubt crept it.

"Coach isn't out on the ice. You are. And maybe he's letting you two work this out on your own. He doesn't want to discourage your aggressive shooting by contradicting himself and telling you to shoot less. I don't know. I've seen moments in the past where you played with Patrick as if you two were in each other's heads, like you were one mind and body. It was sheer poetry in motion to watch the two of you take apart a defense. Now I see two guys out for themselves."

"I'm not out for myself."

"Not on purpose. You're doing what you need to do. All I'm suggesting is you might have overdone your part a little. Not much. But a little and added to Patrick's frustration. Just think about it. You know I've always got your back."

I nodded, but I was resistant to Lex's claims. If I wasn't doing what Coach wanted, he'd have told me. I knew he would've.

"And Naomi. She was upset when she ran out of here."

I heaved a sigh and met Lex's gaze. "She dumped me."

"She did? For Patrick? Is that what's going on?"

"I don't know. I think so." I put my head in my hands and groaned. I had a splitting headache to go with my broken heart.

"Ah, man, I'm sorry. That's brutal."

"Tell me about it."

"I wonder if Kaitlyn knows anything."

"I'd prefer you not ask her. It's over. I saw Naomi and Patrick together."

"Together?"

"Not fucking, if that's what you're thinking. They were hugging and staring into each other's eyes. It was pretty obvious."

"That sucks on all kinds of levels."

"Don't I know it. I've been screwed by my brother and my girlfriend, taken for a fool."

"Did you ask them about it?"

"Nah. She dumped me before I had a chance. Seems like a moot point. Her dad saw them, too, and talked to me. She's torn between my brother and me, and I don't want to be jerked around for God knows how long until she figures out which one of us she wants. From where I'm standing, Patrick's looking like the winner of this game."

I took a long gulp of tequila, hoping the liquor would dull my pain a little. Not that it'd worked well before, but right now it was all I had.

36

ALREADY GONE

Naomi

I was inconsolable. I hid out in my dorm room all weekend and didn't travel with the team to their last weekend of away games before Christmas break, claiming to have the flu.

I hadn't planned on watching Pax play, but I tuned in anyway for a good torture session, reminding me of what I'd lost.

Paxton's play on Friday night was unremarkable. What glimpses I saw of his face revealed frustration and futility. In the second period, Coach Keller moved him to the second line. Without Patrick scowling at him, he settled down and played decently. On Saturday night, Pax came out red-hot. I saw the determination on his face, as if during the last twenty-four hours, he'd had an attitude adjustment. He was everywhere on the ice, with power and gutty resolve. He took a few brutal hits and didn't back down. He scored one goal on Friday and two on Saturday, while Patrick had one on Friday and none on Saturday.

Several times, I punched out a text to Pax and didn't send

it. We'd vowed to remain friends, yet we weren't communicating. I'd hurt him when I'd broken it off, thinking I was doing the best thing for him. Now I wasn't so sure. Perhaps I'd made a rash decision based on pride rather than logic. Maybe I hadn't been protecting him but protecting myself.

Kaitlyn was with the team that weekend, so I wasn't able to get her unfiltered opinion. Instead, I was a pathetic hot mess. I barely got out of bed and hadn't taken a shower since Friday morning. Finally, Sunday afternoon, I dragged my sorry ass out of bed, took a shower, and washed my hair. I felt a little better. Even tried to study, but I couldn't concentrate.

Instead, I did something completely out of the ordinary. I called my dad. If anyone knew about juggling hockey and a relationship, he did, even if he hadn't done it well. He'd met my mom in the minors and married her his first year in the league.

He might be able to shed some light on what was going on in Paxton's head. My dad didn't pick up, so I left a message. He usually called back within a few hours.

Still restless and unable to crack the books, I called Kaitlyn. She also didn't pick up, but she texted me within ten seconds.

Kaitlyn: At Biscuit. Join us. Pax is here.

I resisted the urge to ask if he was with anyone, but she read my mind.

Kaitlyn: He's alone and looking like a whipped puppy. Really pathetic. What's going on?
Me: I'll explain later.
Kaitlyn: Are you coming to the Biscuit?
Me: I can't tonight. Catch up with you later.
Kaitlyn: Later.

She didn't know about Pax and me?

Or she had a more nefarious plot in mind, such as pushing us back together? Imagining Kaitlyn as a matchmaker made me laugh. That wasn't her style. She didn't get involved in others' problems to that extent.

I went to the dining hall and had a salad from the salad bar, content in the knowledge I wouldn't run into Pax. I slumped down in one of the plastic chairs in the mostly deserted area and toyed with my food.

"Hey, want some company?"

I looked up and sighed. I should've found a more private place so I'd be able to eat in peace. Patrick approached with a tray filled with food. He didn't wait for an answer but sat down across from me.

"I heard you broke up with my brother."

"Who told you that?"

"Actually, he did."

"Oh. Are you two friendly again?"

"No." Patrick scowled, but pain flashed in his blue eyes.

"Maybe it's time you cleared the air and discussed what's bothering both of you." My suggestion was merely as a good friend. I cared about both of them and hated to see them hurting like this.

He shrugged and bit into his burger.

"Your differences are hurting the team."

"We won, didn't we?"

"Yeah, but I watched, and I'm not Gene Smith's daughter for nothing. I saw the rift between you two before Coach moved Paxton to the second line. Your team had to be feeling it. As captain, isn't it your responsibility to seek solutions to grievances among team members? Even if it's you and your brother?"

Patrick stopped in mid-chew. I'd hit a sore spot, and he

didn't like me pointing out where he might've failed as a captain.

He finished chewing and put down the burger, methodically wiping his hands with a napkin and taking a drink of water as he considered my words.

"You know I'm right," I prodded. "You two were so close. This has to be eating you up inside. It's too late for Paxton and me, but it's not too late for the two of you."

Patrick scrubbed his face with his hands. "I guess so," he admitted grudgingly. "He was my best friend."

"He can be again. This is a minor setback based on pressures in your lives."

"Pressures?"

"Yeah, school, going pro, upping your level of play. That kind of stuff."

"Maybe." He wasn't committing to anything.

"He's at the Biscuit. Go talk to him."

"Yeah, I will." Patrick finished his burger and excused himself. He bussed his tray and left the dining hall. I hoped to God I'd done the right thing pushing those two together.

It was time for them to mend fences, even if Paxton and I couldn't.

I returned to my lonely dorm room haunted by the many nights and some afternoons Pax and I had spent naked in this room, cuddled together on the small bed or sitting up and eating popcorn to restore our energy before the next round of sex.

My phone rang, and I answered my Dad's call.

"Hi, Dad."

"Hi, honey, sorry I missed your call. I was working a game tonight." Dad's attitude had improved considerably since he'd started working again. My dad needed a job to be happy, and this temporary gig with the league made him happier than I'd seen him in a while.

"Glad to see you enjoying yourself, Dad."

"Yeah, this has been good for me. Keeps me out of your hair." He laughed and so did I.

"Your team played well this weekend. How was the trip?"

"I didn't go, but I watched on TV."

"You didn't go? Are you sick?"

"Not physically."

"Is something wrong?"

"I didn't...I didn't feel like going."

He was silent for a long while, and I tilted the phone to see the display screen to make sure he was still on the line. "What's going on?" His voice was quiet, as if he were tiptoeing through enemy lines and didn't want anyone to hear him. Alarm bells sounded in my head, but I didn't know why. Something was off.

"I broke up with Paxton." His name came out on a choked sob.

"Oh, honey, I'm sorry. I'm sure it's for the best. You shouldn't have been leading that poor kid on like that when he wasn't the one for you."

I frowned into the phone, as if he could see me. "What do you mean?"

"I saw you and Patrick having an intimate moment."

"What?" I was incredulous and confused. "Are you sure it was Patrick?"

"Absolutely. I spoke with Paxton that evening about it. Seems he saw you two also."

"I don't understand." I racked my brain, trying to remember an intimate moment I'd had with Patrick, but there weren't any. "Where did you see us?"

"Last week, in the hallway by the locker room."

Oh, no. The truth crashed down on me. Paxton had seen me, and he'd planned to set me free to be with his brother, but I'd beaten him to it and broken it off with him first, proving his suspicions.

"He and I met in the rink that night, and we had a heart-to-heart. I told him he should concentrate on hockey and that you'd always loved Patrick. I tried to let the kid down easy."

"Dad, Patrick was consoling me because I was upset about Pax backing off from me. I'm not in love with Patrick. I don't believe I ever was. It's always been Paxton, but I've spent the majority of my life trying to please others. You wanted me to be with Patrick, and I obliged by convincing myself that's what I wanted."

"Omi, I never meant to cause you pain and take away your happiness. I…I thought I was doing what was right for you. I've fucked things up, haven't I?"

"No, Dad, I did. I shoulder the majority of the blame. I didn't have to go along with any of it. I didn't listen to my heart. I didn't fight for what Paxton and I had. I let my pride interfere." I cleared my throat. "I called you tonight to ask you if it was possible to have a good relationship with a profes-sional hockey player. I wanted to know if I'd made the right decision or if I should've hung in there and made this work."

"Do you miss him?"

"I'm brokenhearted. I can't study. I can't sleep. I cry at the drop of a hat. I miss him so much the it hurts like someone ripped open my chest and put a stranglehold on my heart."

"That's how I felt when your mother died." His voice was so soft I strained to hear the words.

"I'm sorry, Dad." Silence stretched between us.

Dad sniffled, or what sounded like a sniffle. "Don't be," he said in a voice suspiciously husky. "I'm the one who's sorry. I shouldn't have interfered. I made things worse instead of better. I've been pushing you in a direction you haven't wanted to go for a long time."

"Especially when it comes to skating?" I joked.

"Especially that." He laughed then sobered. "Naomi, I know I'm a controlling, hard-nosed ass at times, and I haven't been the best father or husband."

"You did the best you could."

"Maybe. Maybe not. Being with a hockey player isn't all glamour and fame. There are a lot of lonely nights where you're left wondering what's going on with the person you love. Wondering if they're being faithful. Your mom and I had our good times and bad times, but through it all, I loved her and she loved me. I wouldn't trade what we had for anything." He blew out a long breath, and I could tell this wasn't easy for him.

"I don't know what to do."

"You know in your heart what you want and how badly you want it."

"Okay."

"Naomi, I want you to know I'm proud of you, and I love you."

I choked up even more than I had before. "I love you, too, Dad." Everything was going to be okay despite what happened with Pax and me.

"If you love the boy, go after him. I chased your mom until I finally caught her."

"How did you catch her?"

He chuckled as if reliving a fond memory. "I made a grand gesture."

"A grand gesture?"

"I spent every penny I had, which wasn't much back then, and rented a rooftop garden in the city, hired a chef, and invited her to dinner under false pretenses. I almost thought she wasn't going to show up, but true to form, she was thirty minutes late. The rest is history. I won her over that night."

"That's so lovely, Dad. Why have I never heard that story?"

"I don't know. Too painful, I guess, or too personal? Naomi, love is something you don't walk away from no matter how many obstacles are in your way. You're facing obstacles. Do you find an inner strength to overcome adversity, or do you give up and walk away? Look, I need to go. Let me know what you decide."

"I will," I promised, but he was already gone.

SHOWDOWN

Paxton

The weekend's games had been a mixture of the good, the bad, and the ugly. The bad was how I played in the first period of Friday's game. The ugly was my further-strained relationship with Patrick on full display for all my teammates to see. The good was what happened after the first period.

Maine had fought tough on Friday night, and by the end of the first period, neither team had scored. I wasn't playing badly, but I wasn't quite right either. I struggled to get in the zone, and my brother wasn't helping things. He barked orders at me like a general. He was on my ass every time we hit the ice. I wanted to pulverize him, but losing my temper wouldn't help the team.

"Paxton, a word." Coach Garf motioned me out into the hall. I followed him.

"What's up, Coach?"

"I've been hearing rumors you're going through some personal issues."

"Yeah, somewhat."

"It's not that I don't sympathize, but you've come too far this year to blow it all in a few weeks. Listen to me, and listen well. You must have a professional mindset. Do you know what that means?"

I nodded. "Yeah, it means that you don't let your personal problems affect your game."

"That's the gist of it." Garf leaned against the wall in a deceptively casual pose that didn't fool me. He was intent on getting his point across. "Whatever is happening to you personally cannot collide with your professional ambitions. You must compartmentalize all else and concentrate solely on hockey. There'll be time for personal healing later, but hockey doesn't wait for your feelings to catch up. Hockey comes now. You must have a single-minded purpose to play your game and keep the crap out of your head. I'm so proud of what you've accomplished. I know you can do this."

"I can," I stated firmly with conviction. "And I will," I added with a grin, knowing my coach hated the word *can*.

He snorted at me and slapped me on the back. "Good. Let's win this game."

I took a step toward the locker room when he called me back.

"One more thing. Coach Keller and I decided we're moving you to right wing on the second line."

"But?" I'd always played left wing on the first line with my brother. Always.

"This isn't a punishment. Maine's goalie is red-hot tonight. We need your scoring ability to hold down the second line, while Patrick can handle the first line. I believe in you, Pax. Trust the plan."

I understood the strategy, and I had to agree with it. I'd have more opportunities to score on the second line, and my brother and I wouldn't be at each other's throats. And right wing? Usually I played left, but Lex played left on the second line. I had more experience, and it made more sense moving me.

We held on somehow and won on Friday night, and I did score a goal from the second line.

I approached Saturday night's game with a single-minded purpose. I was about to be a professional, and professionals did not let their personal relationships affect their play. I mentally prepared using Garf's techniques. I also swapped rooms with Lex's roommate to lessen the friction between Patrick and me.

I couldn't believe it had come to this. He'd always been my best friend, always had my back, and I missed him as much as I missed Naomi.

I stepped onto the ice that night mentally prepared and played a lights-out game. The gamble of moving us to separate lines paid off for me. Patrick not so much. He struggled and missed every shot, while I shined. I braced myself after the game, expecting to be the object of his frustration and anger. Instead, he didn't speak a word to me.

We got home early Sunday morning, and I didn't go home. I slept on the couch at the hockey house. I got up before noon, worked out, and studied at the library until Lex texted me a few hours later. A bunch of the guys were at the Biscuit, and I was starving. Even better, Patrick wasn't there. I couldn't avoid him forever, but I hadn't arrived at any kind of viable plan on how to fix this problem between us.

I'd tossed and turned half the night, rotating between missing Naomi and frustrations with Patrick. I needed a drink and sustenance. Garlic Parm wings sounded like just the thing.

When I got to the Biscuit, our usual table was filled with teammates and no Patrick, thankfully. Maybe he'd decided to study for once. Finals were looming on the horizon, and my brother wasn't known for taking his studies seriously.

I ordered a beer and wings and settled into my seat next to Lex. We talked about the game and gave each other shit, a normal night at the Biscuit with my boys. I was chomping on my sixth wing, enjoying the garlic goodness when our raucous table became oddly quiet. I frowned, put down my wing, licked off my fingers, and wiped them on a napkin. Everyone was staring at me or a point behind me. I turned my head to look over my shoulder.

Patrick stood a few feet behind me, hands on hips and wearing a big scowl. "Move over," he ordered Lex, who looked to me. I nodded, and Lex vacated his chair so Patrick could sit there. The conversation resumed, but our teammates continued to cast wary glances in our direction.

My twin stole one of my wings, but I didn't put up a protest. Normally, he didn't like that flavor, but he was fucking with me. I shrugged and sipped my beer, pretending everything was fine when it wasn't. No one was fooled. The tension between us was thicker than the slop they called gravy in the dining hall.

"Where've you been? You didn't sleep at home last night."

"Slept at the hockey house," I muttered.

We ignored each other for several minutes. Patrick ordered a beer and some wings, striking up a conversation with Tate sitting across from us. We'd diverted a disaster. Or so I hoped.

"Why'd Coach move you to the second line, Pax?" one of the freshmen asked. The second the words were out of his mouth, he realized his mistake.

I stared straight ahead, not looking at my twin. The table went silent again as all eyes turned to me and our team captain —my brother.

Michael, our alternate captain, rushed to fill the silence.

"Pax is having a good scoring year. More scoring opportunities for both Pax and Trick if they're on different lines."

"He's showboating. Hogging the puck. Moving him was punishment," Patrick muttered.

"What the fuck did you say?" My blood boiled, and my head was so filled with rage I couldn't see straight.

"You heard me." He lifted his chin in defiance and looked me straight in the eyes.

"Guys, we're teammates, and you're brothers. Let's get along," Tate admonished us.

Patrick's glower told me all I needed to know. He wasn't through with me yet. He stood and moved to the end of the table. An hour and many beers later, things seemed to have blown over.

But I was wrong.

I got up to leave, and Patrick followed me out the door. I waited until we were away from the windows and prying eyes. I whipped around, ready to take this wherever it needed to go.

"You wanna settle this right here?" I asked.

Patrick shook his head and said in a deadly quiet voice, "Meet me at the rink tonight at midnight. On the ice. Wear your skates. This is between you and me. I don't want anyone else there. We'll settle our differences then."

From the look on his face, he was angling for a fight. I was ready for him. If he wanted a fight, he'd get one, because I was fucking sick and tired of his entitled behavior.

KICKING ASS

Paxton

Several hours later, I strapped on my skates and stepped onto the ice. Patrick was already skating lazy circles in the center of the rink. I skated up to him.

"You're an ass," he said simply, keeping attention on the perfect circles he was skating.

"Better than being a prick," I shot back. All my plans to handle this diplomatically and mend fences flew out the window as emotions overcame any logic.

Patrick ground his skates to a stop and faced me. "You asked to be moved, didn't you? So you could showboat."

Anger and resentment I didn't know I had bubbled to the surface. "You're an entitled prick who thinks every member of our team should do your bidding. We don't play hockey to glorify you or make your game look better."

"Fuck you."

"Fuck you," I said back, knowing on some level we sounded like children rather than twenty-one-year-old men. I had to get away from him and calm down before we ended up brawling on the ice.

This wasn't going as planned. I dug in and sped off, skating a couple feet from the boards. Patrick caught up with me and matched me stride for stride. I skated faster. So did he. I turned on the speed. So did he.

Faster and faster we went, rounding the corners at a dangerous pace and somehow keeping our blades under us. We hit the straightaways with breakneck speed, neither conceding to the other. We'd raced before but nothing like this. We were on a mission to prove who was better. I'd die before I backed down. I was as talented and driven as Patrick, and he'd damn well learn to live with that fact. I'd allowed him to be number one too many times, content to exist in his shadow, not wanting the adulation and star status he enjoyed. Tonight, I wanted the acknowledgment from him that I wasn't second-best.

I'd skate with him until my heart burst, my legs gave out, or I passed out. But I would not stop.

We flew around the rink at a dizzying pace, and I lost track of how many laps we'd made. My heart pounded, and my lungs screamed for air. Sweat ran down my forehead and burned my eyes. I didn't give a shit. I ignored my body and pushed harder.

Chunks of ice flew against the boards as we rounded another corner. I heard Patrick's labored breathing over my own and chanced a look at him. We were mirror images of each other down to my being left-handed and him being right-handed. His face was red, his eyes bugged out, sweat soaked every inch of him. I had to look the same.

I lost a little ground by chancing that glance and dug in, finding some last well of strength to pull even with him again.

We were going to die in this fucking arena trying to prove

which one of us was better when we were identical in physical stature, fitness level, and ability. Regardless, I wouldn't relegate myself to second-best. I'd done that too many times, fulfilling my role as the secondary character in the play of our life. Not this time.

We rounded another corner, not letting up. My lungs screamed for oxygen. My eyes blurred either from sweat or because I was about to pass out. My heart jackhammered against my rib cage.

As we started to come out of the corner, we both faltered from exhaustion and drifted in each other's path. My skates hooked up with his. We went down in a tangle of limbs and skate blades, sliding across the ice on our backs.

And that's where we stayed—in the middle of the ice on our backs. I gulped in air, trying to breathe despite the pain tearing through my chest and thighs. I stared up at the arena lights. A few feet from me, Patrick sounded as if he was struggling as much as I was.

I prayed he didn't find an untapped reserve and scramble to his feet to resume our mad race. I'd have to do the same if he did, and I'd much rather lie here and bleed out, even though I wasn't bleeding. At least not literally.

I was unable to focus and squeezed my eyes shut. The cold from the ice seeped into my overheated body.

I didn't know how long we lay there. At some point in time, I heard the scraping of Patrick's skates and his gasps as he struggled to his feet.

Oh, fuck no. I scrambled to stand, ignoring my abused body's outraged protests.

We faced each other with five feet between us, both bent over at the waist, holding weary upper bodies with hands braced on our thighs.

We eyed each other like two prizefighters sizing the other

up before the big fight. I prayed he didn't start this insane competition over again, and my prayers were answered. Patrick didn't seem any more interested than I was in finishing our race.

He raised his gaze and met mine. I glimpsed a new measure of respect in his blue eyes so much like mine. "I won."

"Like hell you did."

"Why are you doing this?" he gasped, still short of breath.

"Doing what?"

"Changing the way you play. Hogging the puck."

I started to dispute the hogging claim and snapped my mouth shut. Maybe Lex was right. Maybe I'd overdone Coach's instructions. I'd accept some of the blame. I'd never explained what was going on to my best friend in the entire world. Looking back, I'd made a grave error in judgment by not discussing Coach's mandate with him. I hadn't trusted him enough to have my best interests at heart, and I was ashamed I'd been such an ass.

"Because the Sockeyes coach talked to Garf. He wanted to see more out of me, and Coach Garf knew there was more in there. We've been working on my confidence problem. He felt I passed too much when I had a good shot. He challenged me to play to my potential." I spoke between gulps of air.

"Coach Garf was part of this?" Patrick rose to his full height, and so did I.

I nodded. "I wanted out of your shadow. Do you fucking know what it's like being the overlooked brother?"

A muscle jumped in Patrick's jaw. "I thought you enjoyed your role. We had an understanding, this weird twin mojo where you always knew when to pass the puck to me so I could score."

"We did. Did you ever think of passing it to me when I'd

set up a good scoring opportunity?"

Patrick flinched. "It's not like I've never done that."

"Not often. You've been programmed to believe you were the better player by our dad, our coaches, anyone remotely related to hockey in our lives. I was told to play a secondary role as the guy who enabled your greatness and to be happy with that role."

Patrick gaped at me as if dumbstruck. "I never saw it like that. Never knew it bothered you. I thought you were happy with how well we clicked."

"Do you know what it's like living in your shadow, being compared to you, and always coming up lacking?"

"Yes," Patrick said honestly.

I squinted at him, not understanding.

"Do you know what it's like being known as the dumb twin? The one who barely passes his classes? To be told by Dad that I'd better have a hockey career because that's the only thing I'm good at? The only thing I'm smart enough to do?"

My turn to be shell-shocked. "I had no idea you felt that way."

"You know what else? You want the truth?"

"Yeah, I fucking want the truth," I said.

"Here it is, plain and simple. I'm jealous of you. You're graduating early with honors. You're going pro. And you have Naomi."

"I don't have Naomi. Not anymore. Besides, you and Dad are the ones who claimed she was using me."

"We were wrong. You're the one she wants."

I shook my head. "Not anymore. I saw her with you. It's always been you."

"You saw me with her?" He scowled and shook his head. "I've never been with her. She doesn't want me."

"I saw you near the locker room last week, arms around

242

each other and having an intense conversation."

"Fuck." Patrick rolled his eyes and snorted. "Are you really that dense? She's in love with you. I was comforting her because she was upset about you pulling away from her."

"Then why did she break up with me?"

"For a smart guy, you're really stupid. She wanted to do the right thing for your future even if it meant losing you. Everyone was telling her you needed to concentrate on hockey, including you, and didn't have time for a relationship."

"I struggled with that. I still don't know where I am."

"You'll need to figure that out, bro. I can't help you there. You do love her, don't you?"

"Yeah, but the timing is off."

"The timing will always be off. Do you think it'll get any easier when we go pro? When you're gone more than you're home? When you live your life in a fishbowl and belong to your fans? You think then the timing will be right?"

I considered his words for a long moment. He had a point, but right now I had more immediate matters to settle. Naomi could wait. My brother and I were on the verge of mending fences. "I've missed you, bro." I didn't care if my words might be dismissed as mushy or whatever, I'd take the chance.

"I missed you, too. Maybe I've been purposely drawing away so it won't be as painful when we're not together anymore."

"Maybe we both have."

"When you started dating Naomi, I felt sorry for myself. I didn't have anyone."

"You have half the female population of Moo U."

"It's not the same. You know what I mean."

"You'll always have me," I said quietly, but he heard me. His eyes were suspiciously wet, and he swiped angrily at them with his shirt sleeve.

"And you have me. You're my fucking brother, my twin. You're all I've got," Patrick croaked.

"We sure as fuck don't have our dad."

"He's an ass." Patrick's blue eyes were filled with grief and sadness. "I miss our mom."

"So do I." My eyes burned with unshed tears, and I forced them back.

"I've been an ass, and I'm sorry."

"I get it. I really do. It's hard when things change that are out of your control. I should've discussed what Coach wanted. We could've formulated a plan."

"I didn't understand how I was keeping you down. I never meant to. You're my brother, and I'd do anything for you. I'd have helped you."

I knew that now. "I love you, bro," I said in a choked voice.

"I love you, too."

"You're fucking crying," I accused even as a sob escaped my own mouth.

"I am not fucking crying. You are."

"I am not. Your face is wet."

"From sweat, you moron," Patrick insisted.

"Right." I smiled at him, and he smiled back. Next thing I knew, we enveloped each other in a bear hug. I squeezed my eyes shut, trying to stem the flow of the very tears he'd accused me of.

"If you tell anyone, I'll kick your ass."

"I'll kick yours."

"One other thing, if you're playing for the Sidewinders next year, I'm going to wipe the ice with your face."

"I'm counting on you trying, but that's all it'll be."

I threw back my head and laughed. Arms around each other's shoulders, we dragged our weary bodies into the locker room.

THE PLAN

Naomi

After my conversation with my dad, I did some soul-searching. I'd always been one who went where the wind blew me, tried so hard to please my father, and did what I thought I should, instead of what I truly needed. I'd never been honest with myself. I saw that now.

Being honest with myself, this wasn't about Dad as much as it was about me. I shouldered more of the responsibility than he did. Somewhere deep down, I'd wanted Patrick because he was the star of the team. It's every girl's dream to date the big man on campus, and that big man was our hockey team's captain and top scorer. I'd been so intent on pursuing Patrick, I hadn't seen the wonderful guy right under my nose. Paxton had always been there to comfort and listen, even to my pining for his brother. I hadn't wanted to see Pax's interest in me went beyond friends until it was thrown in my face, and I was unable to deny the truth.

Did Pax and I have a future? Should I fight for him? Or

should I let him concentrate on hockey? Was I deluding myself to think he could do both?

What did I really want?

Right or wrong, I knew what I wanted. I wanted another chance. I'd prematurely broken up with him, concerned he was about to dump me, and he had been.

We'd succumbed to the pressures of everyone else's opinions, rather than searching our hearts for the truth. He hadn't asked me about Patrick and me hugging, and I hadn't given him a chance.

I wouldn't be a coward any longer. For starters, I hang out with the team again. I'd finish off my internship by taking stats for the final game before break.

Then I'd develop a plan.

A grand gesture.

Something to show Pax I was serious and in this for the long haul if he was.

While I debated on my options to win Paxton back, I took advantage of every opportunity presented to be around him. Even though he attempted to sidestep me, I didn't let it happen. I sat with Paxton and his twin in the dining hall. I joined the team at the Biscuit a few nights that week. My studying suffered, but I had my priorities, and I'd cram after the last hockey game before finals.

The twins were getting along again, and I was heartened by that. The tension was gone, and they were giving each other shit like they always had.

Thursday night I went to the Biscuit, stalking Paxton. He was there with some of his teammates and Patrick. I walked up to the table and grabbed a chair. Kaitlyn arched a brow in my direction as I motioned for Lex to move over and make room between Paxton and him. Pushing my chair into the spot, I sat down and smiled at Paxton, who studied me quizzically.

"Hey, Pax, how're you doing?" I said brightly and flashed one of my most endearing smiles at him.

"I'm good." He met my gaze for a moment, and I saw regret, longing, and uncertainty in those blue eyes I loved so much. My campaign to win him back was progressing nicely. I'd proceed with caution, fearing Paxton might be gun-shy at this point.

"Are you ready for finals?" I asked.

"Is anyone ever ready for finals?" His smile warmed my heart and gave me hope I might be on the right track.

"Maybe not."

"Finals? What's that?" From the other side of Paxton, Patrick snorted and saluted with his beer.

"You might want to figure it out before next week, bro," Paxton warned, but he clinked glasses with his brother. I reached across the table to fill my glass from the pitcher. My arm touched Paxton's, and I froze. So did he. I saw him swallow, and that muscle ticked in his jaw. I was getting to him and vice versa. One simple touch through our clothes set my body on fire. I briefly debated abandoning my campaign to win him back for a more direct approach—dragging him into the back room, ripping off his clothes, and fucking any doubt about us right out of him.

The moment passed, and I reined in my libido. Patience. I must practice patience. "You haven't been studying, Trick?"

Patrick shrugged, unconcerned. I admired his ability to make light of the most serious issues, even though I worried he'd probably be in trouble when finals came around.

"He's been studying the female anatomy," Tate joked, and the table erupted in laughter.

"You might want to crack the books," Paxton warned him, but Patrick blew him off and laughed.

"Stop nagging. I'll just send you to take my finals. No one will ever know."

Paxton scowled.

"I'm joking. Quit looking so disgusted with me." Patrick gave his brother a soft punch in the air, drawing a smile from Paxton. I loved Paxton's smile. It lit up the room. Since he didn't smile as often as his brother, when he did, a person couldn't help but notice. His smile spread sunshine on a rainy day.

I grinned at him, unable to stop staring. The smile slipped off his face when he caught me gawking at him. I wasn't deterred. I shifted in the chair I'd wedged between Lex and him so our thighs rubbed against each other. He didn't move away, but he avoided looking at me. I was getting to the man, and I'd continue my subtle campaign until I'd worn down all resistance.

The tension on Paxton's face said it all. He was very aware of my thigh rubbing against his, as aware as I was, which was pretty damn aware judging by the wetness and tingling between my legs. A quick glance at Paxton's crotch told me all I needed to know. He wasn't impervious to me.

Call me evil, but I made a point of *innocently* rubbing against him every chance I got, leaning to talk to one of the other guys, moving closer to him, brushing my arm against his. When I reached for the pitcher again, my breast rubbed against his arm. He pushed his chair back and cleared his throat.

"I have to study," he announced in a tone I recognized. I had him on the edge. If I followed him out of here, we'd be in bed in the time it took us to find a place to get naked. Paxton threw a twenty on the table.

Patrick shot him a surprised look. "Now?"

"Uh, yeah, see you guys tomorrow."

"Bye, Pax," I said in my most sultry *I want you* voice.

"Bye." He backed away, tripped over a chair, and almost ran out the door.

Patrick chuckled and winked at me. "You're getting to him."

"You two seem to be getting along." Every time I'd seen them together, they were laughing, giving each other shit, and enjoying each other's company, like they used to. I was happy to see it.

"Yeah, we had it out last Sunday night. Cleared the air. Everything's great between us."

"I'm so happy to hear that."

Patrick sobered and leaned forward, lowering his voice. "He misses you, Omi."

"He does?"

"Yeah, he does. A lot. I can tell. I'm his twin. He's more serious than usual. He might think he's all about hockey right now, but you're on his mind, too."

"I made a mistake breaking up with him. I want another chance, but I don't know how to go about it."

"That's why you're hanging out with us and torturing the hell out of him?"

"Uh-huh. It's that obvious?"

"Pretty much. We're all enjoying it." He indicated the guys at the table. "I don't think Paxton sees things that way. He can be dense sometimes for such a smart guy."

"I need something epic to convince him he's the guy I want. My dad calls it a grand gesture."

"Your dad is on board with this?"

"He is now."

Patrick nodded and grinned. "A grand gesture. I have an idea, but you're not going to like it."

"Try me."

"Okay, this is what I'm thinking…"

We put our heads together, and I listened to his plan.

It was outrageous, frightening, and brilliant.

I didn't know if I had the guts to do it.

But I had to.

MISCHIEF

Paxton

For Friday night's game, Coach had wanted to put us on separate lines, but I begged him to let us play on the same line to cement our rediscovered twinship. Coach Keller finally relented after Garf pointed out being on the same line was good for our chi. I had no idea what the fuck that was, but if it convinced Keller, I was all in.

Last night, Patrick had come home from the Biscuit an hour after me. Something was going on, but he just smiled this secretive smile and denied any mischief was afoot. But it was. I knew my twin, and we were back in sync. *Just trust me*, he said.

I backed off at that point. Despite my claims to be all hockey, all the time, the next twenty-some hours before the game, I'd alternated between hockey and Naomi.

She confused me. The signals she sent conflicted with her previous words. She made every effort to sit close and touch me every chance she got. Her presence drove me crazy, and the little vixen knew it.

As I warmed up for the game, Naomi was once again seated with the statistician. I forced my gaze away from her, but I was super aware of her presence and felt her eyes caress me as I warmed up.

Patrick skated up to me and gave me a poke with his stick. "Head in the game, bro."

"I...I know."

He winked at me and skated away to offer words of encouragement to other teammates. Patrick was a good captain, a far better one than I'd ever be. Captains spent so much time keeping the team in line and dealing with player issues. I just wanted to play hockey, but my brother loved being in charge. He was welcome to it as far as I was concerned.

Patrick and I were in each other's heads from the first puck drop. We played like a well-oiled team along with our line mates. Not only had we repaired our relationship but Patrick trusted me more with shooting opportunities, not keeping the puck for himself or expecting me to pass every time. We had this twin thing going where we instinctively knew which one of us had a better chance of scoring. We'd always had it, and this time we were listening.

We won easily five to zero. I scored twice and so did Patrick, while Lex scored once.

Now for finals week.

But first, I wasn't averse to a good party at the end of a trying semester. The hockey house would be roaring tonight, and Patrick and I headed there as soon as we showered and dressed.

Drunk on a decisive victory against a good team, we were flying high by the time we got to the hockey house. The party was in full swing.

I pushed my way through the crowd to the kitchen, where

there was always a beer keg. Patrick followed, but a couple seniors I'd known him to hook up with in the past waylaid him. After pouring my beer, I turned to look for him. He climbed the stairs with a female on each arm.

I rolled my eyes and shook my head. My brother would never change. Not that I hadn't had my share of hookups since I'd discovered girls at thirteen, but he rolled through them like a runaway train.

I wandered outside to the porch, where a few guys were drinking and discussing the game. I didn't know any of them. They did a double take when they saw me, probably not sure which twin I was. I ignored them and leaned against the railing, sipping my beer.

While feeling good, I was also in a reflective mood. Next week was finals, then the alumni skate and a few weeks off from classes. I had no intention of going home during those few weeks. I'd be miserable being around my dad for that long. Sad but true.

"You look like you could use some company," said a voice I immediately recognized. Naomi slid up to me and leaned on the railing, close enough our sides pressed together.

"I'm fine."

"Great game, Pax. You guys were a joy to watch."

"Thanks." I stared straight ahead, afraid if I looked at her, I'd fall under the spell of her gorgeous eyes.

She put her hand through my arm and leaned her head against mine. The sweet scent of her invaded my senses, and her body brought my body to life. Resisting her took every ounce of strength I had.

All hockey, all the time, I chanted to myself.

"What did you say?"

I hadn't realized I'd spoken out loud. "Nothing." I turned

my head toward her. Big mistake. She was so close her lips brushed my chin. I shuddered from the impact.

"Paxton," she said breathily in her bedroom voice I'd heard so many times while building her to an orgasm. I made the fatal mistake of gazing into her eyes. They sucked me in. Made me forget my convictions. Temporarily erased the painful memory of her breaking it off with me.

She stood on tiptoe when I wouldn't meet her halfway. Her arms snaked around my neck. Her hot little body pressed against mine. I lowered my head and kissed her, unable to resist. Flashes of her and me having sex, laughing together while eating popcorn in bed, playfully arguing which wing flavors were best at the Biscuit. Everything flooded back, washing over me like a rogue wave that could drag me out to sea.

She clung to me, and I held her close as we deepened our kiss, unable to get enough of her. I needed her so badly I tasted the desire and felt the pain ripping through me. I groaned and lifted her onto the railing without separating our mouths. We made out like the horny twentysomethings we were, unmindful of anyone else and protected by a hazy lust.

"Seriously, you two. Go somewhere else."

"Yeah, find an empty room."

The taunting finally reached our ears, and we turned as one. Lex and Kaitlyn smirked at us, along with several other teammates.

Reluctantly, I backed off and so did Naomi. Kaitlyn grabbed her by the hand and dragged her off. She tossed a longing glance over my shoulder as they disappeared into the crowd.

"You two are back together?" Lex asked.

"No, we're not."

"I see," he chuckled, giving me the impression he really did see. I was transparent as hell. "Sorry to interrupt. Kaitlyn has something she wanted to give Naomi."

"Like what?" I almost growled, annoyed they'd cut off my good time while being grateful they'd done the same.

"No idea."

I guzzled down my beer, tossed it in the large garbage can, and slipped down the outside deck stairs. I'd come this close to sleeping with Naomi. Whatever happened between us, I didn't want another half-drunken hookup.

Leaving was for the best, if not cowardly. I'd pledged to dedicate myself to hockey the next three months. She'd dumped me, even if she did love me as my brother claimed. If we'd started something up again tonight, we'd probably regret it in the morning.

I wasn't convinced my regrets weren't happening right now, though. Not one bit.

41

GRAND GESTURE

Naomi

Kaitlyn dragged me away from Pax, claiming she wanted to borrow some mascara, but I knew better. I'd told her about the grand gesture, and she'd prevented an early reconciliation. They were all conspiring to force me to make my grand gesture.

I was pissed yet relieved she'd interrupted my pending good time. When I'd returned, Pax was gone. Multiple times I'd texted him and not hit send.

We both needed to get through finals week, and then we'd have unpressured time to figure out where we were going. He'd mentioned at lunch one day that he was hanging around during break rather than going home. I didn't blame him. If I had a dad like that, I'd stay on campus, too. In fact, I'd fly home on Christmas Eve and return right after Christmas. That's all I would be able to tolerate of my dad's girlfriend.

Regardless, my make-out session with Pax bolstered my courage. He wanted me, too. While rejection was still a possibility, I felt better about it.

Finals week had been long and brutal. I'd done well on my tests, the last one being yesterday. I'd spoken with Pax a few times when I'd run into him on campus. He'd been friendly but distant.

Secretly, I'd met Patrick a few times to plan my grand gesture, which involved skating. Each time, I had a panic attack and was unable to step onto the ice, even with Patrick's promises to hold on to me so I wouldn't get hurt.

Tonight was the hockey alumni skate, and I waffled between carrying out Patrick's plan and forgetting I'd ever agreed to such a terrifying proposition.

Kaitlyn rapped on my door. I opened it, still wearing my bathrobe.

She looked me up and down. "What the fuck is this? The guys are already headed to the rink. Everything's set up for your grand entrance. And you're not dressed."

"I'm not going. I can't do this. I'll freak out when I'm on the ice. I can't do it."

"Oh, no, sister. You're going. If I have to knock you over the head and get security to carry you out to my car."

"I can't do it. I'm not prepared. It's a deep-seated phobia. I need more prep time."

"Guess what? You don't have more time. Tonight is the night."

Kaitlyn crossed the room to my small fridge. She opened the door and looked inside. After grabbing a bottle of wine, she opened it and poured two glasses.

"Drink. It'll help."

Under Kaitlyn's firm eye, I drank a glass of wine, hoping a little liquid courage would go a long way. My intentions of skipping tonight disappeared when I saw her determined expression. One way or another, I was going. I dressed and put on my makeup.

"You look great. Let's go."

"I don't have skates. I thought you were bringing skates." I'd been relieved to see her skateless. I might still get out of this.

"Patrick has them. You're ruining my date with Lex the longer you stall."

Her guilt trip tipped me over the edge. I steeled myself for the inevitable.

We got there a few minutes after the event had started. Essentially, it involved skating as couples to music with mood lighting and Christmas decorations. A banquet table and bar provided refreshments. This event was a huge hit with the alumni, and the players enjoyed it, too. Not to mention, it was a lucrative fund-raiser for the hockey program. My dad would be here, not sure about his girl-friend. Right now, my dad was the least of my worries, though I suspected he'd be humiliated by my paralyzing fear of skating and complete ineptness on the ice. When he'd suggested a grand gesture, I was positive he hadn't had this public display in mind.

This wasn't about my dad. This was about Paxton and proving how much he meant to me, doing something beyond words.

Kaitlyn ushered me to where Patrick waited in a remote part of the arena away from prying eyes. He handed me a box.

I stared at them in surprise. "Are these—?"

Patrick smiled at me. "He never returned them."

Those skates had probably taken the bulk of Pax's monthly budget, and yet he hadn't returned them. Pax didn't forget stuff like that, which meant his keeping them had been inten-tional. Tentatively, I opened the box. The skates were pink, and they were beautiful. I held one up and examined it.

"I—"

"Put them on. We don't have all night," Patrick insisted with a hint of impatience.

I pulled them on. They fit perfectly. Patrick bent down and laced them up tight. He straightened and gave me an encouraging smile.

"You'll be fine," Kaitlyn said.

"Okay, you ready?" Patrick stood and grabbed my hand. Kaitlyn and Lex watched with grins on their faces.

"It'd help to have less of an audience. I appreciate all your support, but please start your evening. Patrick and I have this."

"You aren't going to run, are you?" Kaitlyn narrowed her eyes and gave me her death glare. No one had a death glare like her.

"No."

"I won't let her," Patrick insisted. "You two go have fun."

Reluctantly, Kaitlyn took Lex's outstretched hand and disappeared around the corner, pausing once to look back at me and wink.

"Ready?"

I drew in deep, calming breaths, attempting to tamp down my rising panic. *I must do this. I will do this.*

Patrick hauled me to my feet, and I clung to him as we made our way down the too long hallway. Our blades clacked on the floor. I wasn't wearing guards because Patrick didn't want to impede my progress by having to remove them before I got on the ice.

I hesitated at the gate onto the ice. I surveyed the scene before me to plot out the most direct path to Paxton with the least amount of people in my way.

My dad had been skating with his girlfriend when he saw me. He did a double take and started to skate toward me. I shook my head and pointed to Paxton, still unaware I was here. Dad grinned and nodded. He got it. He knew what I was up to and approved. His nod of endorsement gave me an extra needed boost of courage.

Patrick stepped onto the ice, grabbed me around the waist, lifted me into the rink. He held me until my legs stopped shaking—somewhat.

"You got this." He turned me so I faced in Pax's direction.

Pax stood in the center of the ice, watching people skate around him. His pasted-on smile was forlorn, almost lost. He turned and glanced my direction. His head snapped back around, and he took a longer look. He blinked several times.

"Ready. Go!" Patrick gave me a push across the ice.

I wobbled and wavered and stiffly glided toward Paxton, waving my arms in a desperate attempt to keep my balance. He gaped at me as if not understanding what the fuck I was doing.

He was so far away, and my heart was pounding so hard my legs trembled, and my throat closed off. I began to gasp for air, fighting for control of my panic. My eyes met Paxton's. I never took my eyes off him. Concern was etched on his handsome face, but he held himself back, as if instinctively knowing I had to do this myself.

"Naomi, you don't have to do this," he called to me. But damn it, I was doing it.

Within five feet of him, one skate slid in the wrong direction and tangled with the back blade on the other. Flashbacks hit me. Panic surged through my veins, robbed me of oxygen, and strangled me in its unforgiving clutches. I struggled for control of my mind and my feet.

I floundered, arms waving wildly.

I was going down.

42

PINK SKATES

Paxton

At first, I thought I had to be hallucinating.

But I wasn't. Naomi was very shakily skating toward me on pink skates, the very skates I'd bought her and she'd given back to me when she'd dumped me.

Not that I'd call what she was doing skating, exactly, but she was on skates, and she was upright. I gave her a zero for form and a ten for execution.

Mr. Smith skated up beside me. I didn't take my eyes off Naomi. I feared if I did, she'd panic and fall. Determination and blind fear warred with each other on her beautiful face.

"What's she doing?" I asked.

"The grand gesture. Just like I told her." Mr. Smith beamed at his daughter, not that I chanced a glance at him, but I knew from the tone of his voice.

Grand gesture?

Wasn't that the thing they did often in romances where the guy, usually, did some huge thing to impress the love of his life? Only this time, the guy wasn't the one. I had no problem with that. I wasn't into male-female stereotypes.

"Naomi," I said in a hushed voice. She faltered at the sound of her name, a disaster in the making as one skate decided to rebel and wrap itself around the other. She was about to go down in a tangle of arms and legs.

I wouldn't let her grand gesture end that way.

In one swift stride, I had her in my arms. She clung to me. Sweat beaded on her brow. Her breath came in panicked gasps. Her heart pounded against my chest. I held her tight, barely noticing the cheering going on around us.

"You're going to be okay. I've got you," I murmured in her ear, knowing what I said didn't matter as much as a calming tone. She wrapped her legs around me, spearing my shins with her skate blades, but I didn't care. Nothing mattered but this beautiful, courageous woman in my arms. After a while, her breathing began to return to normal and her heartbeat slowed. She carefully placed one foot on the ground then the other, standing on her blades.

She looked up at me and grinned in triumph. "I did it!"

"You did." I grinned back, so very proud of her.

"I did it for you, Pax. For us."

"I know," I croaked out with misty eyes. The last thing I was going to do was cry in front of this tough crowd. I hugged her tight, pressing my face into her hair, and held her until I had a handle on my emotions. "Do you want me to help you back to the bleachers?"

"No, I want to skate with you."

"You do?"

She nodded. "Just promise you won't let go of me."

"I promise."

Carefully, I turned while holding her waist, keeping her

close to my side. I skated with slow, even strokes around the rink. My teammates made way for us, cheering as we skated past. Some of the women had suspiciously wet eyes and a few of the guys.

Patrick fist-bumped me and winked. He beamed at the two us. "I knew you could do it," he called to Naomi.

"Thank you, bro." I grinned at him, knowing he'd had a part in this.

We skated slowly to several Christmas songs until Naomi begged for a break. I safely sat her down and retrieved hot buttered rums from the bar. I sat next to her, and we sipped our drinks and watched the skaters.

"Why did you do it?" I asked finally.

"Because I was a fool to break up with you, and I wanted to prove how real this thing is between us. Words weren't enough. I needed something bigger."

"And you came up with skating?"

"With the help of your brother. I'll never forgive him for this." She laughed and so did I.

I wrapped her in my arms and kissed her with every ounce of emotion in my body. Drawing back, I framed her beautiful face in my hands.

"I love you, Naomi. There'll always be room in my life for you and hockey."

"I love you, Pax." She leaned forward and showed me how much. "I guess I'm going to have to get used to the rain next fall."

"I guess you are."

Patrick joined us in a group hug, while Naomi's father stood nearby with a happy smile on his face.

Look out, Seattle, here we come.

THE
END

ACKNOWLEDGMENTS

A huge thank you to Sarina Bowen for the opportunity to write in her world with all these amazing authors. I'm humbled by the faith you've put in me to write in your world.

A special shoutout to bestie Kat Mizera for collaborating with me to bring the Graham twins to life.

Thank you to Stacy for always being there when I need you (even when your world has been turned upside down) and giving this a final read-through.